BOOK LOAN

Please RETURN or RENEW it no
than the last

the visual arts to many newspapers and magazines, among them *Blueprint*, *Crafts*, *Design*, the *New Statesman & Society*, *Modern Painters*, *Sight & Sound*, *Time Out* and the *Burlington Magazine*.

Professor Frayling is a Trustee of the Victoria and Albert Museum, Chairman of the Film, Video and Broadcasting panel of the Arts Council of England and a member of the Arts Council itself. He is married and lives in Bath and London.

CHRISTOPHER FRAYLING

STRANGE LANDSCAPE

A JOURNEY THROUGH THE MIDDLE AGES

PENGUIN BOOKS
BBC BOOKS

PENGUIN BOOKS
BBC BOOKS

Published by the Penguin Group and BBC Worldwide Ltd
Penguin Books Ltd, 27 Wrights Lane, London w8 5TZ, England
Penguin Books USA Inc., 375 Hudson Street, New York, New York 10014, USA
Penguin Books Australia Ltd, Ringwood, Victoria, Australia
Penguin Books Canada Ltd, 10 Alcorn Avenue, Toronto, Ontario, Canada M4V 3B2
Penguin Books (NZ) Ltd, 182–190 Wairau Road, Auckland 10, New Zealand

Penguin Books Ltd, Registered Offices: Harmondsworth, Middlesex, England

First published by BBC Books, an imprint of BBC Worldwide Publishing, 1995
Published in Penguin Books 1996
1 3 5 7 9 10 8 6 4 2

Maps by Venture Graphics

BBC ™ BBC used under licence

Set in 10.5/12.5pt Monotype Bembo
Typeset by RefineCatch Limited, Bungay, Suffolk
Printed in England by Clays Ltd, St Ives plc

For Arthur

CONTENTS

Malcolm XII

ACKNOWLEDGEMENTS

Grateful thanks, first of all, to Jim Burge, the series producer of the BBC television series *Strange Landscape*, which this book accompanied; he successfully piloted the series from inferno via purgatory to a well-deserved paradise. Thanks, too, to Derek Towers and Christopher Salt, who directed the television programmes 'The Jewelled City', 'Fires of Faith' and 'The Saint and the Scholar' with such enthusiasm and skill. Also to Peter Firstbrook (executive producer), Kate Macky (unit manager), Rosie Allsop, Barbie MacLaurin and Liz Sugden (production assistants), who were always at the right place at just the right time. Series researcher Mary Cranitch provided me with a lot of help and support – above and beyond the call of duty – without which this book would not only have been very different, it would also have been much more difficult to write. Alexander Murray, Fellow of University College, Oxford, was historical consultant for the television series; much of his excellent, thoughtful advice has found its way into this book as well, although he bears no responsibility whatsoever for the final result: the first section will not, I sincerely hope, consign me to the Inquisition. Malcolm Miller, at Chartres Cathedral, taught me how to 'read' stained glass windows; Kevin Jackson discussed modernism and medievalism; Graham Cox helped me to think twice about courtly love; Terry Gilliam shared his thoughts on his 'warts and all' version of the Middle Ages; and Umberto Eco was very generous with his time when I pestered him about *The Name of the Rose* and matters arising: they all contributed, unwittingly, to the final shape of this book. Gillian Plummer and Barbara Berry processed the text with truly fantastic efficiency and speed. And my wife Helen put up with, and shared, an inappropriately hectic journey through the highways and byways of medieval Europe. *And* she stayed cheerful. The love that moves the Sun is about right.

CHRISTOPHER FRAYLING

PART ONE

THE MIDDLE AGES TODAY

In 1980 Umberto Eco, Professor of Semiotics at the University of Bologna, published his first novel, *The Name of the Rose*. He had been studying the aesthetic ideas of Thomas Aquinas, medieval art in general and illuminations of the Book of Revelation in particular, since the early 1950s, but it was *The Name of the Rose* which brought together his two abiding interests: the thinking of the Middle Ages and the popular culture of the late twentieth century. Above all, his novel was about 'recognizing the evidence through which the world speaks to us, like a great book', and about the deciphering of that evidence – then and now.

The Name of the Rose tells the story of a visit by a young Benedictine novice, Adso of Melk, and his master, a learned Franciscan called Brother William of Baskerville, to a remote abbey somewhere in the mountains of northern Italy, at the end of November 1327. Their visit coincides with heated debates between the papacy and the radical or 'Spiritual' wing of the Order of Franciscan friars about the Church's role in society – whether its institutions should be poor, what were its margins of tolerance and definitions of heresy, and how should it respond to the rise of the profit economy in western Europe.

In the course of a busy week, which eventually turns into a murder investigation, Adso and William discuss with various members of the community a range of issues which could well have been 'in the air' in the early fourteenth century. These include the aesthetics of light and the symbolism of sacred geometry; the 'modern' depiction of the Virgin Mary; the legends of St Francis of Assisi; the origins of the Inquisition and the role of the Dominicans in administering it; the illumination of manuscripts; the latest inventions – including eyeglasses; the debate between Bernard of Clairvaux and Abbot Suger of St Denis on the use of ornaments and graven images in churches; the attraction to youthful monks of the example of the hot-headed intellectual Peter Abelard; the spread of 'heresies from the Orient' – such as Catharism; the popularity of aristocratic soap operas such as *Tristan and Isolt*; the carvings of 'monstrous races' at the basilica of Ste Madeleine at Vézelay in Burgundy and of monstrous intertwined lions at the abbey church of Moissac in Gascony; the significance of relics and reliquaries; and the language of labyrinths. Running through all these, and other, discussions is a series of perspectives on the Book of Revelation and its predictions of the end of the world, which, as one of the characters says, 'offers the key to *everything*'. Young Adso even finds time during that action-packed week to make love with a 'maiden, beautiful and terrible', in the abbey kitchen, during which the novice's response to what is going on is constructed entirely out of quotations from religious texts of the period – from the Song of Songs to the sermons of Bernard of Clairvaux and the visions of Hildegard of Bingen.

It is clear that Eco's novel, the product of over twenty-five years' research into the eleventh to the fourteenth centuries, was deliberately setting out to provide a detailed ideological and intellectual map of the strange mental landscape of the Middle Ages. There are some references to the early Middle Ages, the so-called 'Dark Ages', which ran from the fall of the Roman Empire in the West (around AD 450) to the year 1000. This was the period of the end of the Great Roman Peace, population decline and the revival of tribalism; literate civilization walled itself up in Benedictine bunkers, until there were the glimmerings of the 'Carolingian Renaissance' centred on the Emperor Charlemagne's court in the Rhine valley, and the emergence of what has become known as the 'crucible of medieval Europe' in northern France, southern England, the Rhine and Rhône valleys, and northern Italy. But the main focus of Eco's novel, as indeed of his researches, is on the period between the year

1000 and the era labelled the Italian Renaissance in the fifteenth century, the era that, as Eco says, 'in our schooldays was called Humanism'. A period known as the high Middle Ages, which ended with gunpowder, the printed word and the invention of the artist's ego.

There's a reference in *The Name of the Rose* to Dante's *Divine Comedy* – 'someone had mentioned that the greatest poet of those days, Dante Alighieri of Florence, dead only a few years [he died in 1321], had composed a great poem (which I could not read, since it was written in vulgar Tuscan)'. The poem is treated by Eco as a summary of late medieval thinking on art, theology, cosmology, science fiction and science written in a modern language, rather than as an unwitting precursor of the artist-centred world of Florence a century later. Even the title of his novel refers directly to the final destination of the pilgrim, 'Dante's mystic rose'.

So Eco's period is the high Middle Ages, the 'Light Ages'. But of course none of the inhabitants of his monastery think of themselves as belonging to the 'middle' of anything (a lot of them, in fact, prefer to think of themselves as belonging to the 'end' of everything). It was fifteenth-century humanists who coined the phrase 'Middle Ages' in retrospect, to describe a huge benighted hyphen between the fall of the Roman Empire and the enlightened present, between the 'twin peaks' of Rome and Florence. The thousand years or so between 500 and 1500 became 'the middle time', when art and civilization marked time. The word 'medieval' was invented even later, in the mid nineteenth century, when romantic gentlepeople began to get misty-eyed about the supposed golden age of chivalry and legend because they were bored with the golden age of Greece and Rome. 'Medieval' by then meant a rich and strange assortment of the novels of Walter Scott, the cult of Shakespeare, the study of documents dating from before the invention of printing, the restoration of buildings which were still in use, the myth of the happy artisan and a fashion for early literature such as Chaucer's *Troilus and Criseyde* – where the combatants in the Trojan War of classical times seemed more like jousting knights who proudly wore their fair ladies' colours into battle and where 'dreams became truth and fables histories'.

In France, as in Italy and Germany, the period is known today as '*le Moyen Âge*', the Middle Age – a single, identifiable era with its own identity (even if it is in the 'middle'); in England and America it is known as 'the Middle Ages' – a series of ages or eras in a long historical time span. As historical scholarship extends the fall of Rome further and further towards the origins of the Renaissance (itself extending backwards by the minute), both phrases, whether singular or plural, now tend to be printed between distancing quotation marks. The Middle Ages are being squeezed out together.

Shortly after *The Name of the Rose* was published in English (in 1983), I had a long discussion with Umberto Eco, at his home in Milan, about the novel's significance and in particular about the continuing fascination – in high culture and popular culture – with the Middle Ages. His first book on medieval aesthetics had been published as long ago as 1956 and he had recently said that 'I know the present time only through the television screen, whereas of the Middle Ages I have a direct knowledge', so it wasn't surprising that he should choose the early fourteenth century as the setting for his first novel. The surprise was that *The Name of the Rose* became a best-seller all over the Western world, joining the success of historian Emmanuel Le Roy Ladurie's *Montaillou*, his late-1970s scholarly study of inquisitorial records written in the early fourteenth century about the last of the heretical Cathar sect in the hill village of Montaillou in south-western France, and – more predictably – Barbara Tuchman's 1978 book *A Distant Mirror: The Calamitous Fourteenth Century*, which drew parallels between late medieval Europe and the dark night of the twentieth century. *The Name of the Rose* was to stimulate a craze for 'whodunnits' located in medieval monasteries – the ultimate 'locked room' setting: Edith Pargeter's (alias Ellis Peters) *Cadfael Chronicles*, set in twelfth-century Shrewsbury, were launched in 1977, three years before Eco's novel was published, but only took off in the 1980s. There have been no less than twenty 'Cadfael' novels between *A Morbid Taste for Bones* (the first) and

Brother Cadfael's Penance (the most recent). So why this general fascination with the Middle Ages – evident in the reception of works of scholarship as well as popularizations?

As Eco pointed out to me, in every period there has been an interest in the Middle Ages. In the Renaissance the great poets returned to the themes of knightly sagas. Cervantes' *Don Quixote* of the early seventeenth century told the story of a man who couldn't reconcile the real world with his love of medieval romances. In the Age of Reason, while philosophers were seemingly fighting the last battle against the Dark Ages, these same Dark Ages began to charm the aristocrats, with the Gothic novel and early romanticism. And thanks to such writers as Walter Scott, Alfred Tennyson and Victor Hugo, and the building restoration work of Viollet-le-Duc, the whole of the nineteenth century would create its own Middle Ages. John Ruskin and the Pre-Raphaelites, for example, championed in theory and in practice by William Morris, turned away from the newly industrialized Victorian world where 'shoddy is king' towards a medieval world of bright colours, myth and happy – or unalienated – craftspeople.

Eco continued:

But in fact the real rediscovery of the Middle Ages would be the work of the mass media in the twentieth century, when there has been a renewed and more intense interest. My thesis is that every time Europe feels a sense of crisis, of uncertainty about its aims and scopes, it goes back to its own roots – and the roots of European society are, without question, in the Middle Ages. Everything presently being discussed at the Council of Europe was born in the Middle Ages: the capitalist economy, banks (along with cheques and prime rate), merchant cities, modern languages, the struggle between the poor and the rich, democratic government, the organization of the modern state, and the modern army, the idea of a supernatural federation – and technological transformation. Windmills, horseshoes, compasses, the acceptance of Arab mathematics, not to mention the keyboard – which is fast becoming the way we write and structure our thoughts about anything . . . The basic concepts may have come from ancient Greece and Rome, but in the Middle Ages we learned how to use them. I think that with antiquity, Egyptian or Greek or Roman antiquity, we restore the monuments and then we contemplate them respectfully: in the British Museum, or 'musified' upon a hill as is the Parthenon. While with the Middle Ages we are doing differently, we are still *living* the Middle Ages. I mean we still live or pray in the cathedral, we still live in the Italian square which was a medieval invention, we still live or work in a bank organization which was a medieval invention. We are recycling and re-constructing the Middle Ages, sure, *but by living inside them* . . . The kind of intolerance and dogmatism studied by Le Roy Ladurie in *Montaillou* still explains our own intolerance and dogmatism.

Eco reckons that this concept of 'roots', our questioning of who we are, applies as much to ideas as it does to inventions, institutions and organizations:

Contemporary logic owes much to medieval logicians like William of Occam. The Middle Ages are not the Dark Ages, as many people believe, but a period of great cultural flowering, with much more variety than we think. It may seem that, like Chinese politicians, everybody says the same thing, quotes the same authority, but on a closer look a slight change in an adjective or in an adverb reveals a different world-vision.

A more recent book which draws parallels between tendencies in contemporary politics and society and 'the Middle Age' does, however, equate the period with the Dark Ages. Alain Minc's *Le Nouveau Moyen Âge* (1993) should really be translated as *The New Dark Ages*, a title that captures precisely what Minc seeks to convey. The collapse of the post-Renaissance, post-Enlightenment world of nation states and well-designed cities, of the expansion of Europe and the triumph of the West has led, he argues, to a new tribalism where cities are divided into clans and neighbourhoods – with up-market apartments guarded by mercenaries and no-go areas within inner cities – and where West/East relations are a mixture of the threat of holy wars and a fear on the part of western Europe and America of just how advanced the Pacific Rim has become (just like the paranoia about Arab civilization in the eighth century and about Islam throughout 'the Middle Age'). Italy seems to be leading the way as a model of neo-medieval disintegration, with corruption on a grand scale (robber barons armed with computers rather than broadswords) and the collapse of the nation state. The tribes of the Eurasian steppe are on the move, restless again, and even the modern equivalent of the Holy Roman Empire – the Europe of Maastricht – seems broken-backed and powerless. As the city becomes medievalized, so the plague sweeps the land (the discourse surrounding AIDS is full of the imagery of Armageddon), beggars wander the streets and new madnesses, superstitions or sects catch on overnight.

Minc summarizes:

The New Middle Ages: the collapse of reason as the basic guiding principle, in the face of easy-to-understand ideologies and superstitions which people thought had gone away.

The New Middle Ages: the return of crises and spasms, as a backdrop to everyday life.

The New Middle Ages: the disintegration of the 'ordered' or 'centred' universe in the face of regions and societies which seem to defy our capacity for rational analysis.

At least one reviewer has responded to Minc's apocalyptic thesis by crying 'unfair to the Middle Ages!' They weren't nearly as dreadful as the modern world, at least not the late Middle Ages – and even the Dark Ages, first time around, had more going for them than that! Umberto Eco might agree with this reaction, and he would certainly agree that the closer you look at the Middle Ages, the more you immerse yourself, the more interesting things you see.

But, as Eco has added, the re-invention of the Middle Ages in the twentieth century has happened as much in the fast-food world of popular culture as in the more careful world of historical scholarship, with a lot of stages in between. And there is nothing new about the re-invention itself: the early twentieth century British writer and critic G. K. Chesterton referred to the tendency as looking at 'the Middle Ages by moonlight'. Indeed, Eco has made a loose classification of various re-inventions – a classification which could be applied to virtually any period from the Renaissance to the present day (and to the Middle Ages themselves, when the cult of chivalry was widely supposed to be a revival of the good old days of classical antiquity and when 'heretics' were seeking to live as they thought the original disciples had lived). Of his ten categories (see Appendix One for further details), the four of most interest today are the philological, the philosophical, the barbaric and the romantic. The philological – based on the procedures of the historian 'searching for the roots of the language' among the vast collections of material now available, and attempting to get inside the 'forms of everyday life', the *mentalities* of the period – acts as a counterbalance to all the rest. Sometimes the mass media have shown an interest in this kind of scholarly work, for example when *Montaillou* was translated in 1978, or when Eco's 1959 study, *Art and Beauty in the Middle Ages*, was reprinted hot on the heels of *The Name of the Rose*, or when J. R. R. Tolkien's translations of the fourteenth-century dialect poems *Sir Gawain and the Green Knight* and *Pearl* share shelf space with the latest multinational sword-and-sorcery sagas. But, on the whole, medieval historians have been content to re-invent and re-document the Middle Ages from within history or humanities departments of universities and colleges. (Some of the recent tendencies of academic studies are summarized in Appendix Two.)

Several scholarly historians, in recent years, have stressed the strong connections between the Middle Ages and today: connections with racism, for example, or with ethnic cleansing, or with aspects (sometimes more positive) of contemporary politics and society. But one of the great gulfs between twentieth-century thinking and western European medieval thinking is that today there is an assumption that beneath the surface things are fundamentally incoherent (part of a chaosmos), whereas then there was an assumption that beneath the surface things were fundamentally coherent (part of a cosmos) – a reflection of the will of God. Throughout this century the pastoral and dogmatic pronouncements of successive Popes – influenced by an inter-war 'neo' version of Thomas Aquinas's theology – have tried to bridge the gulf as best they could; after all, Aquinas managed to bring together the Roman Catholic theology of his day and the philosophy of Aristotle (made available from the East). But in secular culture and philosophy, too, the medieval *philosophia perennis* has proved an important source of inspiration and nourishment – not as some unchanging set of eternal questions out there in the stratosphere but as a philosophical larder to be raided.

Modernist authors of the early twentieth century, for example, confronted by signs of what they saw as disintegration and dissonance all around them, where all that was solid melted into the air, seem to have been particularly drawn to the elegant systems of coherence and hidden order espoused in the Middle Ages. Notable among these authors were James Joyce, T. S. Eliot and Ezra Pound. Joyce's fascination ran so deep, Umberto Eco reckons, that 'he remained medievally minded from youth through maturity'. Eco's *The Middle Ages of James Joyce* begins:

The medieval thinker cannot conceive, explain, or manage the world without inserting it into the framework of an Order . . . *Ulysses* demonstrates this same concept of order by the choice of a Homeric framework and *Finnegans Wake* by the circular schema . . . The medieval thinker knows that art is the human way to reproduce, in an artifact, the universal rules of cosmic order. In this sense art reflects the artist's impersonality rather than his personality. Art is an *analogon* of the world . . . This framework of Order provides an unlimited chain of relations between creatures and events . . . It is the mechanism which permits epiphanies, where a thing becomes the living symbol of something else, and creates a continuous web of references. Any person or event is a cypher which refers to another part of the book. This generates the grid of allusions in *Ulysses* and the system of puns in *Finnegans Wake*. Every word embodies every other because language is a self-reflecting world . . . If you take away the transcendent God from the symbolic world of the Middle Ages, you have the world of Joyce.

One way of organizing the objects and events of the universe into a semblance of order is to make an inventory, or list, or catalogue of them – and this was in fact a most characteristic form of medieval scholarship. A list, a recombination of elements, can then be interpreted with reference to standardized images and phrases from much earlier authorities. Eco continues:

[Medieval] authors compile catalogues of objects and treasures from cathedrals and kings' palaces where the seemingly casual accumulation of relics and art objects follows without clear distinctions between the beautiful work and the teratological [i.e. monstrous] curiosity. They obey, instead, a logic of the inventory. For example, the Treasury of the Cathedral of St Guy in Prague listed, among other innumerable objects, the skulls of St Adalbert and St Venceslas, the sword of St Stephen, Jesus' crown of thorns, pieces of Jesus' cross, the tablecloth of the Last Supper, a tooth of St Marguerite, a piece of the shinbone of St Vitalis, a rib of St Sophia, the chin of St Eoban, the shoulder-blades of St Affia, a whale rib, the horn of an elephant, the ash plant of Moses, and the clothes of the Virgin . . . Last but not least, the Treasury of Cologne Cathedral seemingly held the skull of St John the Baptist at twelve years of age (*sic*). These lists curiously resemble the list of the paraphernalia of the various saints in the mystical procession which appears in the 'Cyclops' chapter of *Ulysses*.

The story about John the Baptist's skull was already something of a joke in the late Middle Ages. According to various original accounts, a pilgrim visiting the shrines of France was shown the skull of John the Baptist on two days running at two different places. The pilgrim asked how there could possibly be *two* skulls belonging to St John. 'Ah,' said the quick-thinking keeper of the second shrine. 'The skull you saw yesterday was obviously the skull of John as a *young man*.' Perhaps there was yet another, even younger skull in Cologne Cathedral!

The idea of the list, or the recombination, certainly appealed to Modernist writers, as indeed it did to Surrealist artists with their cabinets of curiosities, ethnographic collections and '*bricolage*', where the apparent randomness became the great attraction – part of the 'archaeology of knowledge', in Michel Foucault's phrase. And in making sense of the list – finding the connections behind the combinations – the medieval scholar, again like the Modernist writer, had recourse to recognizable quotations from authoritative texts or from systems of ideas which might well have been around since between AD 150 and 400. As Bernard of Chartres put it, in a phrase coined about 1130, 'like dwarfs standing on the shoulders of giants, it is possible for us to see slightly farther than they'. Hence the impression that everyone is saying the same thing and the fact that everyone is saying something slightly different; less a case of 're-inventing' than of 're-inventorying'.

Developments in twentieth-century logic and in other forms of secular system-building such as structuralism and semiotics have been heirs to what Eco calls 'the perennial vigour of the Middle Ages'. One interpretation of *The Name of the Rose* suggests connections between the study of images and symptoms in the fourteenth century (sculptures, herbs, medicines, colours, jewels, manuscript illuminations) and theories of meaning (the *how* as much as the *what*) today. In the late 1960s Marshall McLuhan, media analyst and author of the *The Medium is the Message*, speculated about the different sensibilities and perceptions of an era when 'publication meant to read a manuscript aloud to probably no more than thirty people at a time' and the post-Gutenberg era when 'the print man must have felt an access of power, when his image could be multiplied so many times exactly in uniform pattern for so many unseen people'. With the speed up of information by electronic means, such sensibilities would shortly be in for 'an even greater revolution than Gutenberg produced in the Renaissance'.

Philosophers such as Pierre Baudrillard have suggested that this 'ecstasy of communication' – the endless conversation between images – characterizes the post-Gutenberg world, and they have related this 'ecstasy' to the hall of mirrors of medieval symbolism where each symbol was part of an endless cycle and recycle of communication, with God as the key. If our world today is a 'culture of quotations', this would also suggest parallels with ways of thinking in the Middle Ages. The major differences between then and now are considered to be that the invisible world may no longer be the key to the visible one; that we are aware that all lists have a hidden agenda, which is about power; that the culture of quotations is no longer part of a 'shared symbolic order'; and that coherence, so prized by the Modernists, isn't necessarily a valuable thing any more.

Some 'New Age' thinkers have attempted to fill the void by searching for 're-enchantment', for ways of putting the magic back into the late twentieth century, and they have – not surprisingly – been concerned with similarities with the Middle Ages rather than differences. Philosophers of science such as David Ray Griffin are seeking for 'a physics which no longer disenchants our stories . . . but which provides us with a new story which can become a common, unifying story underneath our more particular ones', a physics where matter becomes living and dancing, rather than fixed and inert. Theorists of the 'men's movement' find valuable the metaphor of the medieval knight as an image of masculinity – the 'balanced warrior' who after initiation into psychic openness (as opposed to defensiveness) recognizes his obligation to the feminine but is equally aware that he must draw his sword in the cause of 'warrior responsibility'; James Hillman in his *Eranos: Lectures on the Thought of the Heart* uses the metaphor of the man with the *coeur de lion*, who is not afraid to rage and roar in the desert of today's contaminated culture. And art theorists such as Suzi Gablik argue that the function of art is to 'heal the alienated, vulnerable human consciousness' which has expelled the sacred by losing connection with the wisdom of the body, represented in the archetypal forces of nature and myth.

Others have written of tourism as 'a disenchanted version of medieval pilgrimage', and of what would need to happen for new kinds of enchantment to emerge – New Agers seem particularly fond of processions, communal dancing, chanting and discussing empowerment through magic and mythology. In general, the search for 're-enchantment' or 'centredness' has led back to the basics of cosmology – the science of the universe – and to stories which predate the era of reductionism and disenchantment. These stories

have in turn been consciously reworked – not as institutional religion, but as part of a generalized 'sense of the sacred', an alternative
to believing in nothing.

In this sense, convoys of 'New Age Travellers' would probably
like to see themselves as the 1990s equivalent of the mendicant
orders – living off public charity and providing an example of alternative anti-bourgeois, anti-suburban ways of living; such a self-
image helps to give them the moral high ground in arguments with
local citizens who would persecute them. Like the wandering
medieval friars, they stand for spiritual renewal, herbal medicine and
a new relationship with Mother Earth. But as the convoys converge,
magnet-like, on enchanted places such as Glastonbury and Stone-
henge, the sounds from their ghetto-blasters, or from compact disc
players wired up to their car batteries, may well be of another
Middle Ages – a barbaric era when life was nasty, brutish and loud.

These are the sounds of 'Heavy Metal', a phrase that comes from
William Burroughs' *Naked Lunch*, although the music has been
called – by *Newspeak: A Dictionary of Jargon* (1984) – 'the equivalent
of fantasy's sword and sorcery, and game-playing's dungeons and
dragons'. It is a mixture of explosive drumming, blues-based
power-chords amplified to the limits of human endurance – like a
broadsword trying to carve its way through sheet metal – smoke
machines, coloured light, long hair, leather, a sonic armoury stacked
up like a disused car lot, and an iconography which manages to
conflate Tolkien's Hobbit, the Book of Revelation, Goths and
Vikings, Celtic myth, sorcery, the Black Death and motorbikes. As
such, the Heavy Metal music of the 1970s and 1980s represents one
of the strongest images of the Middle Ages to have emerged from
within contemporary popular culture; a shaggy image, of darkness,
brute force and irrationality.

There are, of course, like the breakaway orders and sects of the
Middle Ages, sub-sects – Black Metal, Christian Metal, Goth Metal
and Medieval Metal – and there are even different weights of Metal.
But perhaps the most appropriate way, in the circumstances, of
finding order behind the ear-splitting chaos is to follow the

medieval tradition and make a list of the bands of the last twenty years with names which chime with 'the Middle Ages': Angelwitch, Apocalypse, Apocrypha, Armageddon, Attila, Avalon, Battle Axe, Black Sabbath, Candlemass, Cirith Ungol (the 'pass of the spider' on the borders of Mordor, in Tolkien's *Lord of the Rings*), Cloven Hoof, Dark Angel, Dark Lord, Dark Star, Dragon, Elf, Elixir, Excalibur, Four Horsemen, Hallow's Eve, Helmet, Heretic, Icon, Iron Maiden, Kreator, Megadeath, Metal Church, Messiah Force, Mordred, Nazareth, Omen, Ostrogoth, Oz, Pandemonium, Pestilence, Possessed, Raven, Satan, Saxon, Shadow King, Shire, Sieges, Skull, Steel Forest, Stormwitch, Sword, Talisman, Tygers of Pan Tan (from a Michael Moorcock fantasy), Voivod, Watchtower, Wolfsbane and Zodiac Mindwarp.

They are names which sound like items from a catalogue of impending disasters in a high-tech book of the hours – *Les très riches heures de Chuck de Berry*, perhaps. I was told by one of my students – who collected the Heroic Fantasy illustrations of Frank Frazetta and the writings of Aleister Crowley, and who at open-air Heavy Metal concerts liked to get her head as near as possible to the *inside* of the nearest amplifier – that the physical experience of the music transported her to a kind of Tolkien Middle-earth, which was a lot more interesting and a much nicer place than this one. She also made connections between the special powers associated with saintly relics of the Middle Ages and the more secular attractions of rock music relics today – Elvis Presley's Graceland, the lamp-post near Chippenham where Eddie Cochran met his death, John Lennon's floral-painted Rolls-Royce, and so on.

The combination of barbarism, heroism, mysticism (up to a point) and technology – amounting to 'a metallic onslaught' as the music critics like to style it – is also a strong feature of comic book culture. A list of titles compiled at random in a local comics emporium goes: *Avatar, Black Dragon, Black Knight, Camelot Eternal, Camelot 3000, Conan the Barbarian, The Demon featuring Merlin, Dragonflight, Dragonlance, Dungeons and Dragons, Elfquest, Excalibur, Groo the Wanderer, Mordred the Superhero, Savage Sword of Conan,*

Slaine the Horned God, Sword and the Atom, Vlad the Impaler. Super-heroes of the skies, often armed with lasers and a barrage of heavy metal weaponry (as well as with a highly self-conscious, almost exegetical knowledge of the history of comics), seem to have colonized the court of King Arthur or taken over from St George.

The settings of these comics are 'medieval' in the generalized sense of the word noted by historian Georges Duby and quoted in a book called *Le Moyen Âge au cinéma*: 'a Middle Age which operates like a mythology, which is simply situated "once upon a time" and which is far enough away for people to project today's fantasies on to it – while at the same time giving them the *weight* and *texture* of a real past'. A real past also, and simultaneously, seems to be happening in a parallel world of outer space. 'Today's fantasies' include a super-hero who relies on physical prowess, animal instincts and skill with technology (and who lacks, entirely, a spiritual dimension). He is a self-made man (rather than emerging from a nobility or an élite), who is usually concerned with personal revenge or a commando-style rescue mission rather than with any cause (the 'rights and duties' of a gallant medieval knight, for example); his initiation is likely to take the form of a training in the martial arts, and he is much more interested in casual sex than courtly love (preferably with a super-heroine who is just as physically tough as he is). There is some mystic-speak, but the prevailing atmosphere of the comics is defiantly materialistic. The spiritual realm – where ethic and aesthetic meet – has gone. As Conan the Barbarian puts it, 'trust no one . . . just the sword'. And the dungeons probably have computers in them. Eco, a little uncharitably, locates such comics 'midway between Nazi nostalgia and occultism'.

It is tempting to search for the origins of this strange reuse of the Middle Ages in the Conan the Barbarian stories written for the pulp magazine *Weird Tales* in the 1920s and 30s by Robert E. Howard (who committed suicide in 1936 at the age of thirty). He liked to provide his stories with a distinguished genealogy – 'you have heard the tale before in many guises wherein the hero was named Perseus, or Siegfried, or Beowulf, or Saint George' – before moving on to more 'barbarian', Ice-Agey forms of adventure. But the origins seem to go back further, to Mark Twain's *A Connecticut Yankee at King Arthur's Court* (or *A Yankee at the Court of King Arthur*) published in 1889. In this story, one Hank Morgan – a supervisor from the Colt arms factory in Hartford, Connecticut – wakes up to find himself in Arthur's Britain:

There was no gas, there were no candles; a bronze dish half full of condemned butter with a blazing rag floating in it was the thing that produced what was regarded as a light. A lot of these hung along the walls and modified the dark, just toned it down enough to make it dismal . . . There were no books, pens, paper, or ink and no glass in the openings they believed to be windows. It is a little thing – glass is – until it is absent, then it becomes a big thing. But perhaps the worst of all was, that there wasn't any sugar, coffee, tea or tobacco.

Eventually, Morgan turns the 'groping and grubbing automata' he sees all around him – the knights with their pointless and snobbish ideas of chivalry, the peasants under 'the hand of that awful power, the Roman Catholic Church' – into a nation of men rather than a nation of worms, by a mixture of Yankee know-how, scientific management, assembly lines and the latest examples of engineering. But the combined power of the Church and aristocratic ideals of chivalry prove too much for him. He retreats to Merlin's Cave with thirteen Gatling guns, a supply of glass cylinder dynamite torpedoes and a dynamo linked to an electric fence, and in a sickening display of mass destruction 'I touched a button, and shook the bones of England loose from her spine . . . Twenty-five thousand men lay dead around us . . . Let the record end here.'

Twain's satire was deliberately intended as a reply to the fashion for 'pastoralism' and the romantic version of the Middle Ages which saw in that world a cosy response to rationalism, industrialism and creeping bureaucracy. *A Connecticut Yankee* is in this sense at the opposite pole to the dreams of John Ruskin (with his unalienated craftsmen building Gothic cathedrals) and William Morris (with his yearning for a shared symbolic order, useful work and an aesthetic dimension in everyday life). For Twain, such romanticism was very wide of the mark. He preferred the Enlightenment view that the Middle Ages, early *or* late, were a time of barbarism, ignorance and counting the number of angels who could stand on the head of a pin. It was a view shared, implicitly, by L. Frank Baum, whose *Wonderful Wizard of Oz* (1900) set out to substitute for the pastoral, regressive, European fairy-tale – as he saw it – an urban, optimistic, American version. (The name Oz came, appropriately enough, from a label on the author's filing cabinet: O–Z.) The Emerald City of his book was a 'wonderful' place to live, a monument to human achievement, and a lot more comfortable than the hard grind of rural life in the Dakotas (or Kansas in the story itself). And if the Emerald City seems today to resemble a shopping mall more than a cathedral, well that may be a measure of the sharpness of Baum's vision.

The high-tech attitude towards the Middle Ages is perhaps mirrored in the pioneering work of American historians such as Lynn White Jr, who have examined the sheer technological inventiveness of Europeans in the later medieval period: spectacles in late-thirteenth-century Italy; the stirrup – which came from 'the barbarian influence'; the button, the implications of which for costume design were not realized until *c.* 1300; crop rotation and the heavy plough; and the horizontal axis windmill which appeared in late-twelfth-century Normandy. White's researches have demonstrated some surprising things: that the so-called Dark Ages 'stimulated rather than hindered technology', that much technological innovation started on the great plains of 'the vast northern world' and that the general belief in western Europe in the incarnation of Christ – as a once and for all opportunity for redemption – helped to encourage the invention of new machines: life wasn't a rehearsal, it was a single, unrepeatable chance to improve one's lot. So there *was* a connection between spirituality and innovation, after all. In an article written in 1965, Lynn White Jr even showed how the key ingredients of the Wild West – the modern harness, the nailed horseshoe, the covered wagon; the stage-coach; gunpowder, smooth iron wire and the windmill; hanging by a rope; the name sheriff or shire reeve; and whisky (alcohol was first distilled in twelfth-century Italy) – all originated in the European Middle Ages. 'To comprehend ourselves as Americans we must recover, and relate ourselves to our deeper past, the Middle Ages.'

Mark Twain wouldn't have agreed at all (he never liked the idea that the crucible of American democracy may have been the Teutonic forests – surely the land of the free came from somewhere much more sensible), although he might have enjoyed the projection of Yankee know-how back on to the medieval period. He would undoubtedly have found more congenial the barbaric Middle Ages which have been so strong in the late twentieth century – through popular music, comics and film. One film-maker who has made this image his speciality, returning to it again and again, is Terry Gilliam. In *Monty Python and the Holy Grail*, made with Terry Jones in 1974, one of the peasants says 'he must be a king because he hasn't got shit all over him' – and *Jabberwocky* (1977) was billed as 'a film for the squeamish, set in the filthiest period of history, as the Middle Ages were collapsing around the well-dandruffed head of King Bruno the Questionable'. The more recent *The Fisher King* is set in modern-day New York but the street level at the base of corporate towers resembles a medieval shanty-town, courtyards are open to peasants and merchants while high-level apartments are the domain of the lords, a frightening Red Knight makes an appearance in Central Park and a medieval history professor becomes a bag-person.

In November 1991, when *The Fisher King* was first released in Britain, I asked Terry Gilliam about his seemingly inexhaustible fascination with the Middle Ages – and with showing them warts and all:

Total infantilism. It may be that I never grew up believing in anything more than fairy-tales. The things I read and was told as a child I believed, and continue to believe in them. It seems a simpler, more manageable kind of world, a more direct world where when there's a problem, you have a knight go out and slay a dragon. The simple hierarchy of the Middle Ages is very neat when it comes to storytelling or film-making: because you've got a king, you've got priests, you've got warriors, and with these archetypes you can then play, and use them in ways they weren't meant to be used.

It seems a form of nostalgia, for a time of magic when – as *Monty Python and the Holy Grail* put it – 'strange women lying in lakes' were the 'basis for a system of government'. But Gilliam thinks it is less a case of nostalgia than a reaction to the gospel according to Hollywood. 'The filth element, the ordure, the smell of the Middle Ages, is something I'd grown up *not* seeing on film. Everything was shining teeth, perfectly combed hair. I thought my incredibly smelly version of the Middle Ages was probably closer to the reality we live in than this manufactured reality that most of us believe in.'

The 'manufactured reality' had its heyday in the mid 1950s, when the major Hollywood studios liked to choose British locations to test out their new widescreen processes on swashbuckling adventures such as *Knights of the Round Table* (MGM, 1953), *King Richard and the Crusaders* (Warner Brothers, 1954) – the one where Virginia Mayo as the pert and over-made-up Lady Edith delivers the deathless one-liner to George Sanders, 'War! War! That's all you think of, Dick Plantagenet. You burner! You pillager!' – *Prince Valiant* (Twentieth-Century Fox, 1954) and *The Black Shield of Falworth* (Universal, 1954). These films were, as Noël Coward said of the musical *Camelot*, 'like Wagner's *Parsifal* without the laughs'. They combined clean-cut American heroes, comic-book colours and fairy-tale costumes with the kind of sub-Walter Scott dialogue which seemed compulsory whenever grown men struggled into suits of armour: 'Prithee my liege permit me to deliver your message to the Knight of the Blue Cross with all convenient speed.' That sort of thing. Tony Curtis, who appeared in *The Black Shield*, called them 'crazy stories about knights in armour and damsels in distress', which is about right. Cinemascope proved to be excellent for showing lances, battering rams and rows of impossibly white teeth.

The punk rockers of the mid 1970s were similarly rejecting what they saw as the over-produced, remote from reality, oppressive world of mainstream pop music. Music critic Greil Marcus, in trying to track down the roots of punk – as an extreme statement of 'freedom and terror' – in his free-association study *Lipstick Traces – A Secret History of the Twentieth Century*, includes references to the Bayeux tapestry, St Bernard of Clairvaux, Montaillou and, above all, the Cathar heretics of southern France in the early thirteenth century. Marcus maintains that the Cathars treated life on earth 'as a horror movie, a medieval *Night of the Living Dead*'; the world was matter and it was vile, human beings were matter and they were vile – so, at their most extreme, they had licence to do whatever they pleased in this world. They were thus the distant ancestors of Johnny Rotten shouting the line 'I AM AN ANTICHRIST'. The phrase 'Kill 'em all, let God sort 'em out' – which originated in the Albigensian Crusade, at the fall of Béziers – was to be seen on T-shirts in the punk era; mercenaries working with government troops in the Third World wore them, too.

The Cathars' ideas about the evil of the material world mean that they have even been considered as long-term inventors of cinema, in which the imaginative adrenalin-like use of celluloid makes bearable the nastiness of everyday life. And of course there is the more direct use of medieval themes in modern films. John Boorman's *Excalibur* (1981), for example, is a retelling of the entire Arthurian cycle – from the birth of Arthur via the saga of the Round Table to the quest for the Holy Grail – which begins in the Dark Ages with Uther Pendragon breaking his solemn promise to the necromancer Merlin. The prologue has a punky, reptilian quality to it, influenced – according to Boorman – by 'the artist Frank Frazetta, who knows how to create an elemental, primitive feeling'. Then, for the scenes involving the young Arthur, there is 'a more bucolic, perhaps more 'conventional', image of the Middle Ages'. For the mythic Camelot itself, 'imagination runs riot, with a castle all in gold and silver, with gleaming armour, with a high degree of stylization in sets and costumes', while for Arthur's death and the decline of chivalry, the film returns to the dark, punky world of the beginning. In other words, *Excalibur* moves from the Middle Ages as barbaric to the Middle Ages as romantic, and back again. The romanticism comes from recreating the myth as a 'golden age'. As Boorman said in 1985:

The historical facts strike me as of rather minor importance. What is at stake is the myth . . . Much of the legend is associated with a twelfth-century setting, with knights in armour and jousting and so on; the poets who wrote about it incorporated the values of their own period. [Malory's] *Morte d'Arthur*, for example, was very much influenced by the Norman invasion and the establishment of a system of laws. I don't think one can go against that . . . [So] what I had to do was to include the iconography and, at the same time, play with it by creating a 'Middle-earth', in the sense intended by Tolkien in *The Lord of the Rings*: which is to say, a parallel world, similar to our own but somehow different, with numerous allusions to the Middle Ages. When you recount a legend, you find yourself speaking more about your own period than you think . . . I know that Malory in *Morte d'Arthur* spoke of the fourteenth and fifteenth centuries and T. H. White in *The Once and Future King* of the Edwardian era. What is essential, then, is not to refute the myth but to refresh it.

Boorman found the source of this refreshment in the idea that 'the legend of the Grail speaks to us of a period when nature was unsullied and man in harmony with it'. The story 'deals with people who are trying not to discover themselves, but their place in the world, a much more humble attitude . . . their destiny, the universe to which they belong and their relations with their fellow men'. So Merlin speaks of the sword Excalibur as forged when the world was young, when birds, beasts and flowers were as one with man and death was but a dream. The Arthurian myth has moved on from the barbarism of Conan and punk rock to a golden age when the forest was still a book to be studied – with trees as the thoughts of God – and human beings were in harmony with the eco-system which surrounded them. As Boorman concluded, 'The Middle Ages, according to Jung, was a period which – like the unconscious – we ought to study in order to gain a better understanding of ourselves.' Hence the narrative importance of the quest.

The most influential medieval quest stories written this century – stories which have been the foundation of an entire sub-genre of popular literature questionably known as 'adult fantasy', as well as of a multinational games industry built upon the success of Dungeons and Dragons – were by two Oxford academics active in the 1930s and 1940s, C. S. (or Jack) Lewis and J. R. R. (or Ronald) Tolkien. Both were historians of medieval literature, one specializing in the romances and their profound influence on subsequent periods, the other in Anglo-Saxon and Middle English. Both had highly romantic conceptions of the Middle Ages, as a 'world we are about to lose'.

Norman Cantor in his book *Inventing the Middle Ages* calls them 'the Oxford Fantasists' and concludes of their legacy:

Of all the medievalists of the twentieth century, Lewis and Tolkien have gained incomparably the greatest audience, although 99.9 per cent of their readers have never looked at their scholarly work. They are among the best-selling authors of modern times for their works of fantasy, adult and children's . . . The novel that Tolkien read bits of to the Inklings [a small society of Oxford dons and their friends, who regularly met at Magdalen College to read chapters from work-in-progress], with mixed response in the early 1940s, was finally published with trepidation by Allen and Unwin in three volumes in 1954 and 1955. It has now sold eight million copies in many languages, with about half the sales in an American paperback edition. This is *The Lord of the Rings* . . . In terms of shaping of the Middle Ages in the popular culture of the twentieth century, Tolkien and Lewis have had an incalculable effect, and the story is far from ended.

Lewis's seven-volume 'Chronicles of Narnia' (published between 1950 and 1956), among them *The Lion, the Witch and the Wardrobe*, tells of a magical land that lies beyond the wardrobe in the bedroom, a deeper sort of land where 'every rock and flower and blade of grass looked as if it meant more' and where the shadowlands of the mundane are left behind. After encountering the ever-present reality of evil, in the form of witches and anti-gods, Lewis's cheerful schoolchildren manage to sustain their robust Christian faith with the thought that it is the *little things* which continue to matter a great deal; they also learn that the world of medieval-style romance was 'a larger, brighter, bitterer, more dangerous world than ours'. Lewis's 'Chronicles' together with his phenomenally successful *Screwtape Letters* (1942) and *Great Divorce* (1945) seem to have come into their own in the 'New Age'.

Tolkien's vast epic has had an even greater impact, perhaps because it is less obviously regressive and tied to the specifics of Edwardian Christianity. He created his mythical world of Middle-earth, he said, out of a mixture of Old English, Old Norse and Celtic languages – which he then rendered into modern English as if translated from a lost original. He did so, he added, because 'I was from early days grieved by the poverty of my own beloved country: it had no stories of its own, not of the quality that I sought, and found in legends of other lands. There was Greek, and Celtic, and Romance, Germanic, Scandinavian, and Finnish; but nothing English, save impoverished chap-book stuff.'

The result was a body of 'more or less connected legend, ranging from the large and cosmogonic, to the level of romantic fairy-story'. This legend was expressed in the form of a quest – a quest by the hobbit Frodo Baggins of Bag End in the Shire, and his fellowship, to deliver the One Ring to the fires of Mount Doom and so prevent it from falling into the hands of the forces of darkness. The landscape of this journey – ruined cities, quiet villages, desolate battlefields, remote mountains – is peopled by dwarfs, elves, giants, halflings, orcs and dragons (the monsters of Middle-earth), and requires a detailed gazetteer to inform readers about its special features, from Aglarond (Caves of) to Zirak-Zigil (Mountain of).

The Lord of the Rings is like a saga, only it is really an everyday story of suburban hobbits; and it has the very un-medieval punch-line – 'without the simple and the ordinary, the noble and heroic is meaningless'. The key point of contact with 'legends of other lands' – apart from the intricacies of the language – is the assumption that the destruction of the Great Danger routinely involves honour, chivalry, service and self-sacrifice (on the part of the fellowship) in generous measure, and the strong implication throughout that there isn't enough of any of these qualities around any more.

Tolkien expressed the hope that in future others might take up the challenge of retelling and embellishing his epic, to give it an organic life within the culture. The mid 1960s era of psychedelic drugs, the curvilinear *art nouveau* revival and hippie communes – especially in America – took up the challenge and turned *The Lord of the Rings* into a runaway best-seller, complete with Mucha-medieval graphics on the cover. This era begat the sword-and-sorcery sub-genre in comics and popular literature. (Tolkien has justly been called 'the virtual inventor of the epic fantasy novel', an honour he might well have turned down.) Another list, culled from the shelves of a local newsagent – not bookshop – runs: *The Books of Merlin, The Death Gate Cycle, The Chronicles of Thomas Covenant the Unbeliever, Star of the Guardian Cycle, The Heritage of Shannara Cycle, The War of Powers Cycle, The Rose of the Prophet Cycle, The Darkswood Trilogy, The Belgariad Saga, The Malloreon Saga, The Riftwar Saga, The Westlands Cycle, The Elenium Saga, The Incarnation of Immorality Series, The Apprentice Adept Series, The Dragonlance Saga, The Songs of Earth & Power, The Mists of Avalon, Magic of Xanth Saga, The Forgotten Realms Saga.* And these are just some of the *series* made up of count-less individual volumes. Most of them belong firmly in the romantic category – nostalgia for a time when there were still dragons to be fought, and when they were still colour-coded. Some of them claim to be part of the Middle Ages of Tradition (to reuse Eco's term) and are available in occult bookshops as well as newsagents and motor-way pull-ins.

In time, the literature begat the board game of *Dungeons and Dragons* and Tolkien's embellishers became countless schoolchildren throwing dice, consulting their Dragon Cards, and generally finding their way (through a mixture of statistics and imagination) out of the grid-pattern of Zanzer Tem's dark dungeon. By now, the embellishment of the legend which Tolkien looked forward to had attracted a new and more prosaic name – fantasy role-playing.

'You are about to enter,' said the instruction sheet, 'a fantastic land where dragons run rampant, where magic works, and where your skill with a sharp sword is all that stands between you and a swift demise. You and your friends are about to become dauntless heroes who brave unexplored labyrinths in search of treasure and adventure. Your journeys will take you into the most mysterious realm of all – that of your own imagination.'

The roles on offer include the Dungeon-Master (part referee, part storyteller), the Fighter ('trained for combat'), the Cleric (who 'has dedicated his life to a great and worthy cause'), the Magic-User (a researcher of 'arcane subjects' and thus 'usually feeble'), the Thief ('useful to adventuring parties'), the Dwarf ('a demi-human . . . with a respect for fine craftsmanship'), the Elf ('mid-way between fighters and magic-users') and the Halfling ('they resemble human children with slightly pointed ears'). The supporting cast includes bugbears, gnolls, goblins, hobgoblins, ogres and orcs.

If the iconography of Dungeons and Dragons is derived from Tolkien, with a smattering of horror movie moments thrown in for good measure, the iconography of Warhammer – a rival role-playing operation, more concerned with fantasy battles – comes, by a circuitous route, from medieval arms and armour. Thus, 'the Empire' is a parallel world to the Holy Roman Empire, while the forces of Bretonnia are make-believe Norman. The armies are partly based on the troops of the Emperor Frederick II, especially the Order of Teutonic Knights, which knocked the disorderly and heathen Prussians into shape from 1226 onwards. Frederick was known in his lifetime as 'the hammer of the world', a title which had earlier been applied to Attila the Hun, no less. This time *The Lord of the Rings* (the battle bits) is supplemented by science fantasy and heavy metal weaponry: armies go into battle led by characters such as the Captain of the Reiksguard Knights, equipped with Hel-blaster Volley Guns, or Steam Tanks, or a crazed unit of Flagellants (who 'fight with outstanding fury and determination'). Well, they would, wouldn't they?

Warhammer combines the high-tech Middle Ages with visuals which are trying hard to look like Dürer but which resemble Victorian book illustrations done over with airbrushes, and its approach to role-playing is via a parallel world in which it is chaos out there, and only a mixture of muscle, magic and manufactures will pull you through. Midway between Nazi nostalgia and occultism? A tempting thought, but the emphasis on collection-mania and the finer points of fantastical regalia and uniform (a kind of medieval train-spotting, with anoraks taking over from chain-mail) – plus the fact that the enemy is the 'dark corrupting world of Chaos' rather than any specific group – makes the game seem more like a shopping-mall version of the romantic urge of the early nineteenth century to fill domestic interiors with chivalric clutter such as suits of armour and coats of arms; an era equally obsessed with games and competitions.

The important thing, says the rules, is the taking part, the team spirit – a distant, diffuse, echo of Victorian schoolchildren learning all about chivalry in order to prepare themselves for the empire on which the sun would never set.

At precisely the same time as Tolkien was putting the finishing touches to his *Lord of the Rings*, in 1949, anthropologist Joseph Campbell was publishing in America his classic study *The Hero with a Thousand Faces*. Using examples of 'mythological hero narratives' or 'quest narratives' from all over the inhabited world, Campbell attempted to piece together what he called, following James Joyce in *Finnegans Wake*, a 'monomyth'. The monomyth always begins with 'the mythological hero setting forth from the world of common day (from his hut or castle), then being lured, carried away, or else voluntarily proceeding to the threshold of adventure'. After various trials and temptations, it ends with 'the hero re-emerging from the kingdom of dread (return, resurrection); the boon that he brings restores the world'. Not surprisingly, a lot of Joseph Campbell's examples were taken from the Middle Ages – 'long, long ago when wishing still could lead to something' – notably King Arthur, the Lives of the Saints and Dante's *Divine Comedy* – and he related the key motifs and symbols of the 'quest narratives' to those discovered in dreams by contemporary psychoanalysis.

Campbell's work has been explicitly used as the basis for more recent neo-medieval fantasies. The story of George Lucas's *Star Wars*, for example, emerged from a close study of Campbell's book, as did George Miller's *Mad Max 2 – The Road Warrior*. There is a double quest within *Star Wars*: the quest of Luke Skywalker to understand and master 'the Force', under guidance from surrogate father Obi Wan Kenobi of the order of Jedi Knights; and the quest of the rebel alliance, or the republic, to destroy the Nazi-helmeted and English-accented armies of the Empire. Luke is a mixture of Arthur and Perceval, Obi is an orientalized Merlin and the light-sabres they wield are laser variations on Excalibur. As in the *Conan* comics, the mysticism seems to be part of the hero's initiation ('may the force be with you') before being dropped when the second quest gets going and the down-to-earth values of the Western movie take over. It was George Lucas who tipped off George Miller about Campbell's book – and in *Mad Max 2* the story of Max's defence of the gasoline fortress in the new Dark Ages following a nuclear holocaust, against the punks and barbarians of the great Australian desert, was an updated version of the key elements in 'mythological hero narratives'.

At one level, Umberto Eco's four categories of the Middle Ages as philological reconstruction, perennial philosophy, barbaric and romantic all overlap these days. They are distinct, and they also converge. As Umberto Eco has asked:

Are there any connections between the Heroic Fantasy of Frank Frazetta, the new satanism, *Excalibur*, the Avalon sagas, and [historian] Jacques Le Goff? If they met aboard some unidentified flying object near Montaillou, would Darth Vader . . . and Parsifal speak the same language? If so, would it be a galactic pidgin or the Latin of the Gospel according to St Luke Skywalker? It does seem that people *like* the Middle Ages.

At another level, these categories provide alternative models for understanding the present. If you want to be negative, there is the Dark Ages model, if you want to be positive, there is the quest narrative. The former group usually, but not always, go for the early Middle Ages, the latter for the high Middle Ages. The same material can be interpreted in radically different ways. Heavy Metal and disenchantment, or New Agery and re-enchantment. Or both at once. The Strange Landscape of the Middle Ages – the landscape around which Umberto Eco constructed his novel *The Name of the Rose* – is of particular interest today, partly because it *is* so strange and partly because on closer inspection it *isn't*.

The Middle Ages have impinged on 1980s or 1990s consciousness in some highly dramatic ways. In Terry Gilliam's *Time Bandits* (1981), a knight in full battle armour – mounted on a white charger – bursts out of a wardrobe into a suburban child's bedroom; the child, called Kevin, has just turned the lights off and put aside *The Big Book of Greek Heroes*. A latter-day version of C. S. Lewis, perhaps. In Rob Reiner's film *The Princess Bride* (1987), a small child who is used to fast-forward video games is gradually wooed into the gentler world of medieval romance by his grandpa's telling of a charming bedtime story: 'Has it got any sports in it?' 'Are you kidding? . . . fencing, fighting, torture, revenge, giants, monsters, chases, true love, miracles . . .' 'It doesn't sound too bad. I'll try to stay awake.' A latter-day version of Joseph Campbell.

In Vincent Ward's film *The Navigator – A Medieval Odyssey* (1988), a group of refugees from monochrome Cumbria at the time of the Black Death emerge into the colourful, well-lit world of a late-twentieth-century city in New Zealand, having dug their way through the very centre of the earth; there, the refugees meet some modern-day craft metalworkers, who are about to be made redundant, and the two groups discover they have a lot in common. A latter-day version of William Morris. And in Sam Raimi's *Army of*

Darkness – *The Medieval Dead* (1992), the American hero Ash is propelled down a time tunnel – with his chain-saw, of course – into Britain in the year 1300, after he has had the temerity to read a spell from the dreaded book of dead names *The Necronomicon*. He forcibly tries to take command of the situation: 'All right, you primitive screwheads. Listen up. *This* is my broomstick. Twelve-gauge double-barrelled Remington. This sweet baby was made in Grand Rapids Michigan. YOU GOT THAT? The next one of you primates even touches me . . . BOOM!' A latter-day version of Mark Twain.

But perhaps the most effective entrance made by the Middle Ages in recent years is in Raymond Carver's dirty and magical short story *Cathedral* (1983). A not very bright, not very pleasant, unseeing narrator is watching television – just to pass the time – with a blind man, a friend of his wife's.

Something about the church and the Middle Ages was on the TV. Not your run-of-the-mill TV fare. I wanted to watch something else. I turned to the other channels but there was nothing on them, either. So I turned back to the first channel and apologized . . . The TV showed this one cathedral. Then there was a long, slow look at another one. Finally, the picture switched to the famous one in Paris, with its flying buttresses and its spires reaching up to the clouds. The camera pulled away to show the whole of the cathedral rising above the skyline. There were times when the Englishman who was telling the thing would shut up, would simply let the camera move around over the cathedrals. Or else the camera would tour the countryside, men in fields walking behind oxen. I waited as long as I could. Then I felt I had to say something. I said '. . . Now I guess they're in Italy. Yeah, they're in Italy. There's paintings on the walls of this one church.'

'Are those fresco paintings, bub?' he asked, and he sipped from his drink. I reached for my glass. But it was empty. I tried to remember what I could remember. 'You're asking me are those frescoes?' I said. 'That's a good question. I don't know.'

Eventually, the blind man asks the narrator to do him the favour of describing a cathedral to him. After a couple of attempts – 'they're very tall', 'they're really big' – he quickly runs out of words. So the blind man suggests that they get a pen and some heavy paper, and try to draw the building together. And the narrator succeeds in drawing a cathedral, with his eyes closed, guided by the fingers of a blind man.

The experience the narrator has, as 'his fingers rode my fingers as my hand went over the paper', seems akin to the experience William Golding described in *The Spire* (1964) – a novel about a medieval dean's obsession with building, against all the odds, a great cathedral spire:

There had been sun before, but not like this. The most seeming solid thing in the nave, was not the barricade of wood and canvas that cut the cathedral in two, at the choir steps, was not the two arcades of the nave, nor the chantries and painted tomb slabs between them. The most solid thing was the light. It smashed through the rows of windows in the south aisle, so that they exploded with colour, it slanted before him from right to left in an exact formation, to hit the bottom yard of the pillars on the north side of the nave. Everywhere, fine dust gave these rods and trunks of light the importance of a dimension. He blinked at them again, seeing, near at hand, how the individual prisms of dust turned over each other, or bounced all together, like mayfly in a breath of wind.

Carver's narrator simply doesn't have the words. But the blind man acts as his guide and helps him experience at least something of the Strange Landscape of the Middle Ages . . .

PART TWO

THE JOURNEY

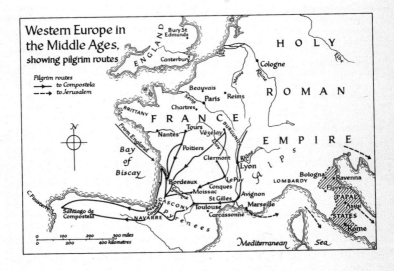

Western Europe in
the Middle Ages,
showing pilgrim routes

Pilgrim routes
⟶ to Compostela
- -▸ to Jerusalem

1

THE JEWELLED CITY

In the strange landscape of the European Middle Ages everything stood for something else, and that something else was God. 'We understand a thing,' wrote a medieval thinker, 'only when we see the divine plan within it.' The visible always pointed to the invisible.

The way to get through this strange landscape, the way to make sense of it, was to follow the light – light which, as the Gospel of St John had put it, 'shineth in darkness, by which all things were made, and that enlighteneth every man'. If, as was generally believed, the world was God's work of art, a work of art which was ordered in measure and number and weight, then light provided the means of understanding it.

And *human* works of art achieved significance, or meaning, only insofar as they managed to reveal the *splendor veritatis*, or the light of Truth, by becoming shadow versions of the Creator's work. The great medieval cathedrals of the twelfth and thirteenth centuries were more than anything else a new architecture of light – a way of reaching out towards God. They were encyclopedias of the latest thought, art and engineering; experimental laboratories where geometry plus craft techniques could be tested out; facsimiles of the Heavenly City itself – which pilgrims believed would descend from the skies at the end of the world – an ordered city, garnished with precious stones. Almost literally out of this world.

The historian Jean Gimpel has written, 'in three centuries – from 1050 to 1350 – several million tons of stone were quarried in France for the building of eighty cathedrals, 500 large churches and some tens of thousands of parish churches. More stone was excavated in France during these three centuries than at any time in Ancient Egypt.' And each building was intended to be an image or reflection of the divine artist and *his* creation. To the medieval pilgrim, who was used to small single-storey houses made of wood and plaster and straw, they must have seemed like glimpses of paradise. No wonder people travelled hundreds of miles, on unpaved roads or Roman roads which had long since gone to seed, to visit them.

Where did all the energy for this construction boom come from? And how on earth did the builders do it? Above all, what was the meaning – at the time – of the Jewelled City? The Jewelled City which had been prophesied in the Book of Revelation.

In the twelfth century the main pilgrim routes across Europe bound the continent together, at a time when not much else did. They overlapped with trade routes – ships carrying French wine to Ireland returned with Celtic pilgrims, for example – and they were used by a surprising variety of people. Historian Morris Bishop has recently written:

On the main highways the traffic was very heavy. Some historians assert that there was more displacement of persons in the Middle Ages than there was in the settled village society of the nineteenth century. Everyone was on the roads: monks and nuns on errands for their community; bishops bound for Rome or making a parochial visitation; wandering students; singing pilgrims following their priests and their banners . . . discharged soldiers, beggars and highwaymen; and sheep and cattle on their way to market befouling the already foul highway.

Well-to-do pilgrims travelled on horseback; everyone else walked, picking their way through the horse and cow dung. The pilgrimage was intended to be a microcosm of the journey through life; it was a penance, an adventure, a party – and often a dangerous way to travel.

Space, time and distance were, like everything else, thought to be governed by their significance in the divine plan. To judge by the Mappa Mundi – an ecclesiastical map of the world dating from the thirteenth century and now in Hereford Cathedral – the world of the medieval pilgrim was round, round like a plate, and at its centre was the Holy City of Jerusalem. The British Isles were at the edge of the world, so pilgrims travelled across Europe from the edge to the centre. Their destinations were the Holy City of Jerusalem, or Rome, or the shrine of St James at Compostela – in the remote north-west corner of Spain, on Cape Finisterre (literally, end of the land). Europe wasn't at the centre of things, it was at the edge, part of the developing world. In the tenth or eleventh centuries a scholar at the great university at Baghdad would have been very dismissive of this Third World backwater.

The pilgrims' stopovers on the road to St James, a road which could be anything up to five hundred miles long, became places on the map and they developed economically and politically as a result. Each major stopover was a holy place in itself, where the human remains of a saint – or bits of material sanctified through contact with the saint's body – could be seen and revered, and where their power could be felt first-hand: around these human remains were built altars, shrines, churches and cathedrals. Travel, at about twenty-five miles a day on a good day, must have been tough – but the end of the journey promised the forgiveness of pilgrims' sins or the intercession of their favourite saint. Whether or not it broadened the pilgrims' minds remains an open question: a *Pilgrim's Guide* written in the 1140s – the earliest to have survived and probably by a priest from Poitou – is full of local patriotism and distaste for the attitudes and behaviour of just about everyone else who might be encountered on the road to Compostela. He seems to have had it in for the people of Navarre in particular:

At a place called Lorca, to the east, there flows a stream known as the Salt River. Beware of drinking from it or of watering your horse in it, for this river brings death. On its banks, while we were going to St James, we found two Navarrese sitting there sharpening their knives; for they are accustomed to flay pilgrims' horses which die after drinking the water. In answer to our question they lied, saying that the water was good and drinkable.

Accordingly we watered our horses in the river, and at once two of them died and were forthwith skinned by the two men . . .

A Navarrese or a Basque will kill a Frenchman for a penny if he can. In some parts of the region, in Biscay and Alava, when the Navarrese become aroused, men show their private parts to women and women to men. The Navarrese fornicate shamelessly with their beasts, and it is said that a Navarrese will put a padlock on his she-mule and his mare lest another man should get at them. He also libidinously kisses the vulva of a woman or a she-mule.

There are also complaints in the *Guide* about inns where pilgrims are forced to pay for an evening meal as well as their bed, where tumblers look large but are in fact small, and where the food is visibly 'off'. The author helpfully includes what has been called 'the first mini-dictionary for travellers', so that pilgrims can – if they must – order a meal in the Basque language ('which is utterly barbarous'). There are tips about the roads, the inns, the key relics and the places which *had* to be visited *en route*. One of these was Vézelay, in Burgundy, south-east of Paris, where 'the most holy body of the blessed Mary Magdalene is above all to be venerated':

There a large and beautiful basilica and an abbey were built; there sinners have their faults remitted by God for love of the saint, the blind have their sight restored, the tongues of the dumb are loosed, the lame are cured of their lameness, those possessed by devils are delivered and ineffable benefits are granted to many of the faithful.

While they were waiting for all these things to happen, or simply passing through, pilgrims could move around the solid, round-arched building at Vézelay – constructed between 1096 and 1136 like a fortress or sanctuary, in common with many Romanesque buildings, in this case on a hill overlooking the Burgundian countryside – on a kind of indoor journey. They could 'read' this space like a three-dimensional book: the walls were the covers; the carved sculptures and reliefs and details were the text. For the main purpose of art – all art – was to reproduce, through human means, the rules and structures that lay behind the order of the universe, an order where every single image reflected, or referred to, every other image in an endless hall of mirrors with God at its centre. The grand narrative which was depicted in this way was of course the Christian story of the world, from the Creation in the Garden of Eden to the incarnation when Christ came down to earth, and to Armageddon when the world would come to an end. It was a continuing story which was seen not as a metaphor or a piece of poetry but as an accurate account of what *had* happened and, chillingly, what *was going* to happen. The pilgrims who visited Vézelay, whether they were literate or not, could 'read' the building; they might need help, in the form of a guide or guidebook, or they might read it as simply as a motorist today reads the red and green of a traffic light. A twelfth-century German Benedictine called Theophilus, author of a work 'On the Different Arts', gives an idea of how the faithful would respond to the visual language of churches; he seems to be referring in particular to Romanesque buildings:

. . . the human eye is not able to consider on what work first to fix its gaze; if it beholds the ceilings they glow like brocades; if it considers the walls they are a kind of paradise; if it regards the profusion of light from the windows, it marvels at the inestimable beauty of the glass and the infinitely rich and various workmanship. But if, perchance, the faithful soul observes the representation of the Lord's Passion expressed in art, it is stung with compassion. If it sees how many torments the saints endured in their bodies and what rewards of eternal life they have received, it eagerly embraces the observance of a better life. If it beholds how great are the joys of heaven and how great the torments in the infernal flames, it is animated by the hope of its good deeds and is shaken with fear by reflection on its sins.

In the waiting-room, or narthex, at Vézelay – a place where pilgrims could if they wished spend the night, as well as a symbolic passageway from the profane outside world to the sacred church within – visitors could see above the central door of the church a half-moon-shaped relief sculpture, showing the figure of Christ at the centre. He is over twice the size of his disciples, depicted on either side of him, and eight times the size of the other figures carved around the arch. He is passing the word to 'every nation under heaven', first to the disciples, who will become missionaries to the known world and eventually the unknown one. Round the outer edge of the sculpture the signs of the zodiac are interspersed with scenes of activities associated with those times of the calendar; between Scorpio and Sagittarius, for example, someone is slaughtering a pig for November, while Capricorn is associated with a man carrying an elderly woman across a threshold – meaning the end of one year and the beginning of the next. On the next ring in, the word is passed on to the known world. A hermit with a stick preaches to a couple of Byzantines and Armenians, while Cynocephali ('dog-heads'), whose natural habitat is within caves in the mountains of India, are having a chat next to some Arabs. The dog-heads communicate by howling and they are fast-moving hunters (one of them has a sword which he rests nonchalantly on his left shoulder).

Along the door lintel are carvings of the inhabitants of the unknown world – based on the Greek texts collected by Pliny the Elder in his *Natural History* shortly after the death of Christ. There are giants ('big-feet' people) and tiny Pygmies from the interior of Africa, one of whom is climbing on to a horse with a ladder: they were supposed to live with miniature cattle but full-sized horses. Then there are the Panotii, the 'all-ears' from the mountains of India; their ears were said sometimes to reach their feet and to double as blankets, and since they were a very shy people they tended to use their ears to fly away when the going got rough.

The homelands of these peoples would have been vague never-never lands with very mysterious names to the medieval pilgrim, but there is no sense in which they are presented as 'primitive' or at an earlier stage of evolution; they are just very different, maybe because they have fallen from grace for some reason. Attempts have been made by historians to explain why the peoples of the unknown world were seen in these ways: maybe the 'all-ears' were in fact elephants and the 'big-feet' were people meditating under palm leaves, and the story improved with the telling. To visitors at the time, though, they were both strange and credible. There were more things in heaven and earth than they could dream of.

On the tympanum at Vézelay the pilgrim thus saw Christ in Majesty, the disciples, the known world, the unknown world and the heavens; the known world is separated from the unknown by carved waves of water, which refer also to the folds of Christ's clothing. It is simultaneously a map, a story, a message – and an uplifting experience for pilgrims as they waited to continue *their* journey. Theirs was a less exotic journey, perhaps, but still one where *difference* would be encountered along the way – and here, as in other church carvings across Europe, they were being given a kind of early twelfth-century Michelin Guide to the conversion of the cosmos.

The next major stopover, according to the *Pilgrim's Guide*, would be Conques in south-western France, where 'the most precious body of the blessed Faith, virgin and martyr, was honourably buried by Christians in the valley . . . Many benefits are granted both to the sick and to those who are in good health. In front of the handsome basilica is a most excellent spring, the virtues of which are too great to be told.'

This was a special place because the abbey church – which has been called 'a prototype of the "pilgrimage road" style of church' – housed the sacred relic of Ste Foy (or Faith), a little girl who had been martyred for her beliefs in the third century. The upper part of her skull had originally been put on display at Agen, Aquitaine, where she died, but in the ninth century a Benedictine monk from Conques had cunningly applied for a job in the rival community and 'after ten patient years' managed to steal the head one night in a sack of vegetables. The *Guide* uses the word 'honourably' to describe this sacred theft, it being agreed at the time that since the relic was a piece of the living saint, she must have wanted the ritual kidnapping to happen so that she could pass on to a new community, her new home in Conques.

There are many surviving accounts, called *translationes*, in the

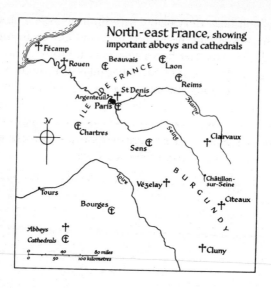

central and late Middle Ages of such ritual kidnappings. Perhaps the strangest involved Bishop Hugh of Lincoln, who, while he was paying his respects to the arm of Mary Magdalene at Fécamp, tried to break off a piece of the arm but failed; he then set about biting off the Magdalene's index finger with his teeth, 'first with his incisors and finally with his molars'. Eventually he succeeded in breaking off two fragments — to the 'utter horror' of the watching monks. It seems clear from these *translationes* that *the* most common motive for pilgrimages was to show reverence to a 'living saint'; that the movement of bones sometimes caused confusion — some pilgrims continued to pray at the original burial site, even though the bones had been translated; and that the cult of relics was by no means confined to any one social class. It is perhaps comfortable to imagine 'simple, working people' believing in such things, but relics were equally visited by those about to be knighted or undergo combat, and kings knelt and wept before the reliquaries of saints. In the thirteenth century King Edward I of England prayed before St

Edmund's shrine at Bury before he went into battle with the Scots and as he was leaving he looked back and bowed to the blessed martyr. A few days later he sent his standard to the prior at Bury asking that a Mass for St Edmund be said over it and that it should be touched by all the relics there.

ABBOT SAMSON OF ST EDMUNDSBURY 'TRANSLATES' HIS PATRON SAINT

Now the coffin was filled with the holy body, and . . . the abbot looking near, found after this a silken cloth which covered the whole body, and then a linen cloth of wonderful whiteness; and over the head a little linen cloth, and another small and skilfully made silken cloth, as it were the veil of some holy woman. And then they found the body wrapped in a linen cloth, and so at last all the lines of the holy body were clearly traceable.

Here the abbot stopped, saying that he dared not go further, and behold the naked body of the saint. Therefore, he held his head between his hands, and said with a groan, 'Glorious martyr, holy Edmund, blessed be that hour in which you were born. Glorious martyr, turn not my daring to my hurt, in that I, who am a sinner and wretched, touch you. You know my devotion and my intention.' And then he touched the eyes and nose, the latter being thick and very large, and afterwards touched the breast and arms, and raising the left hand touched the fingers and placed his own fingers between those of the saint. And going further he found the feet standing upright as though they had been the feet of a man but lately dead, and he touched the toes, and counted them as he touched them.

From *The Chronicle of Jocelin of Brakeland*, Monk of St Edmundsbury

---

The upper part of the skull of Ste Foy, in Conques, was enshrined in a seated golden figure, with piercing glass eyes and a tunic smothered in precious stones, and a sculpted head which evidently came from somewhere else too – it is thought to date from the third to fourth centuries and originally to have belonged either to a

Roman emperor or some Celtic god. The seated figure, made of wood covered with gold and gilded silver, may be the oldest surviving example of large-scale Christian sculpture in Europe. And so the little girl who died for refusing to worship pagan gods ended up looking exactly like one.

The technical definition of an altar in Roman Catholic canon law is, to this day, 'a sepulchre containing the relics of saints', and the word 'shrine' meant the chest or reliquary protecting them, so no church of whatever size could be constructed without a relic at its centre. The *Pilgrim's Guide* is full of references to the heads, bodies and tails of saints which could be viewed at local cult centres all along the journey to Compostela – and to the miracles which routinely happened when the saints intervened, as they often did, in everyday affairs. They were like the Greek gods who lived on Mount Olympus in ancient times, the main difference being that these saints had actually lived and left behind their bones to prove it – so they were *still living*.

One of the seven great pilgrimage churches of Rome was the basilica of Santa Croce in Gerusalemme. According to pilgrim folklore it had been built by Emperor Constantine in the fourth century as an elaborate reliquary for the sacred relics dug up in the Holy Land by his mother Helena. It certainly contained the finest selection of relics in the whole of Rome, displayed in suitably ornate settings. There were three pieces of the True Cross – the biggest pieces on show anywhere – supposedly found in a pit in Jerusalem; two thorns from the Crown of Thorns; a small piece of stone from the manger in Bethlehem; the tablet or notice from above Christ's Cross at the crucifixion – 'Jesus of Nazareth, King of the Jews' – written in Greek, Latin and Hebrew, although the Hebrew bit had been broken off at the top; one of the original nails from the Cross; and, the *pièce de résistance*, the index finger of Doubting Thomas, the disciple who had said of Jesus, 'Except I shall see in his hands the print of the nails, and put my finger into the print of the nails, and thrust my hand into his side, I will not believe' – well, there was the finger he did it with.

What would a twelfth-century pilgrim have made of all this? The pilgrim would have approached the altar with – in a famous phrase – the mixed smell of blood and roses in his or her nostrils, a mixture just like the little bits of bone in their elaborately worked containers which the pilgrim had come all this way to see. These pieces of eternity would have brought the pilgrim face to face with the physical reality of the New Testament and would have concentrated on this particular place an immense power. They would have been far easier to understand than the abstruse debates of theologians – helping to explain, for example, what happened at the Eucharist when bread and wine became body and blood. And maybe miracles and apparitions would happen here as a result of these relics. I say 'maybe', but to the twelfth-century pilgrim there would have been no 'maybe' about it: miracles were part of everyday life – for example, it was miraculous whenever someone recovered from a serious illness or whenever there was a piece of good fortune. The cult of relics was to be much mocked by Renaissance and Reformation thinkers: Boccaccio wrote derisively of one cherished relic – a feather left behind by the Archangel Gabriel at the Annunciation – and John Calvin famously wrote that there were enough relics of the True Cross to build a ship and of the Crown of Thorns to hedge a field. But, questions of authenticity aside, there is no doubt that the cult gives us a key insight into the mind of the medieval pilgrim. It provided simple answers to very difficult questions.

It was at the royal abbey of St Denis just a few miles north of Paris, which housed the ever-popular relics of the patron saint of France and the bones of its kings – and which was visited by thousands of enthusiastic pilgrims every year – that the very first church 'in the French style' or *opus Francigenum* as it was called, was built. It was started in 1136 and it pioneered a brand new architecture, the architecture of light.

One man was the visionary – and the client – who inspired this new style, Abbot Suger of St Denis (1085–1151). He was born into a farming family, went to a monastery school with the future King

Louis VI and eventually became chief minister of France when Louis VII was away crusading. He had been given to the abbey of St Denis as a child so it is little wonder that he saw the Church as a whole and more specifically the abbey (of which he was elected abbot in 1122) as his 'mother'. In a touching sentence in his writings he relates how, when he became abbot, his first work on the church at St Denis was to have the walls repaired and painted 'with gold and

---

ST DENIS ASSISTS WITH THE BUILDING OF HIS ABBEY

On a certain day when, with a downpour of rain, a dark opacity had covered the turbid air, those accustomed to assist in the work while the carts were coming down to the quarry went off because of the violence of the rain. The ox-drivers complained and protested that they had nothing to do and that the labourers were standing around losing time. Clamouring, they grew so insistent that some weak and disabled persons together with a few boys – seventeen in number and, if I am not mistaken, with a priest present – hastened to the quarry, picked up one of the ropes, fastened it to a column and abandoned another shaft which was lying on the ground; for there was nobody who would undertake to haul this one. Thus, animated by pious zeal, the little flock prayed: 'O Saint Denis, if it pleaseth thee, help us by dealing for thyself with this abandoned shaft, for thou canst not blame us if we are unable to do it.' Then, bearing on it heavily, they dragged out what a hundred and forty or at least one hundred men had been accustomed to haul from the bottom of the chasm with difficulty – not alone by themselves, for that would have been impossible, but through the will of God and the assistance of the Saints whom they invoked; and they conveyed this material for the church to the cart. Thus it was made known throughout the neighbourhood that this work pleased Almighty God exceedingly, since for the praise and glory of his name he had chosen to give his help to those who performed it by this and similar signs.

From *On the Consecration of the Church of St Denis* (1144–7)
by Abbot Suger

---

precious colours'; he goes on, 'I completed this all the more gladly because I had wished to do it, if ever I should have an opportunity, even while I was a pupil at school.' He was very short in stature and came from an ordinary background, but he never seems to have felt inhibited by his illustrious surroundings. Indeed, over the entrance of the abbey he rebuilt, a symbol of the gates of heaven, he depicted himself – not *quite* life-size – at the feet of Christ.

It is clear from Suger's writings that he was absolutely devoted to France's patron saint, St Denis, and to his church. The central authority exercised by King Louis, and therefore the unity of France itself, were for him symbolized or even vested in the abbey of St Denis. He particularly enjoyed the fact that many illustrious people attended celebrations in his church. It is also clear that he was a man of boundless energy, full of big ideas, as in the story of how he had been told by his carpenters that no suitable wood for repair work was available in the surrounding area – so, after lying awake all night worrying about it, he dashed off into the forest the following morning, with his carpenters in tow, and personally found exactly what he was after. The local lord had not used up all the large beams for military purposes, after all. But, beyond all this, Suger was obsessed with the subject of light.

His inscription, commemorating the consecration of the rebuilt east end of the abbey, attempted to describe the effect it would have on the rest of the building:

> Once the new rear part is joined
> to the part in front,
> The church shines with its middle
> part brightened.
> For bright is that which is brightly
> coupled with the bright,
> And bright is the noble edifice
> which is pervaded by the new light . . .

The 'new light' could be interpreted at two different levels – in the sense of the actual lighting conditions made possible by the new architecture and also in the sense of the light of the New Testament as opposed to the Old, which was (in St Augustine's phrase) covered with a veil. The word he used for light was *claritas*, meaning the radiance or splendour which flowed from 'the Father of the lights'.

Suger reckoned that he had the strongest possible theological justification for his light obsession – and for his related passion for gold and jewels and all things precious – in the writings of the great St Denis himself, his beloved patron saint. In fact, he – in common with nearly all the other medieval scholars who wrote on the subject – had managed to confuse the French St Denis with Denis or Dionysius the Areopagite, a disciple of St Paul, as well as with yet another Denis or Dionysius, a fifth-century Syrian. But out of this productive confusion came confirmation of the idea that light was the first great principle of life, the most important source of order and value there was. It was the light of the Greek philosophers, which symbolized the goodness and knowledge towards which human beings struggled, and the light of the Gospel of St John 'by which all things were made'. The more a thing had light reflected on to it, the more it became an 'image' of its creator. As Suger wrote, it was light, reflected *through* glass or *on to* precious surfaces which transported him 'to some strange region of the universe between the slime of earth and the purity of heaven'.

So, with a strong sense of theatre and showmanship, Suger put up coloured glass windows of sapphire blue, ruby red and emerald green, to filter the light as it shone down on to the relics, displayed on a sumptuous golden altar which also displayed a great cross studded with jewels and inlaid with emeralds: he was not the first to have used coloured glass; but he was the first to make it central to the experience of entering a church. The glass and the roomy, transparent interior were not however just the result of philosophy. They were also practical exercises in crowd control. Even allowing for Suger's special pleading (as he pitched for the resources to redesign the old abbey church), it is clear there was a problem:

Often on feast days, completely filled, the abbey disgorged through all its doors the excess of the crowds as they moved in opposite directions, and the outward pressure of the foremost ones not only prevented those attempting to enter from entering but also expelled those who had already entered. At times you could see, a marvel to behold, that the multitude offered so much resistance to those who strove to flock in to worship and kiss the holy relics, the Nail and Crown of the Lord, that no one among the countless thousands of people because of their very density could move a foot; that no one, because of their very congestion, could do anything but stand like a marble statue, stay benumbed or, as a last resort, scream . . . Moreover the brethren who were showing the tokens of the Passion of Our Lord had to yield to their anger and rioting and many a time, having no place to turn, escaped with the relics through the windows.

To realize his philosophy of light, and to ease the flow of visitors, Suger remodelled the church by knocking down the dark forests of pillars and cramped walls, to make way for a lighter, more open and more spacious interior.

But some Churchmen, such as the influential Bernard of Clairvaux, were unimpressed by Suger's emphasis on precious metals and glitter – which had become, as Bernard put it, 'so common nowadays'. He continued, in his *Apologia for Abbot William*:

O vanity of vanities, but more folly than vanity! The walls of the church are ablaze with light and colour, while the poor of the Church go hungry. The Church revets its stones in gold and leaves its children naked. The money for feeding the poor goes to feast the eyes of the rich. The curious find plenty to relish and the starving find nothing to eat.

Suger replied, in defence of his love of splendour and of theatre: 'Those who criticize us claim that the sacred function needs only a holy soul and a pure mind. We certainly agree that these are what principally matter, but we believe also that we should worship through the outward ornaments of sacred vessels . . . and this with all inner purity and with all outward splendour.' And on the great gilded doors of the central west portal of the church he rebuilt, he had inscribed – for all who could read to see – a summary of his theology of light:

PORTARVM QVISQVIS ATTOLLERE QVERIS HONOREM
AVRVM NEC SVMPTVS OPERIS MIRARE LABOREM
NOBILE CLARET OPVS SED OPVS QVOD NOBILE CLARET
CLARIFICET MENTES VT EANT PER LVMINA VERA

AD VERVM LVMEN VBI CHRISTVS IANVA VERA
QVALE SIT INTVS IN HIS DETERMINAT AVREA PORTA
MENS HEBES AD VERVM PER MATERIALIA SVRGIT
ET DEMERSA PRIVS HAC VISA LVCE RESVRGIT

[Whoever thou art, if thou seekest to extol the glory of these doors,
Marvel not at the gold and the expense but at the craftsmanship of
   the work.
Bright is the noble work; but, being nobly bright, the work
Should brighten the minds so that they may travel, through the true
   lights

To the True Light where Christ is the true door.
In what manner it be inherent in this world the gold door defines:
The dull mind rises to truth through that which is material
And, in seeing this light, is resurrected from its former submersion.]

Eventually, persuaded by Suger's two treatises on the subject – and by their distinguished pedigree apparently from the mind of St Denis himself – Bernard came to accept the argument that the duller members of the laity sometimes needed the brightness of a work of art, or of a precious jewel, to brighten up their inner thoughts. He never wrote a word of criticism of the new abbey of St Denis, and in fact remained on surprisingly good terms with Suger right up until the abbot died.

It was no matter that Suger's ideas were given immense credibility because of a long-standing case of mistaken identity between three men all of whom answered to the name of Dionysius, or Denis: a follower of St Paul who, according to Acts xvii, 33, heard him preach in Athens, then 'clave to him and believed'; the patron saint of France, who was martyred while converting Gaul in the middle of the third century; and a nameless Syrian writer of seven hundred years before Suger's time, who for reasons best known to himself claimed to have been the follower of St Paul. Without this triple mistake, the new St Denis and the 'French style' it ushered in would never have happened, for it would have had no basis in theology. Today, little remains of Suger's new abbey except the west front with its innovative 'rose window', the ambulatory and the crypt; the present nave and upper sections were added later. And St Denis is well off today's pilgrim route. But what Suger had started was to become – further south – the crowning glory of the Jewelled City.

Within less than a single generation, between 1194 and about 1220, a small community of less than ten thousand inhabitants managed to build on a plateau overlooking their town the great cathedral of Our Lady of Chartres, the grandest and tallest structure Western Christendom had ever produced. It has been called (by the sculptor Rodin) 'the Acropolis of France', but unlike the other greatest hits in the early story of architecture – the Great Pyramid, the Athenian citadel, the Colosseum in Rome – it was not built as a grandiose statement of power and authority. It was built by the people for the presumed benefit of the people, and it was built for the most French of reasons: because an entire community had become devoted, head over heels, to a lady called Mary, who, as a contemporary chronicle put it, 'had chosen Chartres as her special residence here on earth'.

As the cult of the Virgin Mary had developed in the Western Church, and as the image of Mary had changed from being a remote, shadowy figure to becoming first the queen of heaven and then the mother and advocate of everyone, so the association of Chartres with the cult had put the community on the map – not just spiritually but economically as well, with great textile fairs and trade shows which coincided in the calendar with the four great feasts of the Virgin. Chartres had in fact been the focal point of the cult since the middle of the ninth century, when the original cathedral had been destroyed by Vikings. King Charles the Bald, grandson of the Emperor Charlemagne, had presented the church at that time with the sacred relic known as the Sancta Camisia, widely believed to have been the actual tunic worn by Mary when she gave birth to Jesus.

Chartres was also famous for its scholars, associated with the cathedral, who had become in the past two hundred years the most important community for the study of geometry, mathematics and music – and the deep connections between them – in the western world. So the spectacular Royal Portal, built at the west end of the original cathedral in about 1150, following one of several fires, included sculptures of the founding fathers of these disciplines – among them Pythagoras, Euclid and Aristotle – plus allegorical figures representing the Liberal Arts – Music, Astronomy, Arithmetic, Geometry and Dialectics, presided over by the Mother of God herself – and all based on the proportional geometry of the golden section, the ratio (of approximately 5:8) which Plato had called the most pleasing of all.

On the central tympanum of the portal, to the left of these scientists and mathematicians, sat a larger-than-life Christ in Glory, flanked by the winged figures of a man or angel, an eagle, an ox and a lion. This tableau was based on the vision of St John the Divine and it remains an excellent example of the many levels at which the medieval symbolic universe operated. For the four figures are in fact the 'emblems of the Evangelists': the man is St Matthew (because his Gospel opens with a family tree of the ancestors of Christ); the eagle is St John (because the bird was reported to be able to stare at the sun, the very essence of things); the ox is St Luke (because his Gospel opens with the sacrifice of Zacharias and the ox was the archetypal sacrificial beast); and the lion is St Mark (the voice crying, or roaring, in the wilderness). These associations of ideas, or *analogies*, represent one level of meaning: man = family tree, eagle = getting to the heart of creation, ox = sacrifice, lion = roaring, all of them relating to the opening lines of their respective gospels. But the four creatures also represent four great moments in the grand narrative of the universe: Incarnation (man), Ascension (eagle), Redemption through sacrifice (ox), the Redeemer lives (lion, who was thought to sleep with his eyes always open). And they represent, at a human level, the aspects of character which are most needed for salvation: intelligence, vision, sacrifice and courage.

So the three simultaneous levels – the opening lines of the Gospels, the holy story, the human drama – are all embodied in the figures which surround Christ, and a full understanding of them would require a comprehension of the Bible, of interpretations by the early Church Fathers, and of the illustrated texts of mythical and real beasts known as Bestiaries based on pre-Christian thinking. Take the lion as an example: the pilgrim would need to know the opening verse of St Mark's Gospel, the sleeping habits of the beast and the fact that the lion wasn't a cowardly lion but a courageous one. Interpretations of these 'emblems' had become, and were to become, some of the great achievements of Christian art, including the *Book of Kells* which was illuminated in about 800. Indeed, the emblems may have entered the visual bloodstream through decorations on parchment of the opening words of the Gospels in the early Middle Ages.

The Royal Portal, the crypt and the foundations are just about all that survive of the original cathedral, for in 1194 yet another fire destroyed most of the town centre of Chartres and engulfed its emblematic building. It seemed to be a sign from heaven that the Virgin Mary had deserted the town – which would now go into terminal decline. Three days after the fire, on 13 June 1194, a visiting cardinal and papal legate called an assembly of the townspeople of Chartres – in the open space in front of the Royal Portal, which was still surrounded by smouldering embers.

The cardinal had just begun his speech about how important it was – for the spiritual and economic survival of the town – somehow to muster the energy and raise the funds for the rebuilding of the cathedral, when a solemn procession suddenly appeared carrying the sacred tunic of the Virgin Mary. This was a great piece of timing, and it was also a miracle because the relic had survived the

A MIRACLE SAVES THE RELIC FROM THE FIRE AT CHARTRES CATHEDRAL

And there was another miracle, which surpassed all the others, and which happened when the holy Reliquary was taken into the crypt, when the cathedral first caught fire. Those who had devoted themselves to saving the Relic, finding themselves unable to get back into the church, rushed down into the crypt again and shut the iron door behind them. They remained there for two or three days without eating. But the Holy Virgin confronted them and ensured that they were not injured by smoke, fire or hunger . . .

When the fire was finally extinguished, these generous sons of Our Lady managed to come out of the crypt, full of joy and health, to the great amazement of all their fellow citizens who thought they must have expired under the smoking debris of the church. Everyone embraced them, everyone wept and thanked God and his Holy Mother for having protected them from all evil by a definite miracle.

From *Chronicle of the Miracles of the Blessed Virgin Mary of the Church of Chartres (c.* 1210)

fire after all – it had been salvaged from the cathedral crypt. This was interpreted by everyone present as a sign that the Lady of Chartres herself had permitted the old church to be burned down, not because she had deserted the town, but because she wanted a new and even more worthy church to be built in her honour. And she had expressed her wish in a particularly dramatic way.

The community's despair turned – instantly, if the author of the *Chronicle of the Miracles of the Blessed Virgin Mary of the Church of Chartres (c.* 1210) is to be credited (and in the chronicles moods do tend to change, irrationally, on the instant) – into a swell of enthusiasm. There was chanting and praying and singing in the streets. There was no doubt about it now, the new cathedral just had to be the finest building in the Christian world. It would be an encyclopedia of this world and the next, waiting for the end of time; an experience which would be something like entering the city of God through the gates of heaven itself. The world might come to an end at any time and its life story − from the Garden of Eden to Armageddon, from the beginning to the end − would be there for all to read in limestone and glass. Above all, the new building would be an embodiment of the words of St John, in the Book of Revelation xxi:

I saw the Holy City, new Jerusalem, coming down out of heaven from God, made ready like a bride adorned for her husband . . . In the spirit an angel carried me away to a great and lofty mountain, and showed me Jerusalem, the Holy City, coming down out of heaven from God. It shone with the glory of God; it had the radiance of some priceless jewel, like a jasper, clear as crystal. It had a great and lofty wall with twelve gates . . . The wall was built of jasper, while the city itself was of pure gold, bright as clear glass. The foundations of the city wall were adorned with special stones of every kind, the first of the foundation-stones being jasper, the second lapis lazuli, the third chalcedony, the fourth emerald, the fifth sardonyx, the sixth cornelian, the seventh chrysolite, the eighth beryl, the ninth topaz, the tenth chrysoprase, the eleventh turquoise, and the twelfth amethyst . . . The city did not need the sun or the moon to shine on it, for the glory of God gave it light, and its lamp was the Lamb. By its light shall all the nations walk . . .

At the beginning of the great adventure the people of Chartres gathered in their thousands at the quarries of Berchères, five miles from the town. (The site today is 20 ft (6 m) below the surface of the fields.) Although overgrown, the limestone faces where they hacked at the rocks, the chisel marks they made and the pieces they left behind can still be seen. The stones were dragged to the building site in ox-drawn wagons, a process which took a full day per load − and was, incidentally, one of the most costly aspects of the whole enterprise. Some of the wagons were even manhandled by nobles and merchants, who slaved away in silence pausing only to ask for forgiveness. This strange 'cult of the carts' was believed at the time to have originated in Chartres with the building of the previous cathedral in 1144–50 (although there is a surviving account of the phenomenon of nearly a century before) and it clearly had great emotional significance for the region. The Abbot of Saint-Pierre-sur-Dives, in Normandy, wrote of the cult:

Who ever saw, who ever heard, in all the generations past, that kings, princes, mighty men of this world, puffed up with honours and riches, men and women of noble birth, should bind bridles upon their proud and swollen necks and submit them to wagons which, after the fashion of brute beasts, they dragged with their loads of wine, corn, oil, lime, stones, beams, and other things necessary to sustain life or to build churches, even to Christ's abode? Moreover, as they draw the wagons we may see this miracle that, although sometimes a thousand men and women, or even more, are bound in the traces (so vast indeed is the mass, so great is the engine, and so heavy the load laid upon it), yet they go forward in such silence that no voice, no murmur is heard . . . When they pause on the way, then no other voice is heard but confessions of guilt, with supplication and pure prayer to God that he may vouchsafe pardon for their sins.

The charred area around the cathedral would have been transformed into a gigantic building site, as master masons, rough masons, freemasons and artisans of all descriptions – under guidance from the cathedral chapter, one of the wealthiest in France through its income from land, harvests, mining and taxes – gathered for their grand project. Contemporary written sources, and artists' impressions, have surprisingly little to tell us about the processes of construction of a cathedral. Artists more usually depicted moments from the Gospels, or from saints' 'Lives', but because they made no attempt to put biblical construction projects – Noah's Ark, the Tower of Babel – into any kind of 'historical' setting, their drawings can sometimes reveal something about the techniques and details of their own day. And just occasionally a document gives the flavour of what it must have been like to witness the building of one of these giants. Lambert, parish priest of Andres, describes in his Chronicle how in about 1200 his town walls were rebuilt:

. . . many oftentimes came together to see these great earthworks; for such poor people as were not hired labourers forgot their penury in the joy of beholding this work; while the rich, both knights and burgesses and often-times priests or monks, came not daily only, but again and again every day, to refresh their bodies and see so marvellous a sight. For who but a man stupefied or deadened by age or cares could have failed to rejoice in the sight of that master Simon the Dyker, so learned in geometrical work, pacing with rod in hand and with all a master's dignity, and setting out hither and thither, not so much with that actual rod as with the spiritual rod of his mind, the work which in imagination he had already conceived?

Under the direct supervision of contractors or masters, the masons at Chartres would seem to have worked in loosely organized gangs – of maybe seventy or eighty journeymen apiece – for the next quarter of a century. There are no documents to tell us who any of these people were but the material of the building itself contains some clues. If you look very closely at the masonry, different styles and techniques begin to emerge. The quality and cutting of the stone, the units of measurement and even some design features reveal the different standards of workmanship of the various separate gangs – and the building isn't at all the harmonious unity it at first appears but, close up, is something of a shambles.

A few of the changes in style and technique are obvious, like the delicate web of buttresses which support the central nave as compared with the more solid ones which support the sanctuary on the eastern section. Less obviously, where the builders' accesses run around the roof level of the whole cathedral, the walkway arches, door lintels and window openings come in all shapes and sizes. And some rare written clues – medieval signatures in stone, which today need detective work to find and decipher – are hidden away in the builders' attics and storerooms, which visitors seldom see. They take the form of a series of masons' marks – triangles, crosses, circles, letters of the alphabet, bow shapes – incised in the stone, probably by the stonecutters back at the quarry in Berchères to keep a tally

WILLIAM OF SENS, MASTER MASON OF THE CHOIR OF CANTERBURY CATHEDRAL, HAS A SERIOUS ACCIDENT

After he had prepared to vault the great vault, suddenly the beams broke under his feet, and he fell to the ground, stones and timbers accompanying his fall, from the height of the capitals of the upper vault, that is to say, of fifty feet. Thus sorely bruised by the blows from the beams and stones he was rendered helpless alike to himself and for the work, but no other person than himself was in the least injured. Against the master only was this vengeance of God or spite of the devil directed.

The master, thus hurt, remained in his bed for some time under medical care in expectation of recovering, but was deceived in this hope, for his health amended not. Nevertheless, as the winter approached and it was necessary to finish the upper vault, he gave charge of the work to a certain ingenious and industrious monk, who was the overseer of the masons; an appointment whence much envy and malice arose, because it made this young man appear more skilful than richer and more powerful ones. But the master reclining in bed commanded all things that should be done in order. Thus the vault between the four main piers was completed.

From Gervase of Canterbury, *On the Burning and Rebuilding of the Church of Canterbury* (*c.* 1184)

of how many stones they had cut. Marks such as these were the only signatures of any kind in the entire cathedral, the closest we can get to the individual human beings who actually built the place.

From the masons' marks, and from the close-up evidence of the stonework, we can reconstruct in detail – albeit speculatively – the probable organization of the workforce and the order in which the cathedral was built. Although scholars have argued for centuries about whether construction took place from west to east, or vice versa, it now seems likely that the building went up from its existing foundations – one reason why it took only twenty-five years – horizontally, in layers, in about twenty-five to thirty separate campaigns. Each horizontal section may have been the work of a combination of gangs, for they left behind their distinctive signatures in stone as they went along. The builders would not have worked from measured drawings, though, and the engineering would have been based on proportional rather than structural principles. But with design advice from the cathedral chapter, and with wooden or metal templates and jigs supplied by the master masons, they were able to complete each section in turn; there was a measure of autonomy (hence the signatures) but only a measure.

Separate campaigns were essential, not only because they allowed time for the mortar made of lime to dry, shrink and settle (a process which could take six months or more), but also because the financing of the project was a question of raising the money, with help from the relic, spending it, and then waiting for another infusion of capital into the cathedral coffers. It would have been particularly difficult to work in winter, a time of high winds and downpours of rain. At each stage in the process a temporary wooden roof would probably have been added, to allow the usual church services to continue on site.

As the building progressed higher and higher, the work-groups would have used sturdy scaffolding and hoisting machines powered by huge wooden wheels attached to ropes, some large enough for five men to walk inside them. It would have taken about three hundred steps to raise any load, even a hundredweight, to the first floor – let alone to the main roof – and if one of the men happened to miss his footing, the stone would fall and the big wheel would turn the wrong way at double-quick speed, breaking everyone's legs in the process. That is if they were lucky. Other tools would have included water-powered saws and hammers, block and tackle pulleys, winches, drills and lathes, but the basic tools would have been jigs, adzes and axes, and for the masters, compasses, straight-edges, angles and string. And, of course, faith – 'the spiritual rod of the mind'.

The great wooden wheel would have come into its own when the masons were installing the vaults just below the roof, once the columns and walls and an outer triangular roof had been completed. First of all, a wooden frame was constructed and huge curved bows hoisted up and mounted on scaffolding. Next, mud was poured on to the bows and moulded into the shape of the vault. Each stone rib was raised on ropes – in sections – set in the mud, supported by the bows, and locked in place by a keystone. Finally – the most dangerous part – the stone webbing was carefully put into place, the mud and wooden bows removed, and the finished vault covered in a 4 in (10 cm) layer of mortar from above to avoid cracking between the stones. Then they waited for it all to dry.

The basic design decision had been that the dimensions of the new cathedral should match those of the previous structure. The only expansion would therefore be upwards, to a staggering 120 ft (36 m) high – the greatest space ever to have been enclosed up to that time. The geometry worked and the masonry was stable now that it had settled, but proportional thinking, as distinct from structural engineering, did have its practical limitations. Was the building stable enough?

To bind together its central section – 54 ft (16 m) across, 120 ft (36 m) high – the master builder or mason at Chartres used a new type of arched vault, where the supporting ribs travelled all the way down to the ground via shafts surrounded by clusters of thin columns, so the visual line from the centre of the ceiling right down to the floor was unbroken. The *energy* of the building was thus there to be seen and marvelled at. This was a revolutionary break with both the traditional solid wall approach of Egypt, Greece and Rome – walls holding up roof – and the forest of clumsy pillars supporting early medieval arched roofs.

The ceiling itself was a series of rectangles which stretched from wall to wall, crossed by ribs, with a keystone in the centre locking it all in place – like pushing up an umbrella made of stone, locking it and then taking the handle away. Contemporary chroniclers simply could not believe their eyes: since the columns, instead of the walls, seemed to be taking all the strain, the walls could simply be opened up. One of them expressed the hope, rather apprehensively, that the effect might 'last until the end of time' – which, given contemporary views on the apocalypse, may not have been a particularly optimistic thought.

The downward weight of the vaults, with the stress they placed on the delicate columns or piers, meant that the whole structure at the top was continually pushing outwards. But that couldn't be seen from the inside. From the outside – at the level of the builders' accesses around the roof – the problem of pressure and counter-pressure was much more evident. Because the stone vaults tended to push the supporting piers outwards, stone towers or buttresses were constructed in parallel to the main building and linked to its walls with flyers, attached to the walls just above the tops of the piers inside. So the force pushing outwards was transferred along the flyers, down the stone towers to the foundations below. These flyers came to be known as flying buttresses and this was the first time they had ever been used as an integral part of a building's overall design. If the walls were like the covers of a book – an image which was often used in the twelfth and thirteenth centuries – and the windows were like the text, then the flying buttresses were like book-ends which prevented the books from falling over. Although they had no means at all of testing it – again, their knowledge of structures seems to have lagged far behind their knowledge of geometry – the system on the whole seemed to work.

The last thing to be added was the stained glass, which – following Abbot Suger's philosophy at St Denis – was the main purpose of the building: walls made up of jewel-like fragments of coloured glass which bathed the interior with light as if from another world. Once the windows were securely in place – and it was discovered with relief that the rose-windows *could* resist high wind pressures, perhaps because they were based on the sturdy model of the cartwheel (the only available model) – the building was virtually complete. Originally it was to have been crowned with nine towers, but in one of the many changes of mind which happened during construction, this number was reduced to two. The huge roof was made of wood, covered in grey lead. The present-day copper roof, which has turned green, was added after a fire in the 1830s.

Of all the medieval cathedrals, Chartres today has the most complete set of original stained-glass windows, 176 in total, forty-three of which were donated by the merchants and craft brotherhoods of the town – carpenters, wine merchants, cloth merchants, furriers, bakers, money-changers, teamsters and so on. They have been called, like films or comic strips in the twentieth century, 'books that even the illiterate can read', one basic difference being that the windows date from 250 years or so before the invention of printing. St Gregory – no less – had written 'for that which writing supplies to him that can read, that does a picture to him that is unlearned and can only look'.

But the stories the windows tell are sometimes more complex than they appear, so the average medieval pilgrim may well have needed a guide in the form of a clerk to show him or her around. To take just one example, in the south aisle the 'Good Samaritan' window – where the details are clearly visible, provided the light outside is at reasonable levels – tells at least three interlocking stories at once. It needs to be read starting at the bottom and working upwards, from left to right.

The bottom line, symbolically enough, has a message from the sponsor: the shoemakers. The first two panels show the shoemakers at work, and in the right-hand panel a group of shoemakers offer the window to the cathedral. Shoemakers of course had something of a vested interest in the pilgrim business – it was a good way to wear out shoes – and they would also have gained redemption points for their generosity.

Then comes the first of the four-leaf shapes which resemble a flower. On the bottom leaf, Christ – with raised right hand – talks to two listeners, who have asked him, 'Master, what must we do to gain eternal life?' By way of an answer, he tells them the parable of the Good Samaritan. In the left, middle and right leaves, a man leaves the walled city of Jerusalem, through a red door, to go to Jericho; on the Jericho road he is mugged by a robber who pulls a sword on him – against a red background; and the gang of robbers thoroughly beat him up. In the top leaf the victim is lying there, while a priest and a Levite walk by without offering to help him; they just watch.

In the next three shapes, a man from Samaria discovers the victim and binds his wounds; puts him on a white donkey; and settles him down in an inn. At the bottom of the next flower shape, the Samaritan takes care of the victim, promising to come back later and settle his debts. At this point, another story begins, from the Book of Genesis in the Old Testament.

In the left-hand leaf, God – who looks exactly like Christ, is wearing the same clothes and has the same facial expression – breathes life into Adam, the first man. Adam sits in the Garden of Eden surrounded by trees, again against a red background, and, as he sleeps, God creates Eve from his spare rib. At the top, God shows the forbidden fruit of the tree of knowledge to Adam and Eve, complete with red serpent entwined around the tree-trunk. The next three shapes depict Eve trying to persuade Adam to eat of the fruit of the tree of knowledge, which he does – in red – and, as he eats, chokes on the fruit. Adam has his hand on his throat, clutching his 'Adam's apple'. Adam and Eve are now aware of their nakedness, and so they wear fig leaves to cover themselves. In the top flower, an angel expels them from paradise, through a red door.

Adam and Eve are now shown being forced to work for the first time – 'when Adam delved and Eve span' – while on the right leaf, the consequences of their original sin are depicted: Cain bashes Abel on the head, the first murder which puts the mark of Cain on all of us. At the top, Christ sits on a rainbow flanked by two angels, with an orb or globe in one hand and his other raised in blessing – in an exact visual parallel of the first gesture of the first story.

So the window finishes where it began, connecting the three stories: the Good Samaritan, Adam and Eve, and Christ in His heavenly city at the end of time. The connections had been made – in writing – not in the Bible, but in scholarly commentaries written by the early Church fathers, notably St Augustine and the Venerable

Bede. And they were connections at a symbolic, or analogical, level.

The man leaving Jerusalem is also Adam expelled from paradise. The robbers on the Jericho road also represent human temptation, original sin. The priest and the Levite passing by are Old Testament religion which can no longer heal our wounds. The inn is the Church itself, where the Samaritan promises to come back one day, and the Samaritan is also Christ, who synthesizes the two stories at the top where He sits in paradise regained at the Last Judgement. These connections are like another stained-glass image at Chartres, in the south rose-window: four Old Testament prophets carry on their shoulders the four New Testament evangelists. The evangelists are smaller and yet they are empowered to see further; and between them stands Mary, holding her baby son – completing both the Old Testament prophesies and the message of the New.

But beyond the parallel stories in the 'Good Samaritan' window, other things are happening as well. There is the colour coding – nasty things tend to happen in red, the colour of forbidden fruit; and there is the geometry of the window, based on variations of the circle, which relates to the geometry of the cathedral and of the largest single decorative feature in the building, the 1000 ft (305 m) labyrinth on the floor below. The Cathedral School of Chartres was, of course, famous for its researches into geometry. Above all, there is the symbolism of light: light as a glimpse of the perfection of its creator which human beings in the shadows cannot confront directly or they would be dazzled; light which has to be mediated or filtered – hence the stained-glass window.

This window is just one of 176 in the cathedral of Chartres and a specialist historian such as Malcolm Miller could provide an equivalent exegesis of any one of them. Other cathedrals of the building boom might have contained as many, but in the unique case of Chartres the collection is, miraculously, still almost complete – thanks to restoration, repainting, releading and removal during the two world wars of the twentieth century. Each window is at the same time a book with several stories, a commentary, an educational aid, an exercise in applied geometry, a message from the sponsor and an experience – just for a moment – of what it might be like to live in the heavenly city, a city 'of pure gold, bright as clear glass', a city filled with the colours of precious stones. There aren't many films or comic strips that can do all that.

How much of this would have been comprehensible to the medieval pilgrim is still a much-debated question. As indeed is the question of the laity's involvement in religious practices of medieval cathedrals in general. The idea of a service which involves sitting down in pews, listening to a sermon, and full participation on the part of the congregation does not seem to 'fit' the medieval experience. The congregation usually stood or knelt; there was very little preaching (preaching did not become widespread until the arrival of the friars in the thirteenth century); and the Latin of the Mass would have been unintelligible to most people. The service was more like a dialogue between the priest and God, the priest celebrating Mass with his back to the congregation. Attendance at weekly Mass was expected, but a papal decree of 1215 which made once yearly Communion mandatory would suggest that the expectation was more honoured in the breach the observance. Maybe the laity showed their devotion to the Eucharist when the bread was elevated at the Consecration, rather than by actually receiving Communion.

As to the use of the cathedral by local townspeople, it is clear that the building was an integral part of everyday life – and that many of today's divisions between 'religious' and 'secular' activities had not yet been invented. Inside the walls of Chartres, people would gossip, exercise their dogs, parakeets and falcons, play ball games, go courting, shelter from the rain, and buy wine and food from merchants who had set up shop on prime sites all along the nave; the merchants were only prepared to move when the chapter offered them another equivalent 'pitch', this time in the crypt. Some of these activities were frowned upon – we only know about them because of decrees which tried to put a stop to them – but some of them were not, provided they kept to their own 'zones' of the building. It is clear that the cathedral of Chartres was a social and economic – as well as a religious – centre. The cathedral's floor has a gentle slope to it, probably to make the place easier to sluice out after pilgrims had turned it into a mass bed-and-breakfast.

In this century historians have tended to place Chartres Cathedral on a pedestal, to treat it as if it is one huge sculpture in an exclusive art gallery called Civilization. In fact, this extraordinary building was deeply embedded in the everyday thoughts and actions of the twelfth-and thirteenth-century people who planned, built and used it, as well as in the most advanced philosophy and theology of the age. Even at the time the chroniclers were quick to pick up on the success and coherence of the building. 'None is to be found in the whole world,' wrote one of them, 'that shines so brightly.' And it still does. Chartres Cathedral stimulated Church authorities, and their master builders, to engage in a kind of building race, rather like the space race in the twentieth century. The great aim was to build higher and lighter, onwards and upwards, to boldly go where no man had gone before. And about 100 miles north of Chartres, at Beauvais, there was to be the most ambitious cathedral of all.

The building of Beauvais Cathedral was begun just as Chartres was completed in 1225. The idea was to build the most colossal and the tallest structure imaginable; masonry buildings were, in fact, never to reach such heights again. It was to be the ultimate reflection of God's work of art, for pilgrims to experience and 'read' with utter amazement.

Funds poured in at the start of the project but by the middle of the thirteenth century the money had begun to run out. By that stage only the vaults of the choir had been completed, and they were so daring – at 150 ft (45 m) – that in 1284 they collapsed, leaving just the eastern end of the cathedral standing. (It has been estimated that a fourteen-floor building, of the modern skyscraper type, could have been erected in the choir of Beauvais without even reaching the vaulting.)

The geometrical proportions had worked but the underlying structure had not, and this time the practical engineering knowledge was just not there. Chartres, too, had been built without the benefit of a knowledge of structural mechanics, a detailed design to scale and even an agreed and precise unit of measurement; the building had shown that it was possible to achieve stability through proportional rather than structural analysis, through getting the shape right rather than calculating the stresses placed upon it. But Chartres had depended on stability (rather than strength) and the plain fact was that Beauvais was unstable. Pairs of extra buttresses, and new fliers, were added to prop up the tottering edifice and the choir was rebuilt, using extra columns which divided the original arches.

Work on the rest of the building proceeded slowly, until another collapse in the sixteenth century. And so Beauvais, which was to have been the last word in 'the French style', was never completed. It was simply too large, too light. And it was a cathedral built of chalk – rather than the limestone of Chartres – a soft stone which, it transpired, wasn't up to the job. Amid all the geometry and the philosophy of light, this basic fact had somehow been forgotten. Beauvais, in the end, didn't succeed in 'challenging the stars', as the chronicle hoped, or in reaching God.

If it had been completed, Beauvais would have been three times as big as it is today – stretching right out into the city centre. The original intention had been to replace a squat and dark little tenth-century church, on the same site, which had been damaged by fire. As it turned out, the church of the Basse Oeuvre – still standing, next to the cathedral – could well outlive the extraordinary chalk structure which replaced it.

One of the last sections of Beauvais to be completed, in the sixteenth century, was the southern façade, which was built in a later, much more flamboyant version of the original style, by then commonly called 'the Gothic'. With the fate of Beauvais, the intense religious and intellectual enthusiasm – not to mention the funds – which had underpinned pure 'Gothic' architecture seemed to be exhausted. Churches which had taken one or perhaps two generations to build now took centuries. Technical innovations, of the kind which had been stimulated by the cathedral boom, were at a standstill. 'Gothic' came to be treated as just another style in the style wars that followed the Middle Ages. And yet Gothic architecture wasn't just or even mainly a matter of flying buttresses or pointed arches or cross-ribbed vaults or dizzying heights. Those were means not ends.

The ends were a set of beliefs which expressed themselves through a new use of light and a new emphasis on structure and

---

ON 'READING' A CHURCH BUILDING

The church consisteth of four walls, that is, is built on the doctrine of the Four Evangelists; and hath length, breadth, and height: the height representeth courage; the length fortitude, which patiently endureth till it attaineth its heavenly Home; the breadth is charity, which, with long suffering, loveth its friends in God, and its foes for God; and again, its height is the hope of future retribution, which despiseth prosperity and adversity, hoping TO SEE THE GOODNESS OF THE LORD IN THE LAND OF THE LIVING.

Again, in the Temple of God, the foundation is Faith, which is conversant with unseen things: the roof, Charity, WHICH COVERETH A MULTITUDE OF SINS. The door, Obedience, of which the Lord saith, IF THOU WILT ENTER INTO LIFE, KEEP THE COMMANDMENTS. The pavement, humility, of which the Psalmist saith, MY SOUL CLEAVETH TO THE PAVEMENT . . .

The glass windows in a church are Holy Scriptures, which expel the wind and rain, that is all things hurtful, but transmit the light of the True Sun, that is God, into the hearts of the Faithful. These are wider within than without, because the mystical sense is the more ample, and precedeth the literal meaning. Also, by the windows the senses of the body are signified: which ought to be shut to the vanities of this world, and open to receive with all freedom spiritual gifts . . .

From William Durand, *The Symbolism of Churches* (c. 1286)

---

geometry – in short, a form of see-through architecture which was a machine for worshipping in. It was not so much a question of form following function, although that was part of it, as form following faith, which was itself a kind of function.

Renaissance commentators called all this 'Gothic' – which was intended as a term of abuse (deriving from the word Goth or Barbarian), rather like the word Modernism today. Barbarian architecture. Barbarian, because there wasn't enough ornament; because there was something faintly disgusting about relics; and because the architect had not put his name and his ego in capital letters all over the building. One can only react by saying that 'barbarity' like 'civilization' is in the eye of the beholder.

2

FIRES OF FAITH

In three out of the four Gospels Christ had said 'it is easier for a camel to pass through the eye of a needle, than for a rich man to enter the kingdom of heaven'. And yet the twelfth and thirteenth centuries saw Europe's first commercial age – with the development of trade, business and the profit economy, and with the spread of prosperous towns and cities. One of the great questions of the time was how to reconcile religion with these fast-changing facts of everyday life.

'Holy lives' of simplicity and austerity were increasingly admired – even if most people stopped short of actually wanting to copy them. Up to then, such 'holy lives' had been lived mainly in monasteries, set apart from the wider society, but there was a growing space for an inspiring spiritual force within ordinary communities, for thoughtful people to preach in market-places and at crossroads, and make religion seem a lot less distant.

Should Christ's words be taken literally; did they describe a state of mind, or did they just refer to the *reckless* getting and spending of wealth? Where was the line of orthodoxy to be drawn? Did the rise of the profit economy mean that the end of the world, the Apocalypse, was at hand? After all, the Book of Revelation had been full of dire warnings, which seemed in the twelfth and thirteenth centuries to be coming true:

And the kings of the earth, and the great men, and the rich men, and the chief captains, and the mighty men, and every bondman, and every free man, hid themselves in the dens and in the rocks of the mountains; And said to the mountains and rocks, Fall on us, and hide us from the face of him that sitteth on the throne, and from the wrath of the Lamb: For the great day of his wrath is come; and who shall be able to stand?

There was a growing sense of urgency, a need to put the world's house in order, to prepare to face the day of judgement. Time was, literally, running out. For on the last day, the wheat would be separated from the chaff – the godly from the ungodly, holy lives from unholy.

The end of the grand narrative of the universe, according to the Bible – which provided a helpfully detailed description of it – would come after a series of battles and disasters and plagues: God's will is fulfilled and the new Jerusalem comes down from the skies. There wasn't a specific date put on this, but some scholars who studied Revelation tried to fill the gap by calculating it. The obvious candidate had been the turn of the millennium in the year 1000 – but that had come and gone, to everyone's intense relief. A Cluniac monk, writing three years after the great non-event, said 'it was as if the whole world, having cast off its age by shaking itself, were clothing itself everywhere in a white robe of churches'. The second favourite, thanks to the visions of the southern Italian, Joachim Abbot of Fiore (c. 1132–1202), was the year 1260 – which wasn't *that* far away. Joachim reckoned that the third great epoch of human history, the epoch of 'the new spiritual order', as predicted by Revelation, would begin in that precise year, and his very specificity attracted a great deal of anxious attention.

Whatever the exact date, much of European society in the 1100s and 1200s lived under the constant threat of Armageddon – not unlike the threat of the nuclear bomb in the second half of this century. At the same time the Church in Rome – which was trying hard to consolidate its power-base, get its own house in order, renew and reform itself and lay down some workable ground rules – became increasingly alarmed by signs of fragmentation and disorder. It was still a developing organization and if things really did fall apart, the centre wasn't yet strong enough to hold. And in some places it began to look as though things were falling apart.

From the 1100s onwards, as long-distance travel became more feasible – bringing contact with other points of view, with *difference* – there grew up across the whole continent of Europe a series of new movements led by self-styled prophets and strange holy men. They spread the word to more isolated communities, and wandered the countryside preaching the gospel and attracting people away from the institutions of a Church which, they argued, had grown old and distant. The criticisms were already familiar – ill-educated priests, slothful monks, conspicuous consumption – and indeed they had also been made from within the Church itself. But in many of the cities, towns and villages of France, northern and central Italy and the Rhineland of Germany, these unorthodox sects – some of them originating from further east in the Balkans, in Bosnia, Serbia and Bulgaria – began to spread. Among them were the Petrobrusians, followers of Peter of Bruis, who rejected all external forms of worship; the Henricians, followers of Henry the Monk, who rejected the doctrine of original sin; and the Arnoldists, followers of Arnold of Brescia, who wanted to make apostolic poverty an obligation for all Churchmen.

In Lombardy the Humiliati (or Humble Ones) tried to live and work as the original disciples had done. From Lyon came the Waldensians, followers of Waldo, later known as Peter Valdes – a prosperous cloth merchant who gave most of his wealth away to the poor and became a wandering preacher. But it was the Cathars (also known as the Pure Ones) of south-western France who more than any other group would challenge the authority and the very existence of the Roman Catholic Church.

The Languedoc was the region where Occitan – the medieval language of Oc used '*oc*' instead of '*oui*' – was spoken. It was the heartland of the Cathars, or the Albigensians – named after the town of Albi, which had become a centre of Cathar belief. They were also known – by enemies in northern France – as Bulgars, Bougres or Buggers, in the first recorded use of the word as a term of abuse. This part of the south of France, where feudal bonds were loose, the land was prosperous and new ideas found fertile soil, was fiercely independent from the rest of the country.

When Bernard of Clairvaux went on a preaching tour there in 1145, he noted that:

The churches lack their congregations of the faithful; the faithful lack priests; and the priests lack all honour. All that remains are a few Christians without Christ. The sacraments are abused, and the Feasts of the Church are no longer celebrated. People are dying with their sins still upon them. By refusing children the Grace of Baptism these people are depriving them of all life in Christ.

Roman Catholicism, as he recognized it, had ceased to exist.

The Cathars believed in two opposing principles: the Father of Spirit and Light, who was good and a saviour, and the Prince of Darkness, who created the material world, matter and time. So souls belonged to one god, worldly things to the other – and when Christ came to earth, it could not possibly have been as God-made-Man: he must have been an angel, sent to show the way to salvation. The Cathars rejected the sacraments and the Cross – which they called a 'murder weapon'. One of the great attractions of the Cathar religion was that it explained why vicious devils seemed to be everywhere. They proclaimed themselves 'the true Christians'; it was the Catholics who were the betrayers.

The ministers of this alternative, well-organized church – who could be male or female and who were known as *perfecti* or *perfectae* – rejected all worldly temptations and the eating of flesh: only bread, vegetables and fish were allowed. They devoted their lives to the Father of Light, guided by the New Testament translated into the local language of Oc. Human beings might be imprisoned within their bodies but they could at least aspire to the Spirit. The *perfecti* were baptized by book and words (not by water), a ceremony that was called the *consolamentum* (or consolation). Ordinary *credentes* (or believers) only became consoled just before death: once they had done so, they had to lead perfected lives thereafter. The renunciation of all

A CRUSADING MONK DESCRIBES THE CATHARS

And here is another absurdity: A certain believer of heretics at death bequeathed to them three hundred sous and bade his son to remit that sum to the heretics. But when, upon the father's death, the heretics asked the son for this legacy, he said to them: 'Tell me first, if you please, how it is with my father now.' They replied: 'You may be sure that he is saved and is already gathered with the spirits above.' To which the son smilingly rejoined: 'Thanks be to God and to you! Of a surety, since my father is already in glory his soul has no further need of alms; and I know you to be so kindly that you would not now recall my father from glory. Be assured, therefore, that you will receive no money from me . . .'

Nor do I think the remark of certain heretics that no one can sin from the waist down should be passed over in silence. They called the placing of images in churches idolatry; insisted that church bells are trumpets of devils; averred that one sins no more grievously in sleeping with mother or sister than with anyone else; and, among the most extreme heretical follies, they affirmed that if one of the perfected should commit mortal sin (for example, by eating the very smallest morsel of meat, cheese, egg, or any other food forbidden to them), all those consoled by him lose the Holy Spirit and must be reconsoled; and they even said that those already saved fall from heaven because of the sin of the one who consoled them.

From Peter of Vaux-de-Cernay, *Hystoria albigensis* (1213)

sexual activity perhaps explains the many myths about their private lives. They did not sleep with their wives: they must be Bougres.

In the eyes of the Church in Rome, the Cathars were heretics whose perfected élite had chosen to be enemies of the properly ordained clergy and whose network of Believers challenged the established bureaucracy. But it was more than just a question of who was to have control. The Cathars' beliefs went back to a third-century teacher in Persia named Mani, who had interpreted evil not as a perversion of good (the devil as fallen angel) but as a form of anti-matter which battled it out on a cosmic scale with its opposite. Manicheism, as the religion came to be known, had reached the Balkans via the Byzantine empire, whence it had travelled along trade and crusader routes into southern France. This belief system denied the Creation, the Incarnation *and* the Resurrection. So the Roman Church was afraid for the Cathars' immortal souls. The Cathars were a deadly disease which had to be wiped out.

Into this turbulent and confusing Europe, across the Alps in Italy, came a man who has been called the greatest Christian reformer the West has ever produced – and, second only to Christ, on whom he modelled himself, the most famous Christian super-hero in history. 'No one in the world,' wrote a friend, 'was so greedy for gold as he was for poverty – which he embraced in everlasting love.' He was baptized Giovanni Bernardone but his father – a wealthy business-man in the cloth trade – preferred to call him Francesco, which sounded more fashionably French. That is why he is known today as Francis of Assisi.

He had a lot in common with other visionaries of the time. Like the Cathars, he wanted to return to the purity and simplicity of the early Church – before it grew weary and class-conscious. Like the Waldensians, he wanted to go out and preach the gospel in the streets, rather than shut himself up in a monastery. But there was a big difference. Francis never once faltered in his loyalty to the Roman Church, which he aimed to reform from within. 'We have been sent as a *help* to the clergy,' he wrote, 'not to win people only by the *scandal* of the clergy.'

Francis had been named after the country where his father made most of his money and the boy was brought up in an upwardly mobile, privileged household. At the age of fourteen he joined the family business and soon became a dedicated follower of fashion; he was fond of marzipan, he enjoyed French troubadour songs and, according to one of the early biographies, his main interests were singing, drinking, dancing and wenching. If all this sounds too clichéd for words – well, the chronicles did tend to dramatize his story as a series of larger than life, symbolic gestures.

When neighbouring Perugia went to war with the town of Assisi, the twenty-one-year-old Francis was kitted out, at great expense, as a cavalry officer, only to be captured and sent to prison until his father bailed him out. He then talked of going on a crusade, but his heart didn't seem to be in it any more. 'All that had once seemed sweet,' he was quoted as saying in the earliest biographies, 'now seemed bitter to him and his existence was empty.' According to his own testament, two incidents would change the whole direction of his life, and help him overcome his pride.

The first happened in about 1205, when he came face to face with his worst nightmare – a man riddled with leprosy. Francis had been terrified of going near this disfiguring disease in his youth, his stylish phase, but this time he not only went up to the man – whose fingers were dripping with blood – he also gave him some money and, Christ-like, kissed his rotting hand.

The second incident which helped seal Francis's fate took place at San Damiano near Assisi. The chapel was in a terrible state of repair at the time and, as Francis prayed before the Byzantine-style crucifix above the altar, it seemed to speak to him: 'Francis, go and rebuild my house which is falling into ruin.' He took the message literally and began to repair the building with his own bare hands, even selling some of his father's stock of cloth to pay for the expenses. But he later came to realize that the voice from the crucifix was setting him a far more ambitious task – not to rebuild churches but to rebuild *the Church*.

This story was typical of the sort of legends, or parables, many of them highly sentimental, with which early biographers – not to mention the painter Giotto di Bondone – surrounded Francis. But, then again, to try and separate the legends from the reality would be to misunderstand the sort and extent of the impact he made.

His next move, having been publicly disowned by his father, was to reject all material possessions and to embrace what he called 'Lady Poverty' as ardently as the troubadours courted their ladies; to be like the poorest people of the region whose lives contrasted so vividly with the affluence of his own family. 'Since I have chosen holy poverty as my lady, my delight and my spiritual and bodily treasure,' he wrote, 'I feel the greatest shame when I find someone poorer than myself.' He took to living in caves or hermitages like a wild man, starving himself, begging for his daily bread, praying rather than reading, and dressing in cast-off rags, 'having', as he said, 'no longer any father but him who is in Heaven'. The early biographers sometimes made his leaving of the world seem easy. It can't have been. And it can't have been easy for his parents either.

When he went into town, people turned him away – because he looked like a robber – or threw mud at him, or put dice into his hands and asked if he'd like to have a gamble and improve his lot. Nevertheless, he didn't stay on his own for long. A few men from Assisi and its surroundings gave away or sold everything they owned and came to share his poverty, living as they thought the original disciples had lived. Francis called them Little Brothers or Friars. The townspeople of Assisi, though, wrote a contemporary, 'took these men of the woods for knaves or madmen and gave them bad usage'. Others, intrigued by their preaching methods, began to be drawn to their tough-minded mission to rebuild the spirit of the Church, and joined the congregation at San Damiano.

The first woman to join the Brotherhood was Clare Offreduccio, who at the age of sixteen ran away from a wealthy home and an arranged marriage. She may well have heard Francis preach in the cathedral of San Rufino in 1210, for her family lived just across the street. Francis had to improvise on canon law to accept her, as well as her two sisters; he advised them to turn away from affluence and embrace a life of 'chastity, penance and prayer'. At first, unable to imagine women taking part in his travelling hand-to-mouth existence, Francis took Clare to some Benedictine nuns; eventually he established her as head of a community of nuns in a house next to San Damiano, where they were known as the 'Damianites' – the female branch of the Fratricelli. She stayed there for forty years, fasting, mortifying her flesh, living the Gospels and trying to persuade successive Popes to allow her and the sisterhood the distinctive privilege of absolute poverty and total obedience, which were contained in the first Rule ever written by a woman. She eventually succeeded, two days before she died in August 1253. Later, the 'Damianites' came to be called the 'Poor Clares' of Assisi.

The new movements of the twelfth and thirteenth centuries, in general, attracted a high proportion of women into their ranks, from noblewomen and merchants' wives right across the social scale. Some have suggested that this may have given them a status and individuality they otherwise would not have achieved; others, that self-mortification was a response to a general lack of opportunity for advancement. These may both be anachronistic judgements, but there is no doubt that Clare imposed on her body an extraordinarily strict regime. She was ill and confined to bed for most of her life; when Pope Gregory IX visited the sisters at San Damiano and saw 'their highest poverty' first-hand, he was moved to tears.

Many women of Clare's class must have entered religious houses in the Middle Ages in order to flee from unsuitable marriages, but it was one thing to become a nun and quite another to become a Damianite. The texts of four supportive letters written by Clare to another woman who rejected her upbringing and renounced worldly wealth – Agnes of Prague – have survived. Agnes was the daughter of the King of Bohemia, no less, who, according to a contemporary chronicle, 'entered the order of the Poor Ladies of the Rule of the Blessed Francis at Prague, rejecting for Christ's sake the Emperor Frederick [II] who had earlier asked for her hand in marriage'. Clare gave Agnes much spiritual encouragement and in her third letter begged her 'to refrain wisely and prudently from an indiscreet and impossible austerity in the fasting that I know you have undertaken'. For Clare to have written this, Agnes must in effect have gone on to a full-scale hunger strike.

As with Francis, Clare's life was highly sentimentalized at the time, creating the impression that all about it was sweetness and light. One of the early official biographies, by St Bonaventure, re-ferred to her as 'the first flower in Francis' garden, who shone like a radiant star, fragrant as a flower blossoming white and pure in spring-time', and a favourite subject of popular late medieval art was Clare of Assisi being carried to the walls of the city, sacrament in hand, to keep the macho imperial armies at bay.

Francis, too, like Clare many years later, would need the backing of the Pope if he wanted the legality of his preaching to be put beyond question. Otherwise he ran the risk of being condemned as a heretic, because of local bewilderment and hostility. He had the support of the Bishop of Assisi, who had probably told him that he was more likely to be understood at the centre of things than locally: the Pope's backing would ensure that Francis's opponents became heretics if they continued to attack him. He would just have to pay a visit to the centre, to Innocent III in Rome.

Meanwhile, Pope Innocent himself watched as all southern France seemed to be slipping away from Christendom. A campaign of preaching missions had had only a limited effect. Even the threat of force did not have the impact it should have had – because local politicians and noblemen were by no means certain to back him. 'Rome', like the 'rest of France', was another country.

It was the brutal stabbing to death of the papal legate Peter of Castlenau in January 1208 which finally tipped the balance. The time for preaching was over. Innocent III declared a crusade – a holy war – against the Cathars and appealed to the lords of northern France to raise an army in his name. French forces, about 25,000 of them, gathered in June 1209 to answer the summons, under the command of Arnold Aimery, Abbot of Cîteaux and papal legate. They had been promised the spiritual reward of a plenary indulgence for forty days' service, and the less spiritual reward of free land and a moratorium on debts – benefits which, whether they were to survive or perish, must have made them feel better about the whole business. Normally, they would have had to travel all the way to Palestine to earn them.

Arnold Aimery proudly wrote that this was the greatest army Christendom had ever assembled. Innocent III expressed the hope that this 'affair of peace and faith' – peace by the sword – would have a successful result. In the event, the Albigensian Crusade turned into one of the most violent and horrific episodes of early European history.

On 22 July 1209 the crusading army arrived at Béziers and stood looking across the River Orb at the Cathar stronghold. The Christian warriors were bishops, barons and knights – with their retinues – and foot-soldiers, sergeants and mercenaries from abroad known as '*les Routiers*', the men of the road. They asked the inhabitants of Béziers to hand over any Cathars who were known to be in the city. There was a period of stalemate during which it looked as though there would have to be a lengthy siege. But the crusaders' heavy cavalry managed a surprise attack across the bridge – knights in chain-mail and iron helmets wielding broadswords and battleaxes – and they simply mowed down anyone who got in their way. 'How will we know who to kill?' a knight was later said to have asked Aimery. The cynical reply was, 'Slay them all – God will recognize his own.' Eventually, about three thousand of the inhabitants crowded in terror into the church of Mary Magdalene – only to have the church burned down around them; some of their skeletons are still under the floor. The indiscriminate slaughter which followed – it has been estimated that upwards of nine thousand people died – was clearly intended to warn the surrounding regions that the crusaders meant business, rather like a terrorist of today who explodes a bomb in a city centre, only it was the heretics who up till then were supposed to be the terrorists. It set the tone for the war which followed.

News of the fall of Béziers and the subsequent atrocities spread like wildfire across the Languedoc and at first led other towns to a quick submission: Carcassonne, Montréal, Mirepoix, Castres and Albi itself. Southern France was clearly pole-axed by the massacre: about a hundred castles surrendered to the crusaders without struggle, and the wide circulation of stories such as the 'kill them all' one shows just how shocked contemporaries were. Then the crusaders turned to the more heavily fortified strongholds of Minerve and Termes and crushed them as well. Any captured heretics could expect to be burned on a mass funeral pyre – between two and three hundred of them after the siege of Lavaur, about 140 at Minerve. 'A great fire having been got ready,' wrote an eyewitness, 'these heretical *perfecti* were flung thereon. To tell the truth, there was no need for our men to drag them thither; for they remained obdurate in their wickedness, and with great gaiety of heart cast themselves into the fire.' This incident must have confirmed them in their view that the world was run by the Prince of Darkness and encouraged them to leave it as quickly as possible.

THE SIEGE OF LAVAUR — FROM THE CRUSADERS' POINT OF VIEW

Now that castle was very famous and very large, standing above the Agout River at a distance of five leagues from Toulouse . . .

When our people came up to the castle they besieged it on only one side for our army was not enough to lay siege to it all around. And so, after the passage of a few days while machines were being built, we began to attack the castle in the usual way, the enemy to defend it as well as they could. Indeed, there was in the castle a countless multitude of men, equipped with the best of arms; in fact the defenders were nearly as numerous as the attackers. We should not fail to note that when we approached the castle the enemy sallied therefrom and captured one of our knights and, taking him inside, killed him at once . . .

Now the Count of Toulouse persecuted the church of God and the count [Simon of Montfort] as much as he could, but not openly, for provisions still reached our army from Toulouse. In the course of these events the count of Toulouse came to the army. The Count of Auxerre and Robert of Courtenay, who were his blood relatives, undertook to advise the count to come to his senses and to obey the commands of the church, but, since they had no success, the Count of Toulouse parted from the Count of Montfort in wrath. The men of Toulouse who were at the siege of Lavaur also quit the army . . .

From Peter of Vaux-de-Cernay, *Hystoria albigensis* (1213)

The crusaders were commanded by Simon of Montfort, fourth earl of Leicester. One chronicler, William of Tudela, called him 'this hardy warrior, full of wisdom and experience, a great and gentle knight, gallant, comely, frank and yet soft spoken'. A less friendly – and anonymous – chronicler, who took over from William as co-author of the *Chanson de la Croisade*, wrote, after Montfort's burial in Carcassonne in 1218:

Those who can read may learn from his epitaph that he is a saint and martyr; that he is bound to rise again to share the heritage, to flourish in the state of unparalleled felicity, to wear a crown and have his place in the Kingdom. But for my part I have heard tell that the matter must stand thus: if one may seek Christ Jesus in the world by killing men and shedding blood; by the destruction of human souls; by setting the torch to great fires; by winning lands through violence . . . by slaughtering women and slitting children's throats – why yes, then he must needs wear a crown and shine resplendent in heaven.

Montfort's army, with a large contingent of riff-raff from the north, tended to serve for the regulation forty days, then go home, at

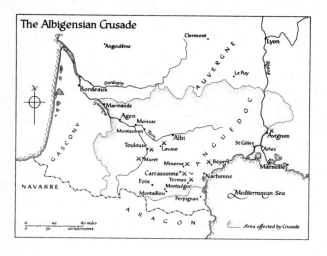

which point the towns which had surrendered took up arms all over again. The many acts of terror, instead of destroying the resolve of the strangers in the south, actually stiffened it and made matters worse by prolonging the agony. Both sides mutilated and blinded their prisoners of war, and were said even to have used them for target practice. There were recognized laws of war, formed by knightly custom and ecclesiastical research, but in this 'internal' crusade they usually seem to have been forgotten.

MASSACRE AT MARMANDE, JUNE 1219, FROM THE CATHARS' POINT OF VIEW

The days of the besieged of Marmande are numbered.
They cannot hold out. They know it. Even more so,
when Prince Louis of France appears on the scene.
He arrives, with splendid barons by his side.
On their well-groomed horses there are 25,000,
of which 10,000 are dressed, men and mounts,
in armour of blue metal and iron saddle-cloths.
Of the footsoldiers, the crowd seems to go on for ever.
Pushing their cartloads of weapons and provisions,
they pitch camp in gardens and orchards . . .

Louis stands firm, before his great tent.
Imagine the terror of the townspeople,
recognizing, in the distance, the son of the king of France!
All of them, at that moment of truth, regret being born.

The French knights, at the first assault,
occupy the ditches, get inside the fences,
destroy the bridges, smash the stockades . . .

        . . . But suddenly a
deafening storm seems to break. They run, they yell, they grab
   weapons.

The crusading juggernaut invades the city.
The massacre begins. Babes in arms, maidens,
noble ladies, barons, stripped of their clothing,
are put to the sword, chopped to pieces.
The ground, everywhere, is covered with chunks of flesh,
flowing blood, breasts and brains,
limbs, bodies ripped from top to bottom,
guts, livers, hearts, trunks.
It looks as though they have all fallen from the sky, like rain.
Blood runs in flowing streams right through the town,
the fields and the rivers. No woman, or man,
or child, or grandparent escapes.
No one, except perhaps (who knows?) some well-hidden child.
Now that the carnage is over, they torch Marmande.
And sire Louis, pious as ever, strikes camp, and takes
the road to Toulouse . . .

From *La Chanson de la Croisade Albigeoise* by William of Tudela and an
anonymous poet from Toulouse (late 1220s)

And so it went on, relentlessly, for over fifteen years, forcing the
heretics either underground or up into their mountain strongholds.
The crusaders had hoped to destroy all trace of the Cathar Church
from off the face of the earth – bishops, *perfecti* and *perfectae*, believers
and mercenaries alike. But instead of destroying them, the crusade
penned them into little pockets of resistance which tried, against all
the odds, to keep the flame of their faith burning. The overall papal
strategy seems to have been to transfer land ownership from Albigensians to orthodox members of the nobility; after all, it had been
the weakness of the secular authority – combined with the laxness
of local clergy – which had created the breeding conditions for
heresy. It looked at first as though this transfer of power would
happen quickly. It didn't, but by 1226 the Languedoc was for the
first time in the control of the French crown. It was the ferocity of

the crusaders, the massacres and the burnings which boosted the Cathars' morale and enhanced their common cause. That, and the confusion of secular with religious motives. A citizen called Jean Tisseyre ran through the streets of Toulouse, according to the *Chronicle of William Pelhisson*, shouting at the top of his voice:

'Listen to me, fellow citizens! I am no heretic: I have a wife; and sleep with her, and she has borne me sons. I eat meat, I tell lies and swear, and I am a good Christian. So don't believe it when they say that I am an atheist, not a word of it! They'll very likely accuse you too, as they have me: these accursed villains want to put down honest folk and *take the town from its lawful master.*'

At about the same time as the Albigensian Crusade began, Francis and his Little Brothers made their way to Rome and the papal palace at the church of John Lateran to ask for permission and authority to found a recognized Order of Friars. They arrived with a recommendation from the Bishop of Assisi.

The meeting of Francis and Innocent III at the Lateran Palace turned out to be momentous. When Francis first arrived, with his twelve 'disciples', he was almost turned away by the cardinals in the outer office. They tended to take some of his remarks about poverty a little personally. Then, when he had gained access to the Pope – a remarkable achievement in itself since he had no religious training and was only known in the Assisi area at that stage – Innocent III in all his splendour and finery opened the proceedings by looking at the enthusiastic young man, who resembled a bag person, and asking him if he'd been anywhere near a pigsty recently. He then showed him the door.

But when Francis returned the next day, clutching a simple rule of life culled from various passages in the New Testament, the two men began communicating with one another. Legend – stemming from the early biographers – has it that Innocent had had a dream in which he saw a starving beggar propping up the tottering edifice of the Lateran Palace, and he recognized Francis as that beggar. Still, the meeting could easily have gone wrong and Francis could well have been treated as a heretic. But the Pope was by now convinced that Francis was simply asking to be allowed to live as he thought the original disciples had lived, and he could not say 'no' to that. So he gave his verbal permission for Francis to found a new Order of Friars, dedicated to absolute poverty and the preaching of repentance to all.

Was this a beautiful moment or was it a shrewd political move? It was probably a bit of both. Innocent III was a gifted politician – a canon lawyer as well as a theologian – and in some senses Francis was the answer to his prayers. He had the potential for enormous popular appeal at local level and demonstrated that you did not

---

FRANCIS AND THE HERETIC

I once heard the following story of the Blessed Francis when he was travelling in Lombardy. One day when he had gone into a church to pray, a certain heretic or manichee, seeing the reputation for holiness which Francis had with the people, ran to him, wishing through him to draw the allegiance of the people to himself, to upset their faith and to make the office of a priest appear contemptible. Now, the parish priest of that place happened to be a man of ill repute who kept a concubine, so the heretic said to St Francis: 'Look here! are we to believe what this man says and to show respect for him while he keeps a concubine and soils his hands with touching a harlot?' The saint, perceiving the malice of the heretic, went, before all the people, to the priest, and kneeling before him said, 'Whether or not this man's hands are as we have heard, I know not; but even if they are, I know that they cannot defile the wonder and efficacy of the Holy Sacraments. And so, because by these very hands great gifts and benefits of God are poured out upon his people, I kiss them in reverence of those things which they administer and of him by whose authority they are given.' So saying, and kneeling before the priest, he kissed his hands and put to confusion the heretics and those who supported them.

From Étienne de Bourbon, *Testimony* (1261)

---

have to found a new sect outside the established Church to live and follow the ideals of the gospel. At the same time, if Innocent represented the authority of the Church, Francis represented its humanity and enthusiasm – a humanity that was prepared to accept and obey that authority. A lucky combination. Francis was both orthodox and radical at the same time. Just what the papacy ordered.

The 'dream' story, legend suggests, was the key to Innocent's decision. He knew that his parish priests, out there at the front line, had difficulty keeping up with the latest developments in theological thinking and were under considerable pressure with the spread of the new towns. They were often conscientious but demoralized; others were less conscientious. The friars, who were well educated, could go into the towns – even set up convents there, in the fullness of time – and preach not only to the people but to the less-well-educated parish priests as well. Since Francis's Order was based on living in groups, not alone, it was in a strong position to sustain morale, enthusiasm and religious example. So the dream of the starving beggar propping up the Lateran Palace was, maybe, a dream about a new grass-roots organization providing support for the long-suffering parish priests who were the Church's foundations. Francis came with the recommendation of the Bishop of Assisi, who knew the problem first-hand. If it had not been for Innocent's judicious – and inspired – decision, and for the support of the bishop, we would never have heard of Francis of Assisi.

Papal inspiration went further, when Innocent gave his support to one other new Order of friars, led by a wandering, red-haired evangelist from Spain, Dominic of Guzman, who had founded the Order of Friars Preachers – soon to be known, after him, as the Dominicans. Their mission was to study theology and preach, especially among communities where heresy had begun to take hold. Dominic himself, who had been involved in trying peacefully to persuade the Cathars of the error of their ways – in the years before the crusade – had also realized from experience that the wealth conspicuously displayed by some members of the clergy only served to make heresy that much more attractive, and the bishop's job more difficult. So he, too, had rejected worldly wealth and his order, imitating Francis, dedicated itself to personal poverty. The Church's doctrine could now be taken out into the community, in support of the established institutions, through the preaching and example of the evangelical friars.

Innocent III's term of office culminated in a great Ecumenical Council, held in Rome in November 1215 and attended by three patriarchs, over four hundred bishops, eight hundred abbots and priors, and representatives of emperors, kings and princes. It was the largest assembly of its kind, ever. The purpose of the council was to reaffirm, through definitions and resolutions, the stability, continuity and orthodoxy of the reformed Church, within a system that aimed to be universal. At its pinnacle was Pope Innocent III. In future, the council resolved, all Latin Christendom – forty to fifty million souls – would owe allegiance to the authority of the papacy. Innocent had, over the previous seventeen years, been placing many of his fellow theology students from the course he had taken in Paris – which had involved the study of scripture, interspersed with prayer, from dawn to dusk, every single day, as well as discussion of its practical implications – into bishoprics. Stephen Langton, who as archbishop of Canterbury would become the crucial figure in the drafting of Magna Carta, was one of them. The council of 1215 attempted to turn the enthusiasm, and practical thinking, of such bishops into Church legislation – an initiative which meshed with Innocent's support for the evangelicals. The key to its success, though, was how it would be implemented in the localities.

Heresy in the south of France had survived and, partly as a result of the council of 1215, a new institution was founded to combat it: a detective agency cum court of law run by the Church and called the 'Inquisition'. At first, after the haphazard horrors which had gone before – the burnings, the brandings, the tortures – this Inquisition, staffed largely by Dominican friars, was welcomed. Heretics who repented were imprisoned, fined, had to go on pilgrimages or – the most common punishment – had large yellow crosses stitched on to their clothing. During the hearings, various pressures were brought on the accused to make him or her confess. Sometimes, though rarely, this involved torture; more usually 'very strict' confinement, which meant a small room, chaining to the wall, and black bread and water.

A characteristic sentence of the Inquisition – in this case, against a colourful citizen of Toulouse who had been an open supporter of the Cathars for many years and continued with his ways despite several warnings, an order to make a pilgrimage (which he ignored) and an attempt to excommunicate him (which went wrong when the arresting officers refused to go through with the sentence) – was entered in the Toulouse records as follows:

Alaman of Roaix, who was condemned for heresy because he saw and adored heretics, both men and women, many times in many places, harboured and sheltered them many times, ate with them and ate of the bread blessed by them many times, was present at many *apparellamenta* [Cathar confessional services] and at the heretications [Consolations] of many persons, often guided and associated with heretics, often gave to and received from them funds, accepted the Peace [the kiss exchanged at the end of Cathar services] from them often, and heard the heretics preaching errors about visible things – that God did not make them, that there is no salvation in baptism and matrimony, that the bodies of the dead will not arise, and that there are two gods, one benign and one malign – and he believed the aforesaid errors just as the heretics uttered them and for thirty years he believed the heretics to be good men; and he abandoned that belief on Thursday after the feast of the Blessed Hillary just past; also, he admitted that all the things were true which were alleged against him in the matter of heretical depravity ... having received the counsel of good men, we command him by virtue of his sworn oath today to enter the prison of St Etienne [the Bishop of Toulouse's prison], there to remain in perpetuity to do penance for the acts aforesaid.

If, after all this, the accused still refused to take the sworn oath, repent or 'give full obedience to the mandates of the Church', then there was the ultimate penalty known euphemistically as being 'relaxed to the secular arm' or 'relinquished to the secular judge-ment'. This meant that the convicted heretic was deprived of the protection of the Church and the civil authorities were granted permission to burn him or her at the stake without themselves committing a mortal sin. The 'relaxation' always had a plea of mercy attached to it – 'we recommend them, as strongly as we may, accord-ing to the prescription of Canon Law, to preserve your life and limbs from peril of death' – but this wasn't worth the paper it was written on. The civil authorities had no option but to proceed with the burning if they wanted to avoid a charge of harbouring and defending heretics themselves. Eyewitness accounts tend to stress the fact that card-carrying Cathars were pleased to leave the domain of the devil and that the crucifix – offered to them at the last minute – was no source of consolation. It was still a murder weapon.

Francis's fame had, meanwhile, been spreading, now with active support from the Church. A student at Bologna, Thomas of Spalato (or Split), saw him preaching one of his improvised sermons at this time, and later recalled in his *History*:

Almost the entire city had assembled. He was wearing a ragged habit; his whole person seemed insignificant and small; he did not have an attractive face. But God conferred so much power on his words that they brought back peace in many a family, torn apart by cruel and ferocious hatreds. The people showed him as much respect as they did devotion.

Unlike the Cathars, who saw in the natural world the work of the Prince of Darkness, Francis in his sermons emphasized the balance and beauty of nature – and criticized those who would dominate rather than respect it. Some of the Franciscan legends – like his famous sermon to the birds, when he preached and they miracu-lously listened; or his taming and befriending of 'brother wolf' in the town of Gubbio; or his plea to give generous Christmas pres-ents to the poor *and* to domestic animals and birds – which long ago became the stuff of greetings cards, actually conceal a tough-minded message. For, in today's terms, Francis was the patron saint of ecology; he was officially adopted as such, by the Pope, in April

1980. In his best-known prayers, and in the animal legends, he constantly stresses that the relationship between humans and creatures should be a balanced one, a relationship of mutual service, and that humans and creatures are 'brothers and sisters' of each other as they perform their functions in the divinely created scheme of things; he deliberately uses the language of chivalry and applies it to animals or natural phenomena. So, for him – and it was an unusual message, at a time when the rise of the profit economy was actively encouraging the exploitation of nature (as the Romans had encouraged it in pre-Christian days) – the physical world was not evil, whatever the Cathars preached, and it did not always represent a temptation, whatever the ascetics might claim.

FRANCIS PREACHES AT BOLOGNA

In the year 1222 on the Feast of the Assumption of the Mother of God, when I was a student at Bologna, I saw St Francis preaching in the Piazza before the Palazzo Publico, where almost the whole town was assembled. The theme of his sermon was: 'Angels, men, devils'. And he spoke so well and so wisely of these three rational spirits that to many learned men who were there the sermon of this ignorant man seemed worthy of no little admiration, in spite of the fact that he did not keep to the method of an expositor so much as of a revivalist. Indeed, the whole manner of his speech was calculated to stamp out enmities and to make peace. His tunic was dirty, his person unprepossessing and his face far from handsome; yet God gave such power to his words that many factions of the nobility, among whom the fierce anger of ancient feuds had been raging with much bloodshed, were brought to reconciliation. Towards him, indeed, the reverence and devotion of men were so great that men and women rushed upon him headlong, anxious to touch the hem of his garment and to carry away bits of his clothing.

From Thomas of Spalato, *History* (*c.* 1240)

His most famous statement of what it *was*, the earliest surviving piece of literature written in the Italian language (the Umbrian dialect), is 'The Canticle of Brother Sun'. 'I want to compose a new hymn about the Lord's creatures,' he said of the 'Canticle', 'creatures of which we make daily use, without which we cannot live, and with which the human race greatly offends its Creator.'

> All praise be yours, my Lord, through all that you have made,
>> And first my lord Brother Sun
>> Who brings the day; and light you give us through him
> How beautiful he is, how radiant in all his splendour
>> Of you, Most High, he bears the likeness.
> All praise be yours, my Lord, through Sister Moon and Stars;
>> In the heavens you have made them, bright
>> And precious and fair . . .
> All praise be yours, my Lord, through Sister Earth, our mother,
>> Who feeds us in her sovereignty and produces
>> Various fruits with coloured flowers and herbs . . .
> Praise and bless my Lord, and give him thanks,
>> And serve him with great humility.

Francis wasn't just tough on himself. He saw the faults of the institutions of the Church, especially at local parish level, only too clearly. But he wanted reform by example rather than by public criticism. So he was also strict on the brothers (whom he sometimes called 'my companions of the Round Table'). When one of them accepted some money, Francis made him take it in his teeth and personally place it in a pile of donkey dung. Others wanted to adopt a more academic or scholarly approach to prayer, but Francis strongly opposed them:

Many are inclined to abandon their true vocation, namely a purely religious simplicity, prayer and inwardness, together with our Lady Poverty. In doing so they believe that through deeper understanding of the scriptures they will come to a more intense piety and love of God . . . In reality they will in this way only become cold and empty.

FRANCIS AND THE RABBIT

Once when he was staying at the town of Greccio, a little rabbit that had been caught in a trap was brought alive to him by a certain brother. When the most blessed man saw it, he was moved to pity and said: 'Brother rabbit, come to me. Why did you allow yourself to be deceived like this?' And as soon as the rabbit had been let go by the brother who held it, it fled to the saint, and, without being forced by anyone, it lay quiet in his bosom as the safest place possible. After he had rested there a little while, the holy father, caressing it with motherly affection, released it so it could return free to the woods. But when it had been placed upon the ground several times and had returned each time to the saint's bosom, he finally commanded it to be carried by the brothers to the nearby woods.

From Thomas of Celano, *First Life of St Francis* (1228–30)

As the Franciscans developed into a more and more complex organization, Francis realized that he was not temperamentally suited to manage or administer the Order, so he resigned its leadership to an assistant, selected by the Pope. In some ways the organization matured not because of him but in spite of him. 'My God, what will happen after my death to the poor family which of your goodness you have entrusted to me, sinner that I am?'

Francis withdrew more and more from his companions, and administrative responsibilities, and retired to the hills around Mount La Verna in the Apennines, about sixty miles north of Assisi. While praying for guidance on the mountainside, he had a vision of an angel who turned into the figure of a crucified man. Suddenly the marks of what seemed like nails began to appear on his own hands and feet, and his right side began to bleed as if pierced with a lance. It was the first time ever that a Christian had received the stigmata, the wounds of Christ, for this is what he and his brothers believed them to be – wounds, interestingly, which resembled the visual treatment of the crucifixion in the art of the high Middle Ages.

Having spent most of his adult life in imitation of Christ – ever since that voice from the cross in San Damiano – he seemed, as an early biographer St Bonaventure, put it, to be turning into his likeness through the sheer intensity of his prayers:

Francis understood that divine providence had shown him this vision so that, as Christ's lover, he might learn in advance that he was to be totally transformed into the likeness of Christ crucified, not by the martyrdom of his flesh, but by the fire of his love. As the vision disappeared, it left in his heart a marvellous ardour and imprinted on his body markings that were no less marvellous.

FRANCIS AND THE BEGGAR

Once it happened that a certain brother uttered a word of invective against a certain poor man who had asked for an alms, saying to him: 'See, perhaps you are a rich man and pretending to be poor.' Hearing this, the father of the poor, St Francis, was greatly saddened, and he severely rebuked the brother who had said such a thing and commanded him to strip himself before the poor man and, kissing his feet, beg pardon of him. For, he was accustomed to say: 'Who curses a poor man does an injury to Christ, whose noble image he wears, the image of him who made himself poor for us in this world.' Frequently, therefore, when he found the poor burdened down with wood or other things, he offered his own shoulders to help them, though his shoulders were very weak.

From Thomas of Celano, *First Life of St Francis* (1228–30)

In his last years the pain of the stigmata, together with malaria and serious eye infections, made Francis an invalid. A physician seared his face from temple to eyebrow with a red-hot iron in an attempt to cure his growing blindness. Francis claimed to feel no pain: 'Brother Fire, I have always been good to you and always will be, for the love of Him who created you . . . The illness of the body benefits the soul if one accepts it with resignation.'

Francis died on 3 October 1226. A few days earlier he had completed a final 'testament and reminder to his brother friars'.

When God gave me some friars, there was no one to tell me what I should do; but the Most High himself made it clear to me that I must live the life of the Gospel. I had this written down briefly and simply and his holiness the Pope confirmed it for me. Those who embraced this life gave everything they had to the poor . . .

The friars must be very careful not to accept churches or poor dwellings for themselves, or anything else built for them, unless they are in harmony with the poverty which we have promised in the Rule; and they should occupy these places only as strangers and pilgrims . . .

This is a reminder, admonition, exhortation, and my testament which I, Brother Francis, worthless as I am, leave to you, my brothers.

As he was dying – laid out, by his own wish, naked on the ground – Francis was surrounded by bodyguards, literally, so that if he did die his body would be sure to be returned intact to Assisi, transforming it into a major centre of pilgrimage. Since word of his troubles had got around, relic-hunters had to be kept at bay. He was buried, intact, in a stone coffin. To encase the coffin, a huge basilica was constructed in the years after his death, and then another huge basilica on top of the original one – one building interlocking with the other.

And about a mile down the hill from Assisi, the little chapel of the Porziuncola – which, like San Damiano, Francis had restored in the early days – was to be surrounded by yet another massive basilica. The Franciscans had become the largest order of friars on the planet and this vast building was needed to shelter the crowds of pilgrims who kept, and keep on, coming to celebrate the man who had begged them 'to put off everything that is of this world'. What he taught, and what he was, seem a long way away from sentimental images of St Francis (he was canonized a mere two years after his death) dressed in gold, sitting on a throne and surrounded by adoring fan clubs of angels.

Towards the end of his lifetime Francis himself was evidently concerned about the legacy he was leaving behind. He had another of his dreams, this time about trying to feed his starving brothers with bread, only to see the crumbs fall through his fingers on to the ground. And after his death tensions within the order – between the organization people and the disciples, the hierarchy and the family – reached crisis point. Some wanted the Franciscans to be university-trained preachers and theologians. Others wanted them to own property and have servants do the dirty work for them. Only a small minority clung to the basic ideas of simplicity and poverty – as Francis would probably have wished them to. In less than a hundred years these so-called 'Spirituals' – the fundamentalist wing – would themselves be branded as heretics and four of their leaders would be burned to death. The Order of Friars Minor had become an essential part of the system and the margins of tolerance had shifted.

By the middle of the thirteenth century the heretics of southern France had all but been destroyed. Just a few communities stuck it out in the hills, refusing to give up hope. The fortress of Montségur, south-east of Foix, perched on a rock more than a 1000 ft (300 m) above the valley below, with only one way in – up the south-western slope – had become a last refuge for Cathar bishops, *perfecti* and *perfectae*, fugitives and Believers who wanted to be among their Good People or their Perfected Ones. The fortress did not control anything – its only value was that it was very remote. In the summer of 1243 a well-planned attack was launched by the Royal Seneschal of Carcassonne with additional troops supplied by the Archbishop of Narbonne and the Bishop of Albi; a rock-throwing machine was dragged near to the summit and there was a long siege.

Morale in the fortress just about survived the winter, but after eight months one of the outer defensive positions fell during a night attack. Negotiations for surrender were begun. Hostages were handed over and armed defenders were promised their lives and an amnesty for past war crimes, provided they had a little talk with the Inquisition first. For the heretics, though, there were to be no deals.

Some of the wives of the defenders, the children and those who were not prepared to die for their faith were evacuated. Two of the *perfecti* managed to escape, to be keepers, it was said, of the secret of where the Cathar treasures had been hidden. The rest were told publicly to renounce their heresy or be burned alive. On 16 March 1244 piles of brushwood were heaped inside a wooden stockade in an open field on the lower slopes and torches were thrown into the tinder. The heretics, over two hundred of them, were shoved or led or carried down the mountainside and herded into the flames. Some of them, the chronicles said, willingly and even ecstatically hurled themselves on to the fire. No Inquisition, no trial, just brute force. The site of this holocaust came to be known locally as the '*prat dels crematz*', the place of those who were burned, the burning field.

There may be something of legend in this: the treasure, the 'kill them all' tactics, the shrine. There is evidence that at least some of the heretics were taken to a nearby town and burned there – following inquisition and sentencing. But the reason it turned into legend was clear: this was the Cathars' last public stand. Montségur, the safe mountain, the rallying place, had fallen. Traces of the faith would remain: it took a long time to track down and question all the people who had been mentioned, after interrogation, by the evacuees of Montségur, and in the little village of Montaillou the Inquisition would still be tidying things up some eighty years later. But Catharism was a spent force.

And yet, looking back, this final defeat was not the unqualified triumph for the Church it should have been. True, southern France had been shepherded into the fold. But the result was a more centralized authoritarian Church which had accepted and sanctioned the use of force and which would no longer tolerate radical reform from within or without. There were now official institutions for channelling that force, legally, against heretics – and the concept of 'heretic' was always a flexible one. As people moved away from their extended family groups and clans to work in towns, there was an increasing need for new, strong identities – a sense of 'us' and 'them'. And as the notion of Christendom began to cohere, so did notions of who were to be 'them'.

Members of the Christian Church were orthodox or they were nothing. In future, if anyone felt squeamish about the market economy or concerned about that camel passing through the eye of a needle, they would just have to express their views somewhere else. In a passage from St Luke's Gospel, which was particularly valued by the Cathars and which continued to trouble everyone else as well, it had been written:

There was a certain rich man, which was clothed in purple and fine linen, and fared sumptuously every day: And there was a certain beggar named Lazarus, which was laid at his gate, full of sores, And desiring to be fed with the crumbs which fell from the rich man's table: moreover the dogs came and licked his sores. And it came to pass that the beggar died, and was carried by the angels into Abraham's bosom: the rich man also died, and was buried. And in hell he lift up his eyes, being in torments, and seeth Abraham afar off, and Lazarus in his bosom. And he cried and said, Father Abraham, have mercy on me, and send Lazarus, that he may dip the tip of his finger in water, and cool my tongue; for I am tormented in this flame. But Abraham said, Son, remember that thou in thy lifetime receivedst thy good things, and likewise Lazarus evil things: but now he is comforted, and thou art tormented. And beside all this, between us and you there is a great gulf fixed . . .

It was that 'great gulf' which the heretics of the twelfth and thirteenth centuries had tried – in vain – to bridge at a time when the market economy was developing fast. By stressing, among other things, the simple lessons of the Gospels rather than the ornate lessons of the Book of Revelation. A great gulf which secular thinkers have been trying to bridge ever since. Peter Damian, the reforming Italian cleric who coined the well-known saying 'avarice is the root of all evil', had summed up the problem in his characteristically outspoken way as early as the mid-eleventh century:

First get rid of money, for Christ and money do not go well together in the same place. If you were to choose both of them at the same time, you would find yourself the possessor of one without the other, for the more abundant your supply of filthy lucre in this world, the more miserably lacking you are in true riches!

But it wasn't, of course, as simple as that . . .

3

THE SAINT AND THE SCHOLAR

One of the great confrontations of twelfth-century Europe – on which, historians have suggested, the immediate direction of western thought depended – was not between kings or knights or armies, but between a saint and a scholar. The saint, who was also a monk, believed that religion was a matter of personal contact with, and experience of, God. The scholar, who was also a teacher, believed that religion was a matter for discussion and explanation and tough-minded argument. The confrontation between the two, between the mystic and the philosopher, was to turn into the theological prize-fight of the century. Indeed, the word 'theology' took on a recognizably modern meaning – the disciplined study of the Bible, drawing on tradition – partly as a result of it.

On the one hand there was Bernard of Clairvaux (1090–1154), later St Bernard, rural, ascetic, spiritual, theologically accepting. 'Believe me, I have experience,' he wrote in a letter, 'you will find fuller satisfaction labouring in the woods than you ever will in books. The trees and the rocks will teach you what you can never hear from any master.' On the other hand there was Peter Abelard (1079–1142) from Brittany, the best-known teacher of his day: urban, arrogant, rational and theologically inquiring. 'Words are useless,' he wrote in characteristic style of a student seminar, 'if intelligence cannot follow them; nothing can be believed until it is first understood . . . The Lord himself criticizes such "blind guides of blind people".'

Between them, these two men represented some of the fundamental choices facing their age – between rural isolation and urban society, monasteries and teaching institutions, contemplation and argument, faith and reason. If the pre-determinate, unwavering, fatalistic, metaphorical, static atom of the twelfth-century world view in the West was ever going to be split, it was going to be split through this choice, for the Einsteins of the Middle Ages were the theologians. So different were Bernard and Abelard in their approaches that they could find very little to say to one another. Bernard wrote of Abelard as 'this man who is content to see *nothing* in a glass darkly, but must behold all face to face'. By the time they *did* meet face to face at the Council of Sens in 1140, a major public clash had become unavoidable.

Peter Abelard was born in the town of Le Pallet, a few miles from Nantes on the Poitiers road in Brittany, some thirteen years after the neighbouring Normans had crossed the Channel and conquered England. His father, a minor country nobleman – of the kind who was finding life increasingly difficult with the advent of a monetary economy – believed that his four sons should have the benefit of a good education before becoming soldiers. Peter enjoyed his education so much that he preferred to soldier on as a student and apprentice philosopher. While his three brothers went to war, he rapidly became bored with provincial Breton society and made his way towards Paris.

'I began to travel about in several provinces,' he was to recall in about 1132, 'disputing, like a true peripatetic philosopher, wherever I had heard there was keen interest in the art of dialectic.' During this period he was taught logic at Loches or Tours under Jean Roscelin of Compiègne. 'At last I came to Paris,' he continued, 'where dialectic had long been particularly flourishing.' But in 1100 or thereabouts the great attraction of Paris was not yet the bright lights and the big city. It was a small town crammed on to the Île de la Cité – with a few houses and markets on the bridges of the Seine and the left bank – whose main claim to fame was that it was near good hunting country, so the kings of France (who had originated as Counts of Paris) liked to look in from time to time. Paris did not even have its own

archbishop: the town came under the jurisdiction of the Archbishop of Sens. The activities of Peter Abelard, as much as anything else, were eventually to make the city famous and help to
populate the Latin Quarter with students and teachers from all
over Europe who actually spoke and wrote in Latin, and who
helped to raise Paris above rival schools in France such as those in
Chartres, Laon, Reims and Tours.

The great attraction in about 1100 was that the schools around
the old church of Notre Dame were becoming centres for the study
of 'dialectic' or the art of reasoning through discussion and debate.
Not cataloguing, or listing, which went on in most centres of learning at the time, but reasoning. The lecturers, or masters, would read
out a text, perhaps of ancient Greek – recently translated into Latin
– perhaps a commentary on the Bible, and the students would then
kick around its possible meanings and test them against the master's
interpretation, a teaching technique that was known as *disputatio*
(rather than *lectio*, a reading, or formal presentation). Nine times out
of ten the master would hold his ground, because he was better
known, more articulate and had had much more practice. But this

---

A TWELFTH-CENTURY STUDENT OVERSPENDS

You are always writing to tell me that times are hard and that you have to
pay your professors. It seems to me, however, that you have no real desire to
learn. To be brief, I shall do nothing more for you than what was agreed.
Why should you alone spend all I possess? I have other relations and friends
to provide for. When I was at school I did not have one obole a day, but I
did not die as a result, God be praised.

Nevertheless I send herewith 10 Angevin sous and 11 Parisian sous, since
I do not want your messenger to return empty-handed. But be assured you
will have nothing more from now until the Calends of May.

From a letter by a canon of Lisieux,
to his student nephew Nicholas (late 12th century)

---

was just the setting for an ambitious and gifted young philosopher – 'aware', as he put it, 'of my own worth' – to make his presence felt by some intellectual jousting in public with a well-known authority.

Such behaviour tended to irritate some of Abelard's quieter fellow students, but after life in rural Brittany and Loches he felt he needed to be stretched. The trouble was, according to Abelard's account, the current 'supreme master' turned out to be a bit of a let-down. He was William of Champeaux, Realist philosopher and head of the Cloister School of Notre Dame, and he proved almost too easy to provoke and defeat in argument. So at the age of twenty-three the apprentice decided to turn teacher – forming small seminar groups at Melun and Corbeil, before returning to Paris where he could 'embarrass' his previous master 'through more frequent encounters in disputation' (*disputatio* again). The debate seems partly to have been about how much the newly translated ancient Greeks, especially Plato and Aristotle, could contribute to modern-day Christian questions, and partly about relationships between the abstract and the particular. Abelard thought the Greeks, especially Plato, could contribute a lot, but at the same time he thought William had boxed himself in with his over-emphasis on 'universals', and by his own account he won the argument hands down – 'with the result that the fame of the master himself gradually declined and came to an end'. Abelard had become a force to be reckoned with, among pupils and scholars:

My own teaching gained so much prestige and authority from this that the strongest supporters of my master who had hitherto been the most violent among my attackers now flocked to join my school. Even William's successor as head of the Paris school offered me his chair so that he could join the others as my pupil . . . William was eaten up with jealousy and consumed with anger to an extent it is difficult to convey . . . [but] the more his jealousy pursued me the more widely my reputation spread, for, as the poet says: 'Envy seeks the heights, the winds blow over the highest things; And thunderbolts strike the highest mountains.'

And yet, however widely his reputation spread, it became increasingly clear – to Abelard, at any rate – that the intellectual games he was playing with philosophy, logic and dialectics were just that: games. His mastery in debate was wasted unless applied to fundamentals, and this meant the discipline of theology – where the real intellectual heavyweights worked. 'Theology' was then in its infancy, it was not even called that yet, and it was taught at Laon, some seventy miles to the north-east of Paris, where Anselm (William's master) was well known for his researches into biblical texts and for his teaching-aids for students reading the scriptures. Abelard's father and mother had recently entered the monastic life and it may be that they had encouraged him to move on to the 'queen of sciences'. Their eldest son certainly hoped that this time he would be both challenged *and* noticed in the right places:

I therefore approached this old man, who owed his reputation more to long practice than to intelligence or memory . . . Anselm could win the admiration of an audience, but he was useless when put to the question. He had a remarkable command of words but their meaning was worthless and devoid of all sense. The fire he kindled filled his house with smoke but did not light it up; he was a tree in full leaf which could be seen from afar, but on closer and more careful inspection proved to be barren. I had come to this tree to gather fruit, but I found it was the fig tree which the Lord

---

A COMPLAINT ABOUT STUDENT DISCIPLINE

What liberty is left for study when we see masters flattering pupils and pupils judging their masters, obliging them according to their pleasure to speak or be silent. It is rare to see a severe master; more often it is the voice and smile of the flatterer. But if someone maintains the severity proper for a master the courtisans flee him like a madman. He is thought cruel and inhuman.

From William of Conches, letter (1140s)

---

cursed . . . Once I discovered this I did not lie idle in his shade for long. My attendance at his lectures gradually became more and more irregular . . .

The problem this time seems to have been less about what Anselm actually said than about how he said it. He gave formal lectures, based entirely within a biblical context, and he thought that dialectics was more appropriately used as a method for philosophizing than for sacred subjects. Abelard, on the other hand, who was singularly unimpressed by the fact that Anselm was a recognized authority on the commentaries of St Augustine (with a special interest in 'Realism', or the spiritual truth which lay beyond mere physical or outward appearances), preferred to pitch in with controversial thoughts: 'Take, for instance, the question whether it is permissible to kill. Identical words may have different meanings, yet the Commandments state "thou shalt not kill". But St Augustine wrote, "if lawful authority commands it we should serve in war". Some sayings seem not just to differ but actually contradict others.'

So Peter Abelard returned to Paris, where the schools were to become better known ('the numbers there increased enormously') partly because of his methods and aggressive personality. He poached several of Anselm's research students and was appointed *magister scholarum* at Notre Dame. Meanwhile, a young nobleman from Burgundy – about ten years older than Abelard – was preparing to renounce the temptations of worldly things.

Bernard of Clairvaux, the greatest and most persuasive mystic of his age, was born on his father's estate at Fontaines, north of Dijon in Burgundy, in 1090, the third of seven children. Again, the pattern was to be a good education (including Latin and verse-making) followed by a military career. Bernard was sent off to Châtillon-sur-Seine, one of the Duke of Burgundy's fortresses supervised by his father. He was, according to subsequent devotional 'Lives', a shy, contemplative young man, especially prone to the temptations of adolescence but preferring to cope with them on his own. He did not enjoy the company of the other soldiers and their attempts 'to make him conform to them'. On one occasion he jumped into a pool of freezing water to 'cool himself down from the heat of carnal longing', for he had resolved that 'chastity was the thing dearest to him in his life'. The chapel of St Vorles at Châtillon was the scene where most of these epic struggles against 'the coiling adder, lying in wait for his heel' were enacted.

Out of these 'temptations', which happened at about the same time as Bernard lost his mother, when he was nineteen, something occurred which became one of the great inspirational legends of the age – often depicted in late medieval and early Renaissance art. Bernard was praying to the wooden statue of the Virgin in St Vorles – asking for her intercession at a time of mental crisis – when he came to the words '*Monstra esse matrem*' (Show thyself a mother). The Virgin then proceeded to appear before him and, pressing her breast, let three drops of milk fall on to his lips. This intimate experience was Bernard's salvation – and from it came his lifelong devotion, unusual at the time, to the cult of the Virgin Mary, as mother, ideal of beauty and mediator between sinful mortals and God.

Bernard returned briefly to his military duties, serving the Duke of Burgundy by taking part in the siege of the castle of Grancey. But the temptations, and the vision which resolved them for him, had made up his mind. He would renounce his worldly career and join a group of monks a little to the south of Cîteaux – Cistercium in Latin. Given his strange behaviour of late, this decision couldn't have come as much of a surprise. What was surprising was that virtually his entire family – uncle, brothers, father: soldiers, members of the nobility, thirty-one of them in all – followed him into the cloister at Cîteaux.

The Cistercians, as these monks were called, were an offshoot – the first of many – of the Benedictine Order, *the* establishment of monastic life whose magnificent new abbey at Cluny – some 50 miles south – had recently been completed. Cluny itself had started out in much the same way, but that was two hundred years earlier and the order had become grand and formalized, with a huge church, elaborate bureaucracy and a liturgy that many thought too long and convoluted. The Cistercians advocated a back-to-basics approach, calling for simplicity in all things – buildings, dress, liturgy, organization, everything – and a *literal* interpretation of the rule of St Benedict. They also expected the monks to do farmwork to support themselves, rather than use tenants or servants. Today we might call this 'low church'. It certainly struck a distinct chord in the increasingly complex and competitive society of the twelfth century. And it was exactly what Bernard – and his followers – were searching for.

Just as well Bernard turned up when he did – for the tough and ascetic life of the Cistercian brothers had led to malnutrition, disease and even death. The order at Cîteaux was in danger of dying on the bough before it had even taken root. Bernard's energy and commitment were responsible for doubling – maybe even trebling – the numbers of the community. His impact was so strong that some people began to call the monks Bernardines. Others wrote stories about how during his first year's novitiate he had managed, through contemplation, to shut out the rest of the world so effectively that he didn't know or care how many windows there were in his church, or whether the ceiling of his cell was vaulted or not; at the end of the year, it was said, 'the peace of his soul shone through his countenance'. (In fact the Cistercians slept in dormitories not cells – but saints' 'Lives' tended to embroider their subjects' *curricula vitae* in the interests of a good moral lesson.)

Whatever the legends, within just four years Bernard was sent out to establish a daughter abbey because Cîteaux was becoming so cramped. Together with about twelve companions, he travelled north to the River Aube (almost beyond the estate boundaries of his father's patron, the Duke of Burgundy), where in 1115 he founded in the marshy reeds his own abbey of Clairvaux. The Cistercians were to make the choice of secluded sites something of a trademark; that way, they could avoid temptation *and* reclaim uncultivated territory through the sweat of their brows. One of the 'Lives' was to say of the twenty-five-year-old abbot: 'For all his fleeing from it, glory chased after him as relentlessly as it always evades those who grasp at it. A proverb he often had on his lips was "doing what no one else does draws all eyes".' At the same time an observer was to write of Peter Abelard's reputation among the schools of Paris: 'No distances on land, no mountain heights, no valley depths, nor the terrible storms of the sea, could prevent the students from flocking to you, attracted by your *fame*.'

A DRINKS PARTY AT CLUNY

What can I say about the drinking of water when even watering one's wine is inadmissible? Naturally all of us, as monks, suffer from a weak stomach, which is why we pay good heed to Paul's advice to use a little wine. It is just that the word little gets overlooked, I can't think why. And if only we were content with drinking it plain, albeit undiluted. There are things it is embarrassing to say, though it should be more embarrassing still to do them. If hearing about them brings a blush, it will cost you none to put them right. The fact is that three or four times during the same meal you might see a half-filled cup brought in, so that different wines may be not drunk or drained so much as carried to the nose and lips. The expert palate is quick to discriminate between them and pick out the most potent. And what of the monasteries – and there are said to be some – which regularly serve spiced and honeyed wine in the refectory on major feasts? We are surely not going to say that this is done to nurse weak stomachs? The only reason for it that I can see is to allow deeper drinking, or keener pleasure. But once the wine is flowing through the veins and the whole head is throbbing with it, what else can they do when they get up from table but go and sleep it off? And if you force a monk to get up for vigils before he has digested, you will set him groaning rather than intoning. Having got to bed, it's not the sin of drunkenness they regret if questioned, but not being able to face their food.

From Bernard of Clairvaux, *An Apologia for Abbot William* (1125)

The reputation of Bernard's community in and around Clairvaux and of Abelard's *tour de force* performances as a lecturer led to the development of personality cults around both of them. Legends – at first carried by word of mouth, through monastic, pilgrim or trade networks, in a form of European whispers – enlarged their characters to fill out their reputations. In the case of Bernard, there were tales of saintliness and miracles, in the case of Abelard, tales of his outlandish behaviour as a lecturer. Somehow their big ideas meant that they had to be larger-than-life people as well. Chronicles refer to Bernard as 'the most famous preacher of holy scripture in France' and to Abelard as 'master of the famous schools to which flock the scholars of almost all the Latin world'.

But it is worth asking what the word 'famous' really meant in the early decades of the twelfth century. Above all, it was based on the spoken word, the gesture, the performance – in short, the rhetoric – and so sermons, lectures, debates, disputations and storytelling were the main ways in which the word, suitably embellished, got around. The labour involved in producing books made them very expensive indeed – not to mention the fact that each volume of lambskin parchment represented a whole flock of sheep – so 'publication', such as it was outside the monasteries, basically meant lending a manuscript to another scholar, handing it on to a copyist or getting a famous person to comment on it. But at precisely this time the spoken word and the written word were coming closer and closer together and Abelard – in his autobiography – has much to say about how *both* contributed to his fame, to his own opinion of himself (which tended on the whole to be high), and thus to his downfall:

Success always puffs up fools with pride, and worldly security weakens the spirit's resolution and easily destroys it through carnal temptations. I began to think myself the only philosopher in the world, with nothing to fear from anyone, and so I yielded to the lusts of the flesh . . . I had always held myself aloof from unclean association with prostitutes, and constant application to my studies had prevented me from frequenting the society of gentlewomen: indeed, I knew little of the secular way of life. Perverse Fortune flattered me, as the saying goes, and found an easy way to bring me toppling down from my pedestal.

He continued this confession with a frank account of his affair with the seventeen-year-old Heloise. Very little is known about her background, except that her mother's name was Hersinde and that – as her own letters implied – she was not of the high nobility but felt herself to be 'raised up' by her relationship with this *magister scholarum*. The story of what happened after they met is best told in the words of the two protagonists – from Abelard's *Historia calamitatum* and Heloise's remarkable personal letters. Some scholars doubt the authenticity of these letters (the manuscripts only surfaced in the late thirteenth century) but most now accept them as genuine.

ABELARD: There was in Paris at the time a young girl named Heloise, the niece of Fulbert, one of the canons [who would have lived in the cathedral square of Notre Dame], and so much loved by him that he had done everything in his power to advance her education in letters. In looks she did not rank lowest, while in the extent of her learning she stood supreme. A gift for letters is so rare in women that it added greatly to her charm and had won her renown through the realm.

HELOISE: What kind of philosopher could match your fame?

ABELARD: I decided she was the one to bring to my bed, confident that I should have an easy success; for at that time I had youth and exceptional good looks, as well as my great reputation to recommend me . . .

HELOISE: When you appeared in public, who did not hurry to catch a glimpse of you, or crane his neck and strain his eyes to follow your departure?

ABELARD: All on fire with desire for this girl . . . I came to an arrangement with her uncle . . . whereby he should take me into his house, which was very near my school, for whatever sum [of money] he liked to ask . . . he was all eagerness for my money and confident that his niece would profit from my teaching . . .

HELOISE: Every wife, every young girl, desired you in absence and was on fire in your presence; great ladies envied me my joys . . .

ABELARD: Her studies allowed us to withdraw in private, as love desired, and then with our books open before us, more words of love than of our reading passed between us, and more kissing than teaching. My hands strayed oftener to her bosom than to the pages . . . To avert suspicion I sometimes struck her . . .

HELOISE: You had two special gifts whereby to win at once the heart of any woman – your gifts for composing verse and song . . . more than anything this made women sigh for love of you. And as most of these songs told of our love, they soon made me widely known . . .

ABELARD: In short, our desires left no stage of love-making untried, and if love could devise something new, we welcomed it. We entered on each joy the more eagerly for our previous inexperience, and were the less easily sated . . .

HELOISE: The pleasures of lovers which we shared have been too sweet . . .

ABELARD: It was utterly boring for me to have to go to the school, and . . . as my interest and concentration flagged, my lectures lacked all inspiration and were merely repetitive; I could do no more than repeat what had been said long ago . . . Separation drew our hearts still closer while frustration inflamed our passion even more . . . we became more abandoned as we lost all sense of shame . . . And so we were caught in the act . . .

HELOISE: I looked for no marriage bond, no marriage portion, and it was not my own pleasures and wishes I sought to gratify, as you well know, but yours. The name of wife may seem more sacred, or more binding, but sweeter for me will always be the word mistress, or, if you will permit me, that of concubine or whore.

ABELARD: I removed her secretly from his [Fulbert's] house and sent her straight to my own country until she gave birth to a boy, whom she called Astralabe . . . In the end . . . I begged forgiveness [of her uncle] and promised to make any amends he might think fit . . . Moreover, I offered him satisfaction in a form he could never have hoped for: I would marry the girl I had wronged.

HELOISE: This marriage would be nothing but a disgrace and a burden to you. Along with the loss of reputation, there are the difficulties of marriage . . .

ABELARD: All I stipulated was that the marriage should be kept secret so as not to damage my reputation.

HELOISE: St Jerome sets out in considerable detail the unbearable annoyances of marriage and its endless anxieties.

ABELARD: [Her uncle] agreed, pledged his word and that of his supporters, and sealed the reconciliation I desired with a kiss.

HELOISE: What harmony can there be between pupils and nursemaids, desks and cradles, books or tablets and distaffs, pen or stylus and spindles? Who can concentrate on thoughts of Scripture or philosophy and be able to endure babies crying, nurses soothing them with lullabies, and all the noisy coming and going of men and women about the house? Will he put up with the constant muddle and squalor which small children bring into the home? The wealthy can do so, for . . . being rich, they do not have to count the cost nor be tormented by daily cares. But philosophers lead a very different life from rich men.

ABELARD: And so when our baby son was born we entrusted him to my sister's care and returned secretly to Paris. A few days later, after a night's private vigil of prayer in a certain church . . .

HELOISE: . . . the name of mistress instead of wife would be dearer to me and more honourable for you – only love freely given should keep you for me, not the constriction of a marriage tie.

ABELARD: . . . at dawn we were joined in matrimony in the presence of Fulbert and some of his, and our, friends . . . But Fulbert and his servants, seeking satisfaction for the dishonour done to him, began to spread the news of the marriage and break the promise of secrecy they had given me.

HELOISE: While we enjoyed the pleasures of an uneasy love and abandoned ourselves to fornication (if I may use an ugly but expressive word) we were spared God's severity.

ABELARD: I removed her to a convent of nuns [called Ste Marie] in the town near Paris called Argenteuil, where she had been brought up and educated as a small girl, and I also had made for her a religious habit of the type worn by novices.

HELOISE: But when we amended our unlawful conduct by what was lawful, and atoned for the shame of fornication by an honourable marriage, then the Lord in his anger laid his hand heavily upon us, and would not permit a chaste union though he had long tolerated one which was unchaste.

ABELARD: At this news her uncle and his friends and relatives imagined that I had tricked them, and had found an easy way of ridding myself of Heloise by making her a nun.

HELOISE: The happiness of supreme ecstasy would end in the supreme bitterness of sorrow . . .

ABELARD: They bribed one of my servants to admit them and there took cruel vengeance on me of such appalling barbarity as to shock the whole world: they cut off the parts of my body whereby I had committed the wrong of which they complained. Then they fled . . .

It was humiliation on a grand scale. Throughout the next day Peter Abelard's house was surrounded by friends, students and clerks publicly weeping for him and his ruined reputation. For, as a senior teacher of divinity with an influence over young people, he would have been assumed, and perhaps expected, to be celibate. He may have been in holy orders (the evidence is ambiguous), in which case he would – equally – have been expected to be celibate: the Church had only just started forbidding senior clergy to get married; maybe celibacy would have improved his promotion prospects. Abelard had broken an unwritten rule about celibacy, so – despite student support – his public reputation was in tatters. But, more than that, he had been humiliated as a private human being. He was a freefloating intellectual and humanist in the tradition of the 'wandering scholar' or goliard – not a soldier, priest or a monk – with an uncertain role in society, committed to defining himself, fully and passionately, as a man. The reason he had wanted a woman by his side, he suggested, was so that he could 'be complete', so that he could achieve his full potential. Well, he could never be 'complete' again.

HELOISE ON 'A MAN'S WORTH'

For a man's worth does not rest on his wealth or power; these depend on fortune, but worth on his merits. And a woman should realize that if she marries a rich man more readily than a poor one and desires her husband more for his possessions than for himself, she is offering herself for sale. Certainly any woman who comes to marry through desires of this kind deserves wages, not gratitude, for clearly her mind is on the man's property, not himself, and she would be ready to prostitute herself to a richer man, if she could. This is evident from the argument put forward in the dialogue of Aeschines Socraticus [a pupil of Socrates] by the learned Aspasia to Xenophon and his wife. When she had expounded it in an effort to bring about a reconciliation between them, she ended with these words: 'Unless you come to believe that there is no better man nor worthier woman on earth you will always still be looking for what you judge the best thing of all – to be the husband of the best of wives and the wife of the best of husbands.'

These are saintly words which are more than philosophic; indeed, they deserve the name of wisdom, not philosophy. It is a holy error and a blessed delusion between man and wife, when perfect love can keep the ties of marriage unbroken not so much through bodily continence as chastity of spirit. But what error permitted other women, plain truth permitted me, and what they thought of their husbands, the world in general believed, or rather, knew to be true of yourself; so that my love for you was the more genuine for being further removed from error.

From Heloise's first letter to Abelard (early 1130s)

The story of the love affair between Abelard, aged nearly forty, and Heloise, aged seventeen, says a lot about the position of both men and women in the twelfth century. It was certainly unusual for a woman to be as well educated as Heloise, but the fact that she had been so well taught as a girl in the convent of Argenteuil shows how relatively well-born women – especially at a top-line convent – could have their own talents and personalities, rather than be just the wicked temptresses of devotional literature and the 'Lives' of the saints, written as they mainly were for frail young men. This was quite a recent development, though. In the middle of the previous century the debate had still been raging about whether women had souls or not! By Heloise's time they were allowed souls – but very little else. If she had never met Abelard, she would probably have

---

AN EARLY-THIRTEENTH-CENTURY SOAP OPERA

Our constant lovers sat there together and told love tales of those whom love had ruined in days gone by. They debated and discussed, they bewept and bewailed how Phyllis of Thrace and poor Canacea had suffered such misfortune in Love's name; how Biblis had died broken-hearted for her brother's love; how love-lorn Dido, Queen of Tyre and Sidon, had met so tragic a fate because of unhappy love. To such tales did they apply themselves from time to time.

When they tired of stories they slipped into their refuge and resumed their well-tried pleasure of sounding their harp, and singing sadly and sweetly. They busied their hands and their tongues in turn. They performed amorous lays and their accompaniments, varying their delight as it suited them: for if one took the harp it was for the other to sing the tune with wistful tenderness. And indeed the strains of both harp and tongue, merging their sound in each other, echoed in that cave so sweetly that it was dedicated to sweet Love for her retreat most fittingly as 'La fossiure à la gent amant'.

All that had been rumoured in tales of old on the subject of the grotto was borne out in this pair. Only now had the cave's true mistress given herself to her sport in earnest. Whatever frolics or pastimes had been pursued in this grotto before, they did not equal this; they were neither so pure nor unsullied in spirit as when Tristan and Isolde disported themselves. These two beguiled Love's hour in a way no lovers surpassed – they did just as their hearts prompted them.

From Gottfried von Strassburg, *Tristan and Isolde* (1200–10)

---

had to marry a nobleman selected by her uncle and her only real chance to cut loose would have been as a rich widow: the odds on a young nobleman getting killed in a battle, a private scrap or a tournament were quite high. Then she could have picked a second husband for herself. As it was, at Abelard's request, Heloise became a nun at Argenteuil – where she remained shut up for most of her life.

A SERMON IN PRAISE OF THE VIRGIN MARY

Let us now say a few words about the name Mary, which means 'star of the sea' and is so becoming to the Virgin Mother. Surely she is very fittingly likened to a star. The star sends forth its ray without harm to itself. In the same way the Virgin brought forth her son with no injury to herself. The ray no more diminishes the star's brightness than does the Son his mother's integrity. She is indeed that noble star risen out of Jacob whose beam enlightens this earthly globe. She it is whose brightness both twinkles in the highest heaven and pierces the pit of hell, and is shed upon earth, warming our hearts far more than our bodies, fostering virtue and cauterizing vice. She, I tell you, is that splendid and wondrous star suspended as by necessity over this great wide sea, radiant with merit and brilliant in example . . .

From Bernard of Clairvaux, *Second Homily in Praise of the Virgin*

There were authors of the time, though, who were beginning to question the traditional role of women – as chaste, simpering creatures whose marriages had to be arranged for them. Adulterous soap operas such as Tristan and Isolt, or Lancelot and Guinevere, sung or said by minstrels in court and courtyard, were to become particularly fashionable in the twelfth century. A tension emerged between authors who implied that it was celibacy, and even chastity, that were wrong – because unnatural – and the new, strict Churchmen, the kind who were themselves celibate, who were highly critical even of noble adulterers; indeed, the Church was insisting on more and more of a role where marriage was concerned. This tension may also have contributed to the cult of the Virgin Mary.

Until this time Mary had remained a remote, majestic figure and there had not been much personal devotion to her in the West. But by the end of the twelfth century every city of consequence on the continent of western Europe had a church or cathedral, sometimes both, dedicated to her name. The Cistercian brotherhood – rapidly expanding under Bernard's influence – was also dedicated to her. Her image appeared in the seals of its abbeys, its members wore white in honour of her purity and began the custom of building a special lady chapel in their churches. In these and other ways Mary was brought closer, more down to earth, as a role model and as an object of devotion. It may be that this change in the image and meaning of Christ's mother in the twelfth century had something to do with noblewomen breaking out of their traditional roles as wives and mothers. Maybe the cult of the Virgin helped to put them back again. Or maybe the cult was simply keeping up with social developments.

The most faithful follower of the cult was Bernard himself – who had helped to create it. His love of the Virgin Mary was as deep a spiritual or religious passion as Abelard's for Heloise had been phys-ical and secular. As he wrote in one of his 'Homilies in praise of the Virgin':

O you, whoever you are, who feel that in the tidal wave of this world you are nearer to being tossed about among the squalls and gales than treading on dry land, if you do not want to founder in the tempest do not avert your eyes from the brightness of this star [Mary meaning 'star of the sea']. When the wind of temptation blows up within you, when you strike upon the rock of tribulation, gaze up at this star, *call out to Mary*.

And as he added in one of his 'Sermons on the Song of Songs', full of rhetorical power:

I love because I love, I love that I may love. A great thing is love, provided that it return to its principle, look to its origin, and flowing back towards its source draw thence the pure waters wherein it may flow unendingly . . . Now I will discuss the highest kiss, that of the Mouth of God. Give all heed to this mystery, for it is passing sweet, but seldom known and hard to understand.

For Bernard, though, it was 'through *austerity* that the Soul can be emptied of self interest and filled with love'.

Peter Abelard, meanwhile, was accepted as a monk in St Denis. He gladly embraced a monastic life, as a way of 'hiding his shame'. But this wasn't to be the end of his misfortune, and it was only the beginning of a life of sheer purgatory for Heloise. From Argenteuil, through her letters, she asked her husband persistently if he could help to write a Rule especially for women or, failing that, if he could become her personal spiritual director:

At present the one Rule of St Benedict is professed in the Latin Church by women equally with men, although, as it was clearly written for men alone, it can only be fully obeyed by men, whether subordinates or superiors. Leaving aside for the moment the other articles of the Rule: how can women be concerned with what is written there about cowls, drawers or scapulars? Or, indeed, with tunics or woollen garments worn next to the skin, when the monthly purging of their superfluous humours must avoid such things? . . . Certainly those who laid down rules for monks were not only completely silent about women but also prescribed regulations which they knew to be quite unsuitable for them.

Hildegard of Bingen (1098–1179), who was an almost exact contempory of Heloise, was on the other hand a committed supporter of the Rule of St Benedict – its spirit rather than its letter. But then again, she had entered a monastery at the age of eight and become an enclosed nun at eighteen. Heloise entered Argenteuil because her husband's – and her uncle's – behaviour left her with no choice. She never pretended to have a vocation.

For Bernard, there were to be no public humiliations of the kind which Abelard had to endure. But he did make some bad mistakes –

usually by going over the top. A year after becoming abbot of Clairvaux he realized that his regime had become so severe that the
community was, quite literally, beginning to fade away. There were
sick and emaciated bodies all around him. An inadequate diet, plus
the demands of physical labour – laid down in the Order's Charter
of Charity and rigidly enforced by Bernard – were proving a killer
combination. Even his most devoted followers were becoming dis-
couraged. His reaction was typically extreme if not wholly helpful:
he ordered that meals in future should be more regular and, feeling
guilty about his thoughtlessness, shut himself away for a year without speaking to anyone.

Shortly after Bernard had decided to start communicating again,
a cousin of his called Robert – one of the original thirty-one disciples – defected to the Benedictines at Cluny, where life seemed a
little easier and life expectancy was a little longer. Bernard took this
as a personal insult.

Does salvation rest rather in soft raiment and high living than in frugal fare
and moderate clothing? . . . If warm and comfortable furs, if fine and precious cloth, if long sleeves and ample hoods, if dainty coverlets and soft
woollen shirts make a saint, why do I delay and not follow you at once? But
these things are comforts for the weak, not the arms of fighting men.

What started, for Bernard, as a family affair was later to become
an all-out attack on the Benedictine Order and its spiritual centre at
Cluny – his first public showdown. Between monks who dressed in
white and monks who dressed in black. His criticisms were to be
described as an overdose of puritanism. 'Wine and white bread,
honey wine and pittances benefit the body not the soul. The soul is
not fattened out of frying-pans! Many monks in Egypt served
God for a long time without fish. Pepper, ginger, cumin, sage, and
all the thousand other spices may please the palate, but they in-
flame lust.'

Once he had cleared his throat, there was no stopping the flow of
Bernard's invective – and he continued to wage war against the
Benedictine monks for some years. He was generally in the right:

the monasteries *had* grown a little lazy and complacent. Peter the Venerable, the next abbot of Cluny, was to take up many of Bernard's suggestions, as was Suger, the great cathedral designer and abbot of St Denis, who re-established regular discipline in the wake of attacks from the abbot of Clairvaux.

'May Christ save you from this,' Bernard had concluded his letter to Robert, 'for at the last judgement you will incur a greater penalty on account of this letter of mine if, when you have read it, you do not take its lesson to heart.' An oft-repeated story goes that as Bernard dictated his famous letter, it began to rain, but that when he'd finished, he discovered that the letter was – miraculously – dry. Another turning-point in the saint's *curriculum vitae*.

Bernard of Clairvaux said in one of his sermons, 'To hear the divine voice is not a matter of hard labour. The labour lies rather in blocking our ears so we *do not* hear it.' He also wrote, 'Believe and you will understand.' So faith, to him, was about personal contact with and experience of God – and he called Clairvaux a '*schola caritatis*', a school of love or charity, rather than a school of debate or scholarship or theology. Today we would call him a 'mystic'. Abelard, on the other hand, argued that 'we can't possibly believe what we don't understand', that it was no use hiding behind famous commentators if you did not personally find them convincing and that 'by doubting we come to inquiring and by inquiring we perceive the truth'. So faith, to him, was about clearing the mind of noise – which could well be a matter of hard labour – and conviction or rational choice, rather than close encounters. Today, we would call him a member of the 'intelligentsia'.

In the twelfth century these ideas – and the personalities who expressed them – seem to have had remarkably wide appeal, in a society which desperately wanted to be saved either by experiencing God direct or by asking the right questions. Received wisdom was no longer enough. The cult of the Virgin Mary, the rise of the universities, the appeal of what came to be known by the name of 'heresy', even popular songs, bear witness to the impact which these two men had on western Europe. And it was inevitable that they would eventually cross swords in the public arena. The language with which they described each other's point of view became more and more extreme, and polemical. Abelard later referred to Bernard's writings as 'poison belched out and vomited in his direction', while Bernard in turn would not dignify what he called Abelard's 'leprous novelties' with the name 'Theologia'. Such bad-mouthing sometimes makes the whole debate seem today like a ping-pong match between two arrogant and not very grown-up undergraduates, but in fact its main concerns – how people perceived God or, indeed, perceived anything, from within – was central to twelfth-century thinking. And both men believed passionately in what they were saying.

It is an indication of how wide Abelard's reputation had spread that within days of his entering the cloister at St Denis – and putting on the black habit of the Benedictine Order – his friends and students were begging him to return to teaching outside the confines of the monastery. Within weeks he was lecturing again, within months he was at work on his theological treatise *On the Unity and Trinity of God* which asked questions about the very nature of knowledge: what is it we know, a lot of individual things, or fundamental principles? Specific examples, or concepts? Abelard especially admired Plato's insight that all real knowledge – not just appearances, which were like a passing fantasy – came to the reflective mind by a kind of illumination, from an invisible world beyond appearances. This seemed close to Christianity and Abelard was so excited by the parallel that he went further and argued that Plato had *almost* discovered the Christian trinity of Father, Son and Holy Ghost in the three fundamental principles of power, wisdom and love. He also argued in *On the Unity* that in the great Aristotle/Plato debate of the time, a mixture of specific examples of things and organizing concepts was the most helpful approach to understanding the nature of knowledge. He wrote:

Now it happened that I first applied myself to lecturing on the basis of our faith by analogy with human reason and composed a treatise . . . for the use of my students who were asking for human and logical reasons on this subject, and demanded something intelligible rather than mere words . . . It was generally agreed that the questions were peculiarly difficult and the importance of the problem was matched by the subtlety of my solution.

Abelard – never one to hide his light under a bushel – reflected that the brilliance of his mind had rescued him from the mutilation of his body. He was certainly at the height of his powers – and irritating his enemies (notably the supporters of William of Champeaux and Anselm of Laon) left, right and centre. He knew that 'philosophizing' carried real dangers for faith – and that faith had always to come first. He must also have known that he was skating on very thin ice indeed; all it needed was for one of those enemies to give him a push.

He was summoned from Paris to away ground at Soissons, to be condemned by a council for writing his book on the Trinity and in particular for implying, with his views about the value of specific examples, that there were 'three Gods'. He was forced to burn the text, in public, with his own hands. He later wrote to Heloise that he suffered more intensely from the shame of having cast his book on the fire, and from the damage done to his reputation, than he had previously suffered from the physical pain of his castration.

As Abelard's star seemed to be falling, Bernard was becoming more and more well known as a religious statesman and negotiator outside his monastery. He preached among Abelard's ex-students in Paris, persuading many of them to 'return to themselves', 'cast off their dirty cloaks' and follow him back to Clairvaux. He, too, published a treatise, *The Steps of Humility and Pride*, which described how dangerous it was for a man to 'think he is better than others. Such a man is always the first to speak, he interferes without being asked. And he is *proud*.'

But Bernard didn't just write about pride. His fundamentalist zeal led him publicly to criticize any bishop or abbot or senior Churchman who was not setting a good enough example. And he didn't mince his words. On one famous occasion he called Bishop Henry of Winchester 'a whore and a wizard'. He would brook no argument or debate; there was one road, and one way to follow it. Chronicles noted that 'his preaching was so persuasive that mothers and daughters and wives hid their menfolk, for fear of losing them to his monastic movement'. When critics complained that a monk ought to confine himself to matters of the cloister, Bernard replied that a monk was a soldier of Christ and ought to defend the honour of God's sanctuary like a crusading knight. In his later years he had his marshals, his garrisons, his storm troopers and his spies everywhere, and his rule – 'leave your body behind when you enter these gates, only your soul is needed' – turned the Cistercians into a phenomenally successful multinational organization. But not before this strictest of lives had taken its toll on its main propagandist.

Bernard was permanently ill – which was hardly surprising given the way he punished his body and the damp surroundings he lived in. He seems to have suffered from a form of extreme anorexia nervosa – rejecting food so regularly that he was sometimes paralysed through lack of nourishment; and he stank continually of stale vomit. 'I have a bad stomach,' he wrote, 'but how much more must I be hurt by the stomach of my memory where such rottenness collects?' The saint's 'Lives' are full of stories about how he very nearly died but came back from the brink. One example was in 1125; in a trance he saw the Devil accusing him before the House of God, and answered the charge:

I confess myself unworthy of the glory of Heaven, and that I can never obtain it by my own merits. But my Lord Jesus possesses it upon a double title; that of inheritance, by being the only begotten Son of his eternal Father, and that of purchase, he having bought it with his precious blood. The second title he has conferred on me and by it I claim the reward of heaven.

The Devil was confounded and went away. Then Bernard saw himself waiting on a sea coast to board a vessel, but it remained out at sea – and left him on land. Finally, the Virgin Mary appeared and laid her hands on him, and when he woke up from his trance the sickness had left him. In the life of this particular saint, she was always there at one minute to twelve to sort out his problems.

After the burning of his book at Soissons, Peter Abelard had been invited back to St Denis (not all Churchmen were happy about the way he had been treated), where he proceeded to make himself even less popular by pointing out to his fellow monks, correctly as it happens, that their patron saint had been wrongly identified. As Abelard had discovered by studying the Northumbrian historian Bede in the monastery library, the saint could not have been the same St Denis as the Areopagite whom St Paul had converted. Since this fond illusion meant a great deal to the abbey – not least in revenues and public credibility – and was actually at the root of Abbot Suger's whole philosophy of how and why to build cathedrals, it was time for Abelard to be moving on again. Actually, Abelard had proved his point about Denis, or Dionysius, by bringing yet another confusion into an already confused story – a *fourth* Dionysius, who was the Bishop of Corinth. But he got to the correct conclusion none the less. Doing the right thing for the wrong reason.

He found refuge with the Bishop of Troyes, who gave him some land four miles outside Nogent on the Seine, on the bank of the River Ardusson. There, he rather provocatively built a chapel of reeds and thatch, and dedicated it to the Holy Trinity – that same Trinity to whom he had dedicated his condemned book. Somehow, whatever he did or said couldn't help but upset the establishment, which in turn made him all the more attractive to young students; his brain would not sit still. Abelard's chapel had to be rebuilt in wood and stone, and extended to accommodate all those who, he recalled, 'began to flock together from all parts forsaking the cities and towns to inhabit the wilderness . . . leaving behind their soft beds to make do with reeds and straw'.

His grass-roots school was thriving – and beginning to attract a lot of attention – when he was elected abbot of a monastery in Brittany, in the diocese of Vannes, whose way of life he described as vulgar and whose inhabitants spoke only a Breton dialect – perhaps a different one from the language he had been brought up to speak, or perhaps he had grown out of his native tongue. He tried hard, he said, to refine these country bumpkins who were 'more savage and wicked than the heathen'. They, by way of thanks it seems, tried to poison him. It is difficult to judge from Abelard's writings whether he was paranoid or they really were persecuting him. It was probably a bit of both. 'God is my witness that I never heard that an assembly of ecclesiastics had met without thinking this was convened to condemn me. I waited like one in terror of being struck by lightning to be brought before a council or synod and charged with heresy or profanity.'

Even his closest associates were not immune. Abelard's enemy, Abbot Suger, having already removed him from St Denis for asking too many embarrassing questions, now expelled Heloise and her nuns from the convent at Argenteuil on the pretext that it belonged to St Denis by ancient right; he also made insinuations about the behaviour of the nuns. Heloise had become the abbess there, with a well-earned reputation for good counsel and holiness – a reputation she continued modestly to deny. Homeless, Heloise appealed to her husband for a safe haven, and he gladly donated his chapel of the Trinity; this was the first time they had met for ten years. Heloise remained there, with some of her nuns, until she died. Abelard returned to his adopted home – and natural habitat – the schools of Paris.

Heloise had written:

Tell me one thing, if you can. Why, after our entry into religion, which was your decision alone, have I been so neglected and forgotten by you that I have neither a word from you when you are here to give me strength nor the consolation of a letter in absence? Tell me, I say, if you can – or I will tell you what I think and indeed the world suspects. It was desire, not affection, which bound you to me, the flame of lust rather than love.

'For me,' she had added in her next letter, 'youth and passion and experience of pleasures which were so delightful, intensify the torments of the flesh and the longings of desire, and the assault is overwhelming.' She went on: 'Even during the celebration of the Mass, when our prayers should be purer, lewd visions of those pleasures take such a hold upon my unhappy soul that my thoughts are on their wantonness instead of on prayers. I should be groaning over the sins I have committed, but I can only sigh for what I have lost.'

Bernard, meanwhile, was busy earning his sainthood by getting involved in Church politics at the very highest level. At a time when Rome had not yet fully established its power-base, he continually drew attention to the need for a head of the Christian world in the West. Despite ill health, he became God's roving ambassador, travelling through France, Italy and Germany, offering his advice to increasingly powerful people. After the death of Honorius II in 1130, two rival popes had been elected. There was nothing unusual about that, but this time one of them, Anacletus, represented the old guard, while the other, Innocent II, who had been elected just as irregularly, wanted to adopt a 'Bernardine' approach to reform. For the next eight years Bernard brought his formidably persuasive powers to bear on the Holy Roman Emperor, on kings and princes, on any of the powers that he could get to listen – to win them over, in the end successfully, to Innocent II's side. From being a contemplative monk, he'd become a pope-maker.

Back in the schools of Paris, Peter Abelard's continuing difficulties would have tried even the patience of a saint. Forbidden by the King of France to teach on his land, he proceeded to lecture his students first from inside a tree – in the air – and then from a fishing boat, on the water. 'The king', says one of the chronicles, 'laughingly confessed himself beaten.' Abelard was becoming a legendary figure.

By the time Bernard finally returned from his missions abroad, Peter Abelard had written a series of even more startling works. *Sic et Non* (or 'on the one hand . . . on the other') gave western thought one of its first discourses on method by listing over a hundred propositions with, beneath each, a quotation saying 'yes' and

PETER ABELARD: *SIC ET NON* (YES AND NO) – ON UNDERSTANDING

Although, amid so great a mass of verbiage, some of the sayings even of the saints not only seem to differ from but also actually to contradict one another, we must not be so bold as to judge those by whom the world itself must be judged, as it is written: 'The saints shall judge nations', and, again, 'And you too shall sit in judgement.' Let us not presume to denounce them as liars or despise them as mistaken, for the Lord said to them: 'He who listens to you, listens to me; he who despises you, despises me' . . .

We should also, when any remarks of the saints are cast in our teeth as being opposed or foreign to truth, take great care that we are not being deceived by a false attribution or by corruption of the text itself. For a great many apocryphal writings were headed with the names of saints, that they might carry authority; and some even of the texts of the Holy Testaments were corrupted through the fault of the copyists . . .

. . . We have decided to assemble various sayings of the Holy Fathers dealing with particular questions, when they occur to our memory, on account of a certain discord which there appears to be between them, so that they may arouse inexperienced readers to the most vigorous activity in seeking out the truth, and that they may sharpen their wits by these inquiries. For assiduous and frequent asking of questions is termed the first key to wisdom. That most penetrating of all philosophers, Aristotle, exhorts scholars to take it up with all their hearts, saying in his work: 'But perhaps it is difficult to make confident pronouncements on matters like this, unless they are frequently discussed. But it will be of some use to entertain doubts about each of them'. For by doubting we come to inquiring and by inquiring we perceive the truth – as the Truth himself says: 'Seek,' he says, 'and you will find; knock and it will be opened to you.'

From Peter Abelard, *Sic et Non* (*c.* 1120)

another saying 'no', from sources of equally high ecclesiastical standing. Other works included *Know Thyself*, which challenged by implication the introspective soul-searching of the monasteries, a systematic *Treatise on the Dialectic* and his *Christian Theology*, the first book to use the word 'theology' in its modern sense. In this he revisited the idea that versions of the Holy Trinity could be found long before Christ in both Hebrew and Greek thought – so by implication it was part of the deep structure of the human mind and by no means unique to Christianity; he also put over his idea in an unusual way – at one point comparing the Trinity with a waxed seal attached to a royal document.

BERNARD: Far be it from us to suppose that the Christian faith has as its boundaries these opinions of the Academicians, whose boast is that they doubt everything and know nothing. But I for my part walk securely and I know that I shall not be confounded.

ABELARD: Assiduous and frequent asking of questions is termed the first key to wisdom. That most penetrating of all philosophers, Aristotle, exhorts scholars to take it up with all their hearts . . . For by doubting we come to inquiring and by inquiring we perceive the truth . . .

Bernard, who had become the most famous individual in the Christian world, was now elected Archbishop of Reims – for the fifth time – and for the fifth time he turned down the dignity. He was, he said, weary after his travels and wanted only to return to the peace and solitude of Clairvaux. Even at this late stage it might have been possible for Bernard and Abelard to avoid a confrontation – not that Bernard was the 'live and let live' type, but they were so different that they could perhaps have coexisted in completely separate worlds. But Bernard's friends and associates – and the small army of people who had been offended by Abelard's methods and his personality problem – had other plans.

'My Lord,' wrote one of them, William the former Cistercian Abbot of St Thierry, 'Peter Abelard is at work, with voice and pen disseminating new doctrines . . . his opinions are said to have found support in the Roman Curia itself. I warn you therefore that you are endangering both your own soul and the interests of the Church by keeping silence under such circumstances.'

In reply to this alarmist letter, which seemed particularly fraught about the fact that Abelard's ideas had reached Rome itself – and might join forces with those of one of his ex-students, Arnold of Brescia, who had dared to argue for an end to the temporal power of the papacy – Bernard wrote: 'To his dear friend William from brother Bernard. In my opinion your misgivings are well called for and reasonable. It is evident from your booklet in which you bruise and close "the lips that mutter wickedness". Not that I have yet had the opportunity to read it with the attention you require . . .'

At first Bernard hesitated. He was sympathetic, but wanted time to consider in detail the 'new doctrines' mentioned by William. He also wanted to be loyal to his friends and supporters, who tended on the whole to be people who had crossed Abelard's path at one time or another. It was probably the reference to Abelard's support in the 'Roman Curia itself' which goaded him to a decision. He wrote to 'the bishops and cardinals in Curia': 'Read if you please that book of Peter Abelard's which he calls a book of *Theology*. Read that other book which they call the book of sentences and also the one entitled *Know Thyself* and see for yourselves how they too run riot with a whole crop of sacrileges and errors . . .'

Abelard, meanwhile, was insisting that a day should be set aside for him to confront Bernard and, in public, to defend his reputation. He contacted his 'beloved friends and associates':

. . . he who has been a hidden enemy for a long time now, who has so far presented himself as a friend, is now inflamed with so much envy that he is unable to hear even the title of my writings, by which things he believes his own glory to have been so diminished and mine so exalted. A short time ago, however, I heard that he greatly lamented because I called that work of ours on the Holy Trinity, composed by us according as God allowed, *Theologia*. He himself, preferring a lesser title, thought it should be called *stultilogiam* [idiocy] rather than *Theologiam* . . . We are confident that his frequent rages will accomplish, God willing, not the suppression of my work, but its elevation: envy seekest the very best things . . .

Abelard finished with a challenge – 'I am prepared to come on the appointed day' – and a request for his associates 'to be present' whenever that happened to be.

Bernard then wrote, more cannily, to 'the bishops of the Archdiocese of Sens':

Word has gone out amongst many and I believe it to have reached your ears that I have been summoned to Sens . . . and challenged to a fight in defence of the faith, although 'the Servant of God must not wrangle but be mild towards all men'. Even if it were only in defence of himself, your child might, perhaps not unreasonably, pride himself on your protection. But now because it is your affair, nay, more yours than mine, I advise and earnestly beg you to prove yourselves friends in adversity. I call you friends, not my friends, but Christ's friends; Christ whose bride [the Church] calls out to you that she is being strangled in the forest of heresy and amongst the undergrowth of errors . . . Do not wonder that I have called upon you so suddenly and at such short notice, for it is a part of the cunning and shrewd design of our opponents to attack us while we are unprepared and to engage us in battle while we are unprotected.

The Council of Sens was arranged for 3 June 1140, the Sunday after Whitsun, when King Louis VII with some of his barons, as well as all the high-ranking Churchmen of the province, were to be in town to view the relics in the cathedral. But the night before the great event, Bernard – who had mobilized his influential friends by presenting himself as a simple child-like David about to do battle with a sophisticated, too-clever-by-half Goliath – called the bishops together and, probably over a dinner where a lot of wine was consumed, tried to stitch up the council in advance. He read them extracts from Abelard's writings, out of context, got them to agree that the writings were both politically incorrect and heretical, and committed the bishops to a verdict before the evidence had even been heard. Abelard, at this stage, was still confident – not quietly confident, since he found it difficult to be quiet about anything – that he had the best arguments and the sharper mind. And some of *his* 'beloved friends' would be at the council as well, rooting for him. So he was looking forward to a very public vindication of his ideas, his methods and his right to express both in the way he chose. It was a chance to clear his name and disassociate himself from 'heresies'. But it is likely that he heard about Bernard's pre-meeting just before he entered the council room on the morning of 3 June. As he walked in he was angry, he wasn't feeling very well, and he now knew that the cards had been stacked against him – that it was to be more like an Inquisition than a sensible debate.

Bernard seems to have opened the proceedings by reading out a list of 'errors' to the assembled bishops, abbots, masters of the schools, monks, educated clerics and, indeed, to the King of the French. These were mainly taken from Abelard's *Theologia*, and in every case but one the quotations were subtly distorted to improve the case against him. The list began:

1 The shocking comparison of the Trinity with a brazen seal and with genus and species.

2 That the Holy Spirit is not of the substance of the Father.

3 That God is able to do what he does, or to refrain from doing it, only in the manner or at the time in which he does so, and not otherwise.

4 That Christ did not take flesh in order to free us from the yoke of the devil.

5 That neither God and man, nor the human person which is Christ, is one of the three persons in the Trinity.

6 That God does no more for a person who is saved before he has accepted his grace than for one who is not saved.

7 That God ought not to hinder evil actions.

And so on, to a total of eighteen '*capitula*' (or headings), each with supporting 'quotations' from Abelard's books. Many of these headings were highly technical, but the fundamental points of conflict between Bernard and Abelard seem to have been threefold: on the

question of the Trinity, Bernard accused Abelard of assigning different powers to the three persons, and was worried about the comparison between the Holy Spirit and Plato's '*anima mundi*' or soul
world; on the Atonement, Bernard's objection was that Abelard
argued that it was not to deliver people from the power of the devil
that Christ was made flesh, but as an example to instruct human
beings in the way of righteousness (to Bernard, the work of Christ
was a 'transaction' or 'ransom'); and, above all, there was Abelard's
insistence on searching for truth using the methods and language of
a *philosopher*. Bernard judged his expressions and analogies to be
very shocking and was deeply disturbed at the thought that faith
could be approached through reason or logic.

Confronted by this barrage of 'errors' – by an Inquisition, in
effect – and realizing that the cards had been stacked against him,
instead of bothering to argue, Peter Abelard stopped the proceedings dead by vowing to appeal (over Bernard's head) to the Pope
himself. He then walked out. Which left the council with little
choice but to condemn his writings *in absentia*. Bernard, for once,
had been seriously wrong-footed. He had been forced into the
position of explaining himself to Pope Innocent II:

To his most loving father and Lord, Innocent, by the grace of God Supreme
Pontiff, the entire devotion, for what it is worth, of Brother Bernard, styled
Abbot of Clairvaux . . .

The dragon is no longer lurking in his lair: would that his poisonous
writings were still lurking on their shelves, and not being discussed at the
crossroads! His books have wings: and they who hate the light because their
lives are evil, have dashed into the light thinking it was darkness. Darkness is
being brought into towns and castles in the place of light . . . Virtues and
vices are being discussed immorally, the sacraments of the Church falsely,
the mystery of the Holy Trinity neither simply nor soberly. Everything is
put perversely, everything quite differently, and beyond what we have been
accustomed to hear . . . He insults the Doctors of the Church by holding
up the philosophers for exaggerated praises. He prefers their ideas and his
own novelties to the doctrines and faith of the Catholic Fathers . . . And so,

in the presence of all, face to face with my adversary, I took certain headings from his books. And when I began to read these, he refused to listen
and walked out, and appealed from the judges he had chosen, which I do
not think was permissible . . . But you, successor to St Peter, will judge
whether this man who has attacked the faith of St Peter should find refuge
in the see of Peter.

To Cardinal Guy, Bernard wrote that 'Master Peter has used in
his books phrases that are both novel and profane in their writing
and in their sense.' To Cardinal Ivo, he added that Abelard was 'a
man at variance with himself' who dared to apply 'the cleverness of
his words to the virtue of the Cross'. And to yet another cardinal, he
described 'one Peter Abelard' as 'a monk without a Rule, an abbot
without discipline, who argues with boys and consorts with women
. . . he has put on record leprous novelties in pen and ink'.

During the frantic lobbying which followed the Council of Sens,
the roles of Bernard and Abelard were – for a brief time – reversed.
Bernard became the angry, disputatious one, while Abelard became
the contemplative one, living at Cluny, convalescing (he probably
had cancer) and trying to shut out the noise. He may have put
together his personal 'Confession of Faith', addressed to Heloise, at
this time. Eventually, after Bernard's concentrated campaign, Abelard was condemned by the Pope as a heretic and sentenced to
confinement in a religious place in perpetual silence. His followers
were excommunicated and some of his books were ordered to be
burned. Abelard and his 'school' had been expelled from the community of Christ, and cut off from the happiness which would
normally come when believers saw God. And yet, as he wrote in his
'Confession' (which was preserved by one of his pupils):

Heloise my sister, once dear to me in the world, now dearest to me in
Christ, logic has made me hated by the world. For the perverted, who seek
to pervert and whose wisdom is only for destruction, say that I am supreme
as a logician, but am found wanting in my understanding of Paul. They
proclaim the brilliance of my intellect but detract from the purity of my
Christian faith. As I see it, they have reached this judgement by conjecture

rather than weight of evidence. I do not wish to be a philosopher if it means conflicting with Paul, nor to be an Aristotle if it cuts me off from Christ. For there is no other name under heaven whereby I must be saved. I adore Christ who sits at the right hand of the Father.

The Abbot of Cluny, Peter the Venerable, took up Abelard's cause and somehow arranged for him to 'make his peace with the abbot of Clairvaux and settle their previous differences'. He also wrote to Innocent II, asking that 'the shield of your apostolic protection cover him'. It seems that the condemnation, and the sentence, were rescinded, for Peter the Venerable – in a subsequent letter – said of Abelard that 'his mind, his speech, his work were devoted to meditation, to teaching and to profession of what was always holy, philosophic and scholarly'. Abelard was moved to the priory of St Marcel, near Châlons, 'since he was more troubled than usual from skin irritation and other physical ailments'. He died in April 1142 at the age of sixty-three and his body was sent for burial to his chapel at Nogent at the request of the abbess there – Heloise.

The showdown between Bernard and Abelard seems somewhat abstract or academic today, but at the time it was very important from many points of view: ecclesiastical party politics – Italy versus France; definitions of heresy; approaches to faith itself; establishing in public the boundaries of what was permissible. The showdown was also inevitable, not because the two contestants were so different, but because in many ways they were so alike. Both of them had dedicated their lives and their intellects to a search for an experience of God which could be communicated; both of them had refined their positions by challenging the received wisdom of the previous generation – Bernard by upsetting the old order of Cluny, Abelard by upsetting the old teachers of Paris. The point of the exercise was to become better men of God. So perhaps the showdown was as inevitable as the better-known one, some thirty years later, between King Henry II of England and Thomas à Becket, who also had a lot in common. It was a matter of a clash of personalities, temperaments and approaches.

Bernard the quiet, reclusive monk had always had the capacity for disputation and lobbying, just as the argumentative Abelard had always coloured his work with humanism and tolerance. In his *Dialogue between a Philosopher, a Jew and a Christian*, he recalled that 'in my father's house there are many mansions'. It was almost as inevitable as their clash that they would eventually be reconciled.

During the last years of his life Bernard in effect governed western Christendom – sending instructions to popes, giving his blessing to crusaders and dreaming of creating a western cavalry, an army for Christ. He died on 20 August 1153, also at the age of sixty-three. He had been abbot for thirty-eight years and no less than sixty-eight monasteries had been founded directly from Clairvaux. He was made a saint in 1174. By then Abelard's teaching was beginning to have far-reaching effects. In the half-century after his death, three of his Italian followers became popes; in the century and a half after his death his principles were so thoroughly absorbed that they became the foundation of Church law – and Thomas Aquinas, in his *Summa Theologica*, succeeded in synthesizing logic and revelation, reason and faith, Aristotle and the Bible, Abelard and Bernard.

Posterity has done some strange things to the reputations of Bernard, Abelard and Heloise. Bernard is remembered as the organization man, always seated in visual representations as he orders everyone about. He has been called, unfairly, the first inquisitor. Abelard is remembered as the hot-headed undergraduate type, always on the move, not so much the man who invented theology in its modern sense, or the pioneer of the 'scholastic' method of bringing religious questions out into the open and debating them, as the great lover who transgressed and paid for it. He would have hated that. Heloise is remembered simply as the object of his affections, when to judge by her letters she was one of the most courageous and humane thinkers of her age.

When Peter Abelard died, the Abbot of Cluny wrote to Heloise saying that one day the lovers would be reunited, for 'beyond these voices there is peace'. We do not know of Heloise's reaction.

We do know that she lived for another twenty years. She had written:

Men call me chaste; they do not know the hypocrite I am. They consider purity of the flesh a virtue, though virtue belongs not to the body but to the soul. I can win praise in the eyes of men but deserve none before God, who searches our hearts and loins and sees in our darkness. I am judged religious at a time when there is little in religion which is not hypocrisy, when whoever does not offend the opinions of men receives the highest praise.

4

CIRCLES OF LIGHT

At the beginning of Canto III of Dante's *Inferno* the poet reads the inscription on a ledge above the gate of hell and hears the shrieks of the damned as they echo across the starless air:

> I AM THE WAY INTO THE DOLEFUL CITY,
> . I AM THE WAY INTO ETERNAL GRIEF,
> I AM THE WAY TO A FORSAKEN RACE . . .
>
> BEFORE ME NOTHING BUT ETERNAL THINGS
> WERE MADE, AND I SHALL LAST ETERNALLY,
> ABANDON EVERY HOPE, ALL YOU WHO ENTER.

'Abandon hope all ye who enter here' (as it has gone into the language) is the best-known line from Dante's *Divine Comedy*. I remember that someone had chalked it above the entrance to the university library when I was at college. And it creates the impression that the *Comedy* is about Dante going to hell, the inferno. But the *Divine Comedy* is about much more than that. It has been in print ever since printing was invented, as the great work of medieval literature – a thrilling adventure about an action-packed pilgrimage from darkness to light; a poem which altered for ever the Italian language; a summary of the religious and scientific beliefs of all the Christian centuries which had gone before; a celebration of the creative process itself, with the artist – for the first time – central to the story; a political tract about unpleasant goings-on in the city of Florence and indeed the rest of Europe. If the *Divine Comedy* had been written a hundred years later, rather than in the early fourteenth century, the author would have been called a 'Renaissance man'. But the whole point is that Dante embedded his odyssey in the sights and sounds and thoughts of the late Middle Ages. So it is not just about Dante going to hell; that is Part One. It is about a journey across the entire universe, from the depths of hell to the mountain of purgatory and to paradise, where the poet travels nearer and nearer to the mind of God.

Dante Alighieri's journey really began on May Day 1274, when he fell head over heels in love with a girl on the streets of Florence. He was nine years old at the time. Dante, who was a fairly well-to-do child, had been taken to a children's party by his father, Alighiero. His mother, Bella, had died when he was very young and Alighiero had remarried in the early 1270s a woman called Lapa di Chiarissimo Cialuffi. Dante was later to go out of his way to avoid mentioning either of them in his work. The one thing that is known of his mother is Boccaccio's later story of a dream she had, just before giving birth to Dante. In the dream, which resembles the dreams of *legendary* heroes' mothers in similar circumstances, she gives birth to a boy who feeds on the berries of a bay tree and drinks from a nearby spring; the boy becomes a shepherd and tries to reach up to the leaves of the tree, but falls; when he gets up again, he has turned into a peacock. Boccaccio's reading of the dream was that the berries meant earlier writers who had influenced Dante; the choice of career meant that the poet was committed to caring for other people; the fall from the tree (of life) meant his death; and the peacock meant that the *Divine Comedy* would only be fully appreciated – and achieve immortality – posthumously, during the Renaissance. Because of enlightened people like Boccaccio. The fact that Donna Bella had this dream at the time she did, wrote Boccaccio, may well have encouraged her to call her son Dante – in other words, the Giver.

Anyway, on May Day 1274 the juvenile Dante found himself at a party given by the Florentine banker Folco Portinari for his daughter Bice (the shortened form of Beatrice), a quiet and well-mannered little girl. She was eight years and five months old and was wearing a bright scarlet dress. After the food had been cleared away, the children started playing party games and . . . it happened. Dante was later to write, in his *La Vita Nuova* (or *New Life – Poems of Youth*):

At that moment I say truly that the vital spirit which lives in the most secret room of the heart began to tremble so strongly that it affected dreadfully the least of my pulses; and in trembling it spoke these words: 'Behold the God who is stronger than I and who in his coming will rule over me' . . . From that moment, I say, love so mastered my soul which was married so young to him, and began to exert over me such care and authority through the power my imagination gave him, that I was forced to carry out all his wishes absolutely. He often ordered me to go and search for this youngest of the angels . . .

From the moment Dante caught sight of Beatrice Portinari, she became the centre of his being – his *raison d'être*. He called this profound emotional experience 'love', although whether someone can fall in love at the age of nine must be questionable. Was it a fantasy relationship? Partly, it seems. But the journey on which 'love' launched him was eventually to take him all the way from the dark night of the soul into the light of paradise: a life's work. One version of male sexuality says that desire usually leads to insensitivity and cruelty; another version – Dante's version, in his maturity – says that sexual desire can be transformed into sensitive and kindly forms of behaviour. What Dante came to mean by 'love' worked on many different levels. At one level it was courtly love, based on the songs and love lyrics of the troubadours of southern France where true masculinity expressed itself by respecting the (usually unattainable) female rather than trying to 'conquer' her. At another, it was full-blooded sexual love – even though Dante never had any physical contact with Beatrice and was eventually to have a settled family life with someone else. At another, it was a mirror image of the love of the Queen of Heaven, the Virgin Mary – whose cult was becoming more youthful and domestic at the time. And at yet another level it was a kind of community spirit, where the private and the public united in support of justice and communal affection. Above all,

Dante's love for Beatrice – or 'she who makes beautiful and blessed' – based on a few fleeting moments of memory, became the focus or distillation of his vision of existence, a perfect example of divine love in an ordinary Florentine girl. As he wrote in the *Divine Comedy* (*Purgatory*):

> . . . I am one who, when Love
> inspires me, takes careful note and then,
> gives form to what he dictates in my heart.

Mere romantic lovers – such as Cleopatra ('who loved men's lusting'), Helen of Troy ('the root of evil woe'), Dido, queen of Carthage, Achilles ('who lost his life to love'), Paris, Tristan and Isolt – were to be consigned by Dante to the second circle of hell, in Canto V of the *Inferno*. There, these 'knights and ladies of ancient times' – these thousand shades 'whom love cut off from life on earth' – are perpetually to be whirled around in a strong wind, the image of their lust, beyond the light of reason. Francesca da Rimini, whose adulterous affair with Paolo Malatesta had, famously, ended in both their deaths – when Dante was about twelve – tries to explain to the poet that her intentions had been strictly honourable. It was a reading of *Lancelot and Guinevere* that had led her and her boyfriend astray ('when we read about those longed-for lips now being kissed by such a famous lover, this one . . . then kissed my mouth'). Dante is at first taken in by this, but it later becomes clear to him that all the lovers are in hell because they confuse love with lust, love with desire, love with self-deceit; their love pretends to be spiritual but in fact it has not developed beyond the physical stage. Francesca's punishment is to be partnered with her lover, exactly as they were discovered *in flagrante* by her husband, for all eternity. Dante's 'Love' that 'so mastered my soul' is a whole universe away from this tacky little affair.

Florence was a rapidly expanding city in Dante's time, full of new building and new confidence; a population of about fifty thousand in 1200 had probably doubled by a century later. While he was growing up, the city was – unusually – enjoying a period of relative peace and quiet. Its textile industry, its eighty banks – based on the gold *florin* – its two hundred shops belonging to the wool guild and its commercial know-how were already creating the kind of prosperity that would eventually make it the powerhouse of the next phase of European history, which liked to style itself as the 'Renaissance'. But Dante's Florence was a medieval city, and so wealth, new building, the tourist trade *and faith* were all linked together.

The Baptistery of San Giovanni was an old building – free-standing in the middle of a graveyard, before the bulky cathedral had been built next to it – but it had remained the heart of the city. In 1266, on Easter Saturday, the great annual baptismal day in Florence, the infant Dante was brought there by his parents. Florentines thought of the Baptistery as the symbol of their city and when they were away from home they dreamed about it. As the wealth and prestige of Florence increased, it was decided to have its interior redesigned by imported Venetian artists and when Dante was eleven the new mosaic ceiling and dome of the Baptistery were unveiled for the first time.

The little boy who loved Beatrice Portinari gazed up at a supremely medieval work of art – a single picture of the story of life, the universe and everything from the Garden of Eden, via the Incarnation, to Armageddon. The origin of the universe; the creation of the first human beings, Adam and Eve; the discovery of good and evil; Adam trying to put the blame on Eve for tempting him; the first human beings expelled from paradise – Dante could see the whole story of the world in candle-lit, glittering mosaic. The souls of the damned being eaten by Satan and his monsters were already in the gruesome setting which Dante would later populate with the nastiest of his contemporaries; the orders of angels circling around. The episodes that the boy saw there could be recognized, and shared, by all who belonged (as the service of the Baptism put it) to 'the faith that makes souls known to God' – that is, by most of the population of western Europe. This picture was quintessentially medieval – all experience unified in one work of art – and Dante was to take it and turn it into a single grand narrative.

By the time he went to Bologna, where he studied politics and taught himself to write poetry, the love of his life had become mixed with day and night dreams and visions until it was already his main preoccupation. A marriage was arranged for him, in his late teens, and his wife, Gemma Donati, was to bear him two sons and a daughter. But he never once mentioned his wife in his poetry. Poetry was for Beatrice, 'the glorious lady of my mind'. They only met, in reality, five times. They may never even have been alone together. When he was eighteen, he happened to brush past her in the street. She was wearing pure white this time and her friendly greeting almost sent him into orbit. He went home, fell asleep in an ecstatic daze and had a dream which formed the basis of a sonnet which he addressed to 'the faithful followers of Love'. It was this sonnet which drew him into the fashionable Florentine circle of poets which he later called *dolce stil nuovo*. The most painful thing that ever happened to him, he was to write, was two years later when he was about twenty and Beatrice refused to 'bestow her smile' on him as he met her again on the streets of Florence. He went into a deep depression. The idea of divine love and his love for Beatrice were beginning to become inseparable.

In 1290, when Dante was twenty-five, Beatrice Portinari died; she was only twenty-four. 'After she departed this life, the city was left as though widowed, despoiled of all life.' But he was not the kind of romantic poet to dwell on her death, or become morbid about it. The miracle that was Beatrice, he wrote, and the 'sign of truth' that she had become, had moved on to their proper place in the universe.

> Beatrice has gone to heaven on high
> Among the angels in the realm of peace.

Dante resolved not to write about her, or the significance of their meeting, any more – after the words he poured out on the occasion of her death. Instead, he would study and search for a new voice, so that one day he would be able to praise and celebrate her as he should. The end of that search – which lasted half a lifetime – was the *Divine Comedy*.

But Dante was also caught up in the day-to-day life of a city which, after he became an adult, was very far from at peace. The year before Beatrice's death he served with the Florentine cavalry in the battle of Campaldino against nearby Arezzo, and he helped to besiege the fortress of Caprona in Pisa that same summer. As was usual for someone of his class, he also took part in city politics, serving on the Council of Priors or magistrates. Florence was not just at war with its neighbours, though: the city itself was divided by fierce and complex sectarian conflicts.

The feuding had started some fifty years before Dante was born, with the brutal murder of a young nobleman called Buondelmonte dei Buondelmonti. There were two rival clans in Florence at the time, the Uberti and the Donati, and Buondelmonte had offended the Uberti by jilting one of their daughters in favour of a Donati girl. On Easter Sunday 1215, as he rode across the Ponte Vecchio dressed all in white, on a white horse – so he was a conspicuous target – the victim was pulled out of his saddle by five assassins and clubbed, kicked and stabbed to death. The assassins had been egged on by Mosca Lamberti, an ally of the Uberti, whom Dante was to depict among the 'sowers of scandal and schism' in the lower hell of the *Inferno*, where he has 'both arms but no hands, raising the gory stumps in the filthy air'. The Uberti clan watched the murder from their tower overlooking the bridge and then saw the Donati parade the corpse through the streets of Florence.

Each side would only be satisfied if the other was put out of action and each side naturally turned to outside help, either from the Pope or the Holy Roman Emperor. The murder was a bloody microcosm of a feud which had paralysed Italy for longer than anyone could remember and, according to Dante, it 'sowed the seed of discord' for many years to come. Both factions proceeded to adopt Italianized versions of German names: the Uberti became leaders of the Ghibelline party (supporters of the Holy Roman

Emperors); the Donati became the Leaders of the Guelphs (supporters of the papacy) – 'Ghibelline' after the German 'Waiblingen', 'Guelph' after the German 'Welf'. The basic division between these parties, made up largely of nobles and powerful merchants, apparently concerned the extent of their allegiance to Germany and secular power. But party warfare was also an excuse for settling old scores, promoting commercial interests and generally regarding 'party labels as flags of convenience' (as Dante scholar William Anderson nicely puts it). In time, the Guelphs were to split up into sub-factions, known as the 'Blacks' under Corso Donati and the 'Whites' under the banker Vieri dei Cerchi. One cause of the split was, of all things, a poisoned black pudding, which killed some of the young Cerchis and with which Corso was suspected to have been involved.

For most of the Middle Ages the whole peninsula of Italy had been claimed by the (mainly German) Holy Roman Empire. But the popes feared being encircled and rallied an opposition among the rising Italian cities. Most of these, especially Florence, had their own reasons for not wanting German domination and were glad to help.

In 1266 the anti-German alliance had inflicted a crushing defeat at the battle of Benevento on the forces of the empire. But then the main allies – Florence and the papacy – fell out. Their quarrel coincided exactly with Dante's lifetime and coloured much of what he wrote. The two still needed each other. The Florentine bankers looked after most of the papacy's business arrangements since the popes had little money – only a lot of land and infinite credit. But how much papal control did that necessarily mean? Florence itself was split on the issue and when in 1300 a papal governor of the city was appointed – a Franciscan friar – one party (and it was Dante's) exploded into revolt.

Dante had, or thought he had, very clear ideas on how Pope and Emperor should relate to one another. Basically, the Emperor should have complete political authority, the Pope should confine himself strictly to spiritual matters – the rulers of the 'Earthly' and the 'Heavenly' being guided as to where these lines should properly be drawn by the 'Divine Will'. Whether this trust in political authority of a kind Dante had never experienced was at all realistic has been a matter for debate ever since. The essay in which he expressed these ideas, 'On Monarchy' (De Monarchia), was put on the Papal Index until 1921, after which time it was officially described as 'a correct analysis' – just in time for Mussolini. But in his own time, with Florence set for commercial expansion, the debate with the city's problematic neighbour flared into crisis. This began in 1294. Many people had been saying the Church should be ruled by a saint and in 1294 the Church had tried just that by electing as pope a bearded hermit, eighty years old, with a reputation for sanctity. He was called Celestine V, the heavenly one. But the Heavenly One had never wanted the job, proved a disaster and after five months was persuaded to resign.

Some later claimed that his successor had spoken to him down a speaking tube, pretending to be the voice of God and suggesting in no uncertain terms that it was time for Celestine to get back into his cave and resign the throne of St Peter. Celestine believed the voice and promptly complied.

To replace Celestine, the cardinals went to the other extreme and chose one of their number who had no pretence to sanctity but was a very experienced, frighteningly skilful and tough-minded ecclesiastical politician. Boniface VIII was stepping into a political hornets' nest and because he himself was something of a hornet he left a mark never erased from contemporary minds, Dante's among them. In Dante's writing, Boniface, and all popes like him – popes who were too political – were to play the role of villains, so the poet's version of events was that Boniface was not concerned in the least about fine distinctions between earthly and spiritual power. Just plain power was good enough for him, and gaining control of the city of Florence was as good a way as any of getting it.

For Dante himself the crisis came in 1300 when Boniface proclaimed a jubilee in Rome, a vast celebration of western Christendom, and – this was the point – of papal leadership. The jubilee was intended to say a collective thankyou for civilization's survival of yet another whole century since the birth of Christ, and through this elaborate piece of public relations the Pope was preparing for some heavy negotiation with the surrounding cities. Dante visited Rome early in jubilee year (he later wrote an eyewitness account of the security arrangements and crowd control on the Ponte Sant'Angelo). His political career had just begun to take off: in 1295 he had a seat on the 'People's Council', the finance and general purposes committee; in 1296 he had made a notable speech in the Florentine 'Council of the Hundred'; a year after he was inscribed as a '*poeta fiorentino*', in the guild of apothecaries (there weren't any specialized guilds for artists); and later in 1300 he was to be appointed one of the six priors on the usual two-month basis.

He was presumably glad of the opportunity to visit Rome: like many of his contemporaries, he took his model of political order from the Roman Empire, the ruins of which – surrounded by very little else – could be seen all around. But there were signs at the jubilee that Boniface was about to make a move. Dante's dream of a balance between Church and Empire was fated never to come true and, where his public life was concerned, 1300 marked the beginning of the end.

By Easter week he was back in Florence, where he had another of his visions – a particularly intense vision which he tried hard to put into words at the very end of *Paradise*:

> Within Its depthless clarity of substance
>   I saw the Great Light shine into three circles
>   in three clear colours bound in one same space;
>
> the first seemed to reflect the next like rainbow
>   on rainbow, and the third was like a flame
>   equally breathed forth by the other two.
>
> How my weak words fall short of my conception,
>   which is itself so far from what I saw
>   that 'weak' is much too weak a word to use!

> O Light Eternal fixed in Self alone,
>> known only to Yourself, and knowing Self,
>> You love and glow, knowing and being known!

The disjunction between this vision of beauty – based, like so much of Dante's poetry, on variations around the number three (trinities, triumvirates, three-line verses) and on the symbolism of light – and the political realities of jubilee year in Rome and Florence led Dante into the dark night of the soul out of which came the symbolic journey of the *Divine Comedy* – a journey which begins on the night before Good Friday in the year 1300, when the poet was thirty-five years old, and finishes a week later.

There had, of course, been comparable symbolic journeys before. There were the depictions of the end of the world, the resurrection of the dead and of the Last Judgement on the portals and tympana of countless churches, usually based on the Book of Revelation, but which also involved a fair amount of artistic licence. There were scenes of cemeteries come-to-life, for example, where everyone was resurrected as a thirty-year-old, because that was the age at which Christ rose again from the dead; or scenes of hellish torment – as much derived from folklore as from theology – where huge reptiles and sharp-toothed creatures tore at the condemned, while demons waited for a diabolical cauldron to come to the boil. In these symbolic, sculptural journeys, hell – on the whole – was fantastical, heaven was more safely biblical, while purgatory did not seem to exist at all yet: life beyond the grave was a stark choice of hell or heaven.

Apart from church art, there was also the well-known literary genre of 'other-worldly visits' or 'visions', which often formed the basis of sermons or devotional tracts in Latin; it was a genre which filled the more than a thousand-year gap between Revelation and the *Divine Comedy*. The story usually involved a person visiting the Other World, having a glimpse of what life was like there and coming back to earth to tell the tale – which had a suitably moral punch line. Then, shortly afterwards, the storyteller died for real.

Medievalist Aron Gurevich has studied the genre in detail and isolated various recurring features: famous historical characters suffering for their vices in hell; diabolical torments specially tailored to the worldly transgression (perjurers having their tongues tortured, gluttons being starved, drunkards being dried out, misers having gold poured down their throats, and so on) – unlike, incidentally, the sculptural versions where the torments were nasty in a more generalized way; a trial over the deceased's soul, with two books containing all his or her good and bad deeds – regrettably often one small book, one very large one; gold and silver chambers, reflecting the brightest of lights, surrounded by the fabulously jewelled wall of the heavenly Jerusalem – for the experience of heaven; the delicate singing of choirs of angels, and the elect, dressed in robes which shone so brightly that they could not be looked at for more than a few seconds.

Where the question of location was concerned, hell tended to be just under the earth or inside the crater of a volcano (Etna and Vesuvius being favourite entrances); heaven was usually described as 'the islands of the blessed', or an enchanted garden, or a place where the deceased could somehow look down not only on to the earth but on to the canopy of stars as well. Again, purgatory did not yet exist in literary odysseys of this kind, although several other-worldly visitors reported that they had to cross a narrow bridge over a dark stream, linking the shores of the blessed and the shores of the condemned, with nasty creatures grabbing and nipping at their ankles – a kind of proto-purgatory. In fact, according to Gurevich, purgatory as such only appeared on maps of the Other World from the late twelfth century onwards, and only achieved widespread recognition in the thirteenth, finally acquiring recognition by the powers-that-be soon after. So a vague idea of a temporary residence between heaven and hell, the length of stay depending on 'good deeds' or remorse, originated in popular medieval consciousness before the academics, and the papacy, got in on the act.

The basic characteristic of these 'other-worldly visits' was that they were intended to be literal: they described an actual, autobiographical experience and as such were of great interest to theologians and Churchmen. Bede's *Ecclesiastical History* describes a particularly detailed one, where an Irishman called Fursey not only visited hell but had scars to prove it – he had burn-marks on his shoulder and chin. Some early readers of the *Divine Comedy* said that Dante, too, must have had scars from the fires of hell on his face. But, although the *Divine Comedy* did grow out of the formulae of such 'other-worldly visions', this was to misunderstand both the work and its author. Dante was never intending to be literal. His Other World is full of detail which encourages the reader to suspend disbelief, but it is explicitly a work of art – a poetic metaphor based on experience and unique to its creator. He isn't saying 'I was there.'

The poet in the *Divine Comedy* is not a detached observer of another place, he takes part in the action and the characters he meets interact with him – in dramatic little interludes which create a brief pause or even break in their timeless destiny. The condemned in hell are not plagued by the reptiles and fanged beasts of sculpture, or even by tailor-made torments; they are plagued for ever by their worldly sins – theirs are mental as much as physical torments, where the sin *is* the punishment lived over and over again. And their torments are individual or personalized to the victims – something to do with their just deserts – rather than a common-or-garden part of the satanic landscape. The stark choice of hell and heaven, with that rickety bridge in between, has turned into the elegant, tripartite division of the Other World into *Inferno*, *Purgatory* and *Paradise*. Apart from the basic idea of the journey – which Dante transformed from the world of folklore to the world of art – and certain details, the main point of connection between 'other-worldly visits' of the fifth to the thirteenth centuries and the *Divine Comedy* was that, whether they admitted it to themselves or not, the travellers found their iconography (and their legitimation) from contemporary art. Gurevich concludes:

[There were] instances where medieval authors 'verified' their visions or the visions of others. The Virgin appeared to the mother of Guibert of Nogent, and she looked like the Virgin of Chartres Cathedral. A blind peasant whose sight was restored by Sainte Foy recognized her in a vision because she corresponded exactly to the statue of the saint in the church. When a young monk from Monte Cassino beheld the archangel Michael carrying off the soul of his dead brother, he saw him 'exactly as he is usually depicted by artists'. Hence it is obviously the wrong question to ask whether descriptions of the Other World are literary creations or a fixation with the visions and dreams of concrete living people. Early medieval man visited the Other World in his dreams and nightmares, attempted to describe these pictures and impressions, and for expressing them had recourse to the only possible and accessible language of traditional forms, which also made these pictures for him simultaneously full of higher meaning, artistically convincing and trustworthy.

The subject of Dante's vision of Easter 1300, he later wrote, 'taken in its literal sense, is the state of souls after death; but if it is taken *allegorically*, its subject is how man by exercise of his free will justly merits reward or punishment'. The allegory begins with the poet regaining consciousness in a dark wood. We are not told where. He is lost, confused and terrified.

> Midway along the journey of our life
> I woke to find myself in a dark wood,
> for I had wandered off from the straight path.
>
> How hard it is to tell what it was like,
> this wood of wilderness, savage and stubborn
> (the thought of it brings back all my old fears),
>
> a bitter place! Death could scarce be bitterer.
> But if I would show the good that came of it
> I must talk about things other than the good.

The poet can see a hill 'in morning rays of light', beyond the wood, which he tries to climb. But three hungry beasts – a leopard, a lion and a she-wolf – keep blocking his path and forcing him in the direction of where 'the sun is mute'. In his confusion, he finds a ghostly guide waiting for him:

'No longer living man, though once I was,'
   he said, 'and my parents were from Lombardy,
   both of them were Mantuans by birth.

I was born, though somewhat late, *sub Julio*,
   and lived in Rome when good Augustus reigned,
   when still the false and lying gods were worshipped.'

It is Virgil, the great poet of Augustus's Rome – born in the reign of Julius Caesar – and the man who was famous for his description of Aeneas's journey to the underworld (as well as, it was alleged at the time, for prophesying the birth of Christ). He is to be the poet's guide for the first part of his journey, which, he explains, will take them to the place of 'tormented shades' and then to the place where 'they have hope of joining the blessed' and finally to the 'city of the blessed' itself – at which point Virgil will have to hand over to another worthier guide, for 'I in life rebelled against His law'.

'But', asks the poet, 'why am I to go? Who allows me to? *I* am not Aeneas . . .' It appears that the soul of Beatrice in heaven has taken pity on the poet and asked 'a gracious lady' if she will allow him to be taken on a journey of spiritual discovery – for 'I fear he may have gone astray'. Beatrice, having got the necessary permission, then descended to visit Virgil among the dead who are suspended in limbo, and asked him if he would guide the poet out of the dark wood. The poet Dante will eventually enter the gates of paradise, but first his soul must be cleansed; the three beasts of his sins are preventing him from going up, so Virgil leads him down to hell.

The details of the geography of hell, and heaven – and the physical nature of the universe – had been studied and refined in the science and literature of the Middle Ages. Dante is at pains throughout the journey to demonstrate his scientific knowledge as well as his spiritual awareness. Hell, for example, is located beneath the visible world, in a conical pit which descends right down to the centre of the earth; the lower the level of hell, the more evil it is, and the poet's quest will take him through successively more miserable circles of hell. The pit was formed when the angel Lucifer fell from grace and was thrown down from heaven and hit the earth: the pit of hell is the impact crater. The dark wood is on the edge of the pit, so the two companions just have to slip beneath the surface of the earth and descend into the inferno.

They go across the first river of hell, the Acheron, to limbo, the first circle – where they meet the virtuous people who through no fault of their own were never baptized as Christians. By the light of natural reason, Virgil introduces Dante to his four friends, Homer, Horace, Ovid and Lucan, and they all enter a seven-walled castle together. Inside, there is a green plain where stand the most distinguished figures of ancient times – Aeneas himself, Hector, Lucrece and Penthesilea, and 'off by himself, I noticed Saladin', the great Islamic opponent of the crusaders. Then, from the light of limbo they travel to the dark of the second circle, the circle of Lust, where the two companions meet the souls of famous romantic lovers, and on to the circles of gluttony, avarice and anger.

At this point, having encountered the sins of incontinence, they have to cross the second river of hell, the Styx, and pass through the infernal iron walls of the city of Dis. The poet, who up to now has felt sorry for some of the damned (such as the adulteress Francesca da Rimini), begins to join Virgil in criticizing and judging them. It is as well that he is feeling more self-assured and confident in his judgements, for the fiendish angels guarding the gates of Dis start howling abuse at the two travellers and staring at them like gargoyles. Virgil is powerless, but a silent messenger from heaven scatters the furies 'as frogs before their enemy the snake, all scatter through the pond and then dive down'. So Virgil and the poet reach the tombs of the heretics within the city of Dis, on the sixth circle, where there is a long conversation about Florentine politics with the late leader of the Ghibellines, Farinata degli Uberti. The seventh circle, the circle of violence, is reached by climbing down the rockfall which happened during the great storm at the moment of Christ's death. There, the travellers cross Phlegethon, the river of blood; walk through the wood of the suicides; and see the plain of burning sand, reserved for crimes against nature and God.

This brings them to the edge of a steep cliff, where Virgil throws down the belt which has been around the poet's waist, to attract the attention of Geryon, a winged, scorpion-like monster. The companions are flown slowly down, in spiralling circles, on the back of the monster to the eighth circle, the circle of Malebolge ('evil pockets') reserved for sins of fraud. Malebolge consists of ten ravines, or moats, radiating outwards, each linked by an arching bridge. They see pimps, seducers and flatterers (who live 'in a ditch plunged into excrement that might well have come from our latrines', where 'I saw someone's head so smirched in shit you could not tell if he were priest or layman'). They reach a ravine which for some mysterious reason is filled with holes which have legs and feet sticking out of them. They resemble baptismal fonts, only it is the soles of the feet which are being baptized – with fire. The holes, it transpires, are reserved for popes who in life were corrupt. They are thrust head-first down into the font and when the next bad pope dies, he is crammed into the same font, forcing his predecessor further down. Flames, meanwhile, burn their oiled soles.

Of the five popes who lived during Dante's lifetime, only one manages to avoid being sent to the poet's version of hell – the mild-mannered Benedict XI, who was a friend of the 'White' faction of the Guelphs and thus of Dante, but who died having achieved next to nothing nine months after being elected to the throne of St Peter. It was said that Benedict died of indigestion after swallowing some poisoned figs served to him by a youth dressed as a nun. So his political correctness on earth did not get him very far.

In the lower depths of the inferno, the poet approaches a pair of legs which seem particularly active:

> 'Whatever you are, holding your upside down,
> O wretched soul, stuck like a stake in ground,
> make a sound or something,' I said, 'if you can.'
>
> I stood there like a priest who is confessing
> some vile assassin who, fixed in his ditch,
> has called him back again to put off dying.

> He cried: 'Is that *you*, here, already, upright?
>   Is that you here already upright, Boniface?
>   By many years the book has lied to me!'

The tortured soul of the late Pope Nicholas III has mistaken the poet for Boniface VIII, newly arrived at the eighth circle of the inferno ahead of his time. But he is mistaken and 'the book' (the book of Fate) is right after all. In 1300 Boniface still had three years of earthly misdeeds ahead of him.

Meanwhile, the Pope's relations with the new establishment in the city of Florence, back on earth, were deteriorating fast. One of Boniface's Florentine bankers had been arrested for embezzlement in April 1300. It was unfortunate for Dante that he happened to be one of the priors who refused to acquit him a couple of months later; he was becoming too well known for making powerful enemies. In April 1301, although he was no longer a prior, he was put in charge of road works in and around Florence – to help protect the city from attack. In June 1301, he spoke at two debates of the Council of the Hundred, trying to persuade them not to give any support to Boniface in his military adventures. Then again in September. The result: even more enemies.

The Pope was by now desperate to maintain control of Florence and to see the city governed by the 'Blacks', the party most sympathetic to his cause. So he decided on a tried and tested remedy for the problems of medieval popes: he turned to the French royal family for help. Boniface had a summit meeting with Charles of Valois, the buccaneering young son of the French monarch, in Siena; a sum of seventy thousand florins changed hands and the fate of Florence was sealed. Dante had been chosen, probably for his oratorical skills, to join a special embassy to the Pope of the 'Whites' from Florence and Bologna. He is said to have remarked, 'If I go, who stays? if I stay, who goes?' A no-win situation. The others in the deputation were sent back home, but Dante was detained at the papal court. It seems that Boniface wanted to keep him occupied in Rome, just in case this trouble-maker spoiled things.

So Dante was not there on All Saints' Day 1301 when the city of Florence was being surrounded by the troops of Charles of Valois. And he was kicking his heels in Rome when the Florentine Corso Donati, known as '*il barone*', champion of the papal faction and friend of Boniface's bankers, actually sacked the city. In several days of violence which were the prelude to a series of purges and show trials, Corso and his thugs turned on their own fellow citizens. They sacked houses, including Dante's, and butchered like hogs any 'Whites' who dared to oppose them.

It is hardly surprising that in Dante's picture of the universal scheme of things, the worst sin of all is not lust or gluttony or anger or heresy – it is betrayal. Those who have turned on their friends are condemned for ever to the lower depths, to the pit of Cocytus, which Virgil and the poet reach by persuading the giant Antaeus to pick them up and place them there. The bottom of the pit, the foulest place imaginable, consists of a vast plain of frozen mud which surrounds the body of the devil, who with his three mouths is busy chewing on the sinews of Brutus who betrayed Julius Caesar, Cassius who helped him and Judas who betrayed Christ. The poet approaches two souls frozen together into a single hole and sees that one of them is sinking his teeth with great relish into the back of the other's head:

> 'O you who show with every bestial bite
>> your hatred for the head you are devouring,'
>> I said, 'tell me your reason, and I promise,
>
> if you are justified in your revenge,
>> once I know who you are and this one's sin,
>> I'll repay your confidence in the world above
>
> unless my tongue dry up before I die.'

It transpires that the living brain of Archbishop Ruggieri is being eaten by Count Ugolino. They had conspired together to betray the town of Pisa in 1288. But the Ugolino story had certain complications, as he explains 'lifting his mouth from his horrendous meal, first wiping off his messy lips in the hair remaining on the chewed-up skull'. Ruggieri turned on Ugolino and locked him up in 'the tower of hunger' together with his four sons and grandsons; in an act of extreme cruelty, he threw away the key, barricaded the door and left the family to its fate. One by one the children died, until Ugolino was forced into an appalling choice:

> The fourth day came, and it was on that day
>   my Gaddo fell prostrate before my feet,
>   crying: 'Why don't you help me? Why, my father?'
>
> There he died. Just as you see me here,
>   I saw the other three fall one by one,
>   as the fifth day and the sixth day passed. And I,
>
> by then gone blind, groped over their dead bodies.
>   Though they were dead, two days I called their names.
>   Then hunger proved more powerful than grief.

The family were, in reality, starved to death eleven years before the year of the *Divine Comedy*, in February 1289. But Dante was to discover to his cost that politics had become no less vicious in the meantime. In Florence the newly elected City Council – which refused to sit in the same room as the 'Whites' – had begun a purge of its enemies, including former priors who were known to have stood in their way. Dante was an obvious target. The trumped-up charge, dated 27 January 1302, was trafficking in offices, bribery, discriminating against the 'Blacks' ('faithful devotees of the Roman Church'); and the original sentence was a fine and exile. But before he had time to return to Florence the sentence had already been increased to death by burning. He heard the news on his way home, while in Siena. Now, he could never go home again.

The companions in the *Divine Comedy* make their way across the frozen plain to the very lowest part of the universe. The poet must purge himself of sin in a place which is as far from the light as it is possible to get, where Virgil points out the massive figure of Lucifer, stuck since his fall from grace into the very centre point of the earth.

He stands 'with half his chest above the ice', and he has one head with three faces: the front one is bright red, the side ones are light yellow and black respectively. Beneath each face a pair of bat-wings flaps continuously to create a freezing wind. So Lucifer appears like an inversion of the Trinity, and a fallen angel – vampiric rather than angelic. The poet compares his first sight of him to a piece of brand-new technology:

> A far-off windmill turning its huge sails
>   when a thick fog begins to settle in,
>   or when the light of day begins to fade,
>
> that is what I thought I saw appearing.

The only exit route is down Lucifer's furry body to the very centre of the earth. The poet clings on to his friend Virgil for dear life:

> I held on to his neck, as he told me to,
>   while he watched and waited for the time and place,
>   and when the wings were stretched out just enough,
>
> he grabbed on to the shaggy sides of Satan;
>   then downward, tuft by tuft, he made his way
>   between the tangled hair and frozen crust.

Then suddenly, Virgil asks the poet to start *climbing*: for up has become down, and vice versa:

> I raised my eyes, expecting I would see
>   the half of Lucifer I saw before.
>   Instead I saw his two legs stretching upward . . .
>
> 'Before we start to struggle out of here,
>   O master,' I said when I was on my feet,
>   'I wish you would explain some things to me.
>
> Where is the ice? And how can he be lodged
>   upside-down? And how, in so little time,
>   could the sun go all the way from night to day?'

The two poets have moved, in an instant, from evening in the northern hemisphere to morning in the southern, and are headed for the mountain which was formed by the displaced material when the devil hit the earth. Virgil explains:

> When he fell from the heavens on this side,
>> all of the land that once was spread out here,
>> alarmed by his plunge, took cover beneath the sea
>
> and moved to our hemisphere; with equal fear
>> the mountain-land, piled up on this side, fled
>> and made this cavern here when it rushed upward.

Now, at last, they can see the stars again. And they cross the shores of the hemisphere of water to the mountain of purgatory where souls wait for their sins to be cleansed, a mountain which is situated at the opposite pole of the globe to the Holy City of Jerusalem. The two companions are greeted by Cato the Younger, the Roman statesman and guardian of ante-purgatory, who needs a lot of persuading that they are not spies from hell. The poet notices for the first time, in the morning light, that he casts a shadow – while Virgil does not; for a second, he is 'seized by the fear that I had been abandoned'. He also notices that the 'mount that grew out of the sea toward heaven's height' seems endless, terraced in levels which get higher and higher as they approach the summit of purgatory: a kind of Tower of Babel, made out of waste products.

Eventually, the two travellers make the tiring climb up the two terraces of ante-purgatory (the excommunicated and the late re-pentant) and visit the Valley of the Princes where the souls of rulers – who must as a penance sing the 'Salve Regina' – are cured of their negligence on earth. The rulers include Henry of Navarre ('the kind-looking person') and Henry III of England ('sitting there all by himself, king of the simple life'). The poet falls asleep, dreaming of flight through fire in the claws of a golden-feathered eagle, and wakes up at the gates of purgatory proper. It seems that Beatrice and the 'gracious lady' have again interceded on his behalf, to get him to the right place at the right time.

After the two companions have passed through the gate – and an angel has scratched the letter 'P' seven times on the poet's brow with the tip of a sword, saying that he must erase the scratches as he climbs the mountain – they pass a series of terraces, at each one of which a 'P' is removed when a guardian angel's wing brushes against the poet's forehead. There is pride (where souls, as a penance, have to carry heavy stones), envy (where souls have their eyes sealed together) and anger (which is smothered in a thick black cloud of smoke). Here, the poet has a seminar about freedom of choice with a gentleman from Venice called Marco Lombardo. Marco, it tran-spires, has *avant-garde* ideas:

> 'You men on earth attribute everything
>   to the spheres' influence alone, as if
>   with some predestined plan they moved all things.
>
> If this were true, then our Free will would be
>   annihilated: it would not be just
>   to render bliss for good or pain for evil.
>
> The spheres initiate your tendencies:
>   not all of them – but even if they did,
>   you have the light that shows you right from wrong.'

Marco concludes with some thoughts about the balance of Church and state, a subject he knows to be dear to the poet's heart:

> 'On Rome, that brought the world to know the good,
>   once shone two suns that lighted up two ways:
>   the road of this world and the road of God.
>
> The one sun has put out the other's light;
>   the sword is now one with the crook – and fused
>   together thus, must bring about misrule . . .'

Not the sun and the moon, with the empire existing in the reflected glory of the papacy, but *two suns*. 'Well argued, my dear Marco,' says the poet – somewhat predictably.

The travellers then watch the sun clearing the 'mountain fog', and reach the terraces of middle purgatory – the terraces of the slothful (where hyperactive souls have to run and shout) and of the avaricious (whose souls are stretched out, in chains, on the ground). Here, as the poet stumbles 'with cautious steps' among the flattened souls, he meets Hugh Capet, founder of the dynasty of 'rulers of France up to the present day', who criticizes some of his descendants for their greed, land-grabbing and general obsession with material wealth. It seems an ideal opportunity to chat about Charles of Valois, even though he did not surround Florence until a year *after* 1300, and did not die until 1325. Hugh seems a remarkably accurate prophet:

> 'I see a time, and not too far away,
> > when there shall come a second Charles from France,
> > and we shall see what he and his are like.
>
> He comes bearing no arms, save for the lance
> > that Judas jousted with and, taking aim,
> > he bursts the guts of Florence with one thrust.
>
> From this he gains not land but sin and shame!
> > And worse is that he makes light of the weight
> > of all his crimes, refusing all the blame.'

Suddenly, the discussion is interrupted by an earthquake – which 'shakes' the whole mountain – and a rousing chorus of '*Gloria in Excelsis Deo*'. This is a sign that a soul is ready to be released from purgatory and ascend to paradise. The soul in question belongs to the Roman poet Statius, a fan of Virgil and – according to Dante, anyway – a convert to Christianity as a result. He will be the poet's third guide, in the journey from the mountain to heaven itself, and he starts by leading the travellers along the path to the terraces of upper purgatory.

First comes the terrace of the gluttonous, where souls are starved of food and drink in sight of a sweet-smelling apple tree with a waterfall playing on its leaves, and where the poet discusses how love has inspired his poetry. He meets his friend and relation by marriage, Forese Donati, with whom – back on earth – he had engaged in a rude (to modern tastes) but well-intentioned 'battle of the sonnets' in the late 1290s. (Dante had accused Forese, in very fruity language, of neglecting his wife who was for ever coughing and spluttering, and Forese had replied by saying snobbish things about Mr Alighiero's money-lending business.) On the sixth terrace of purgatory, Forese explains that it was in fact his wife Giovanella who selflessly prayed for him to be 'raised from the slope where souls must wait and set me free from all the other rounds', so there were obviously no residual hard feelings between them. The poet asks Forese about his brother Corso, '*il barone*':

> 'because the place where I was born to live
>   is being stripped of virtue, day by day,
>   doomed, or disposed, to rip itself to ruin.'

> He said 'Take heart. The guiltiest of them all [Corso]
>   I see dragged to his death at a beast's tail
>   down to the pit that never pardons sin.

> The beast with every stride increases speed,
>   faster and faster, till it suddenly
>   kicks free the body, hideously mangled.'

Corso Donati in reality died in 1308 (again, after the story's year of 1300: hence the need for the prophecy) after falling off his horse and having his throat slit as he lay on the ground. Forese's prophecy turns this gruesome death into a form of punishment suitable for the man who sacked Florence.

Then, on to the terrace of the lustful, where souls are purified by a wall of flame as they cry '*Virum non cognosco*', in honour of the chastity of the Virgin Mary. And finally, after some understandable hesitation, the poet walks into the scorching fire –

flanked by his two guides Virgil and Statius. 'Don't you see, my son,' says Virgil reassuringly, 'only this wall keeps you from Beatrice?' He has reached the summit, and the garden of the earthly paradise. Virgil, who after all was only a pagan, is not allowed to go any further:

> 'I led you here with skill and intellect;
>   from here on, let your pleasure be your guide:
>   the narrow ways, the steep are far below.
>
> Behold the sun shining upon your brow,
>   behold the tender grass, the flowers, the trees,
>   which, here, the earth produces of itself.
>
> Until those lovely eyes rejoicing come,
>   which, tearful, once urged me to come to you,
>   you may sit here, or wander, as you please.'

The poet can now be trusted to explore for himself, without a guide, because *his* 'skill and intellect' have become sufficiently developed. He catches sight – across a stream, which is like 'flowing transparency' – of a woman gathering flowers, who welcomes him into the garden. Who this 'lovely lady, glowing with the warmth and strength of Love's own ways' was, or who Dante intended her to be, no one knows for sure. Perhaps she was a friend of Beatrice. She certainly has the qualifications. She explains that the light breeze in the earthly paradise 'moves as the primal revolution moves', from east to west, the direction of the heavenly spheres: it comes directly from the will of God. She adds:

> 'Perhaps those poets of long ago who sang
>   the Age of Gold, its pristine happiness,
>   were dreaming on Parnassus of this place.
>
> The root of mankind's tree was guiltless here:
>   here, in an endless Spring, was every fruit,
>   such is the nectar praised by all these poets.'

So this *is* the Garden of Eden, moved to a safe place nearest to heaven. It was here that Adam ate the apple, here that he told God that Eve had tempted him – acts of disobedience which brought murder into the world. And it is here that the poet is to be cleansed of evil so that he can experience the ultimate happiness.

The woman reveals to him a heavenly pageant of the history of religion: seven golden candlesticks resembling 'trees of gold', carried by people 'in garments supernaturally white'; then twenty-four elders wearing crowns of lilies (the books of the Old Testament), followed by four beasts wearing crowns of forest green (the four beasts of the Apocalypse, and four Gospels); then a triumphal two-wheeled chariot pulled by a griffin (the Church); then 'three ladies circling in a dance' who represent the virtues of faith, dressed in snow-white, hope, in emerald green, and charity or love, in flame-red – the other virtues of prudence, justice, strength and temperance are all dressed in purple robes. Finally, there are seven men, including an 'old man, by himself, who moved in his own dream, his face inspired' (the rest of the New Testament, with the old man as Revelation). The procession stops when the chariot is level with the poet and there is a peal of thunder. One hundred spirits appear in the sky, dropping a rain of flowers. And then, in what must be the grandest entrance in all literature, a woman appears through the angelic flower festival dressed in a white veil, a green cloak and a red gown. These are the colours of the theological virtues and the entrance made such an impact on the Italian psyche that they were later chosen to make up the national flag.

> And instantly – though many years had passed
>   since last I stood trembling before her eyes,
>   captured by adoration, stunned by awe –
>
> my soul, that could not see her perfectly,
>   still felt, succumbing to her mystery
>   and power, the strength of its enduring love . . .

In a flash, the poet is taken back in his mind to the time 'before I quit my boyhood years'. He turns to Virgil for comfort. But Virgil has gone. The poet starts to cry, as the woman continues:

> 'Yes, look at me! Yes, I am Beatrice!
>> So, you at last have deigned to climb the mount?
>> You learned at last that here lies human bliss?'

Beatrice, for it is she, scolds Dante – also by name – for crying, and tells him that he will soon have a *real* reason to shed tears. He feels 'like the guilty child facing his mother'. She continues to be severe with him, even though angels have begged her to back off:

> 'There was a time my countenance sufficed,
>> as I let him look into my young eyes
>> for guidance on the straight path to his goal;
>
> but when I passed into my second age
>> and changed my life for Life, that man you see
>> strayed after others and abandoned me;
>
> when I had risen from the flesh to spirit,
>> become more beautiful, more virtuous,
>> he found less pleasure in me, loved me less,
>
> and wandered from the path that leads to truth,
>> pursuing simulacra of the good,
>> which promise more than they can ever give.'

The poet, 'shattered by the intensity of my emotions', falls into a dead faint, during which he is dipped by the mysterious lady into the waters of forgetfulness. On waking up, he sees Beatrice unveil herself and looks at her face for the first time since she died ten years before. He can find no words to describe the experience. She is surrounded by the seven virtues and is sitting at the foot of the tree of knowledge. Beatrice reveals to him another vision, this time involving a chariot, an eagle, a dragon and 'an ungirt whore' – a series of tableaux which are probably intended to depict the

Church's work on earth from the ascension of Christ up to the year 1300. The whore represents the corrupt papacy, and in particular Boniface VIII, who had recently hopped into bed (as it were) with the king of France. In explaining the vision, Beatrice uses a code made up of numbers. She then expresses the wish that Dante 'from now on free yourself from fear and shame, and cease to speak like someone in a dream'. They are ready, with Statius, to rise to the stars of paradise.

The poet is about to travel through the medieval equivalent of outer space – a coherent and well-worked-out picture of the universe. And it is the details of the journey – the colours, shapes, distances and geography – which make it so tangible and credible, plus its elegant symmetry, which has already been apparent in the circles of hell and the terraces of the mountain of purgatory. These details were in fact based on the latest ideas about how the universe functioned. There is nothing unsophisticated about Dante's cosmos.

Centred on a round earth – no one since the Greeks had seriously thought it was flat – the geometry of the whole cosmos is based on circles and spheres. Everything about this circular universe is made up of four elements – earth, water, air and fire – which are ranked in a social scale of nobility. Earth is the least noble, so it sinks – all the earth in the universe sinks to form a muddy ball at the centre, *the* earth. Next up the scale is water, which sits on the surface of the earth and sometimes finds its way into the sky where it falls as rain. Nobler still is air, which rises and stays there. Fire is the noblest element of them all, always reaching up to where it can be seen as light – the brightness of the sun in daytime, the stars at night. And each of these elements corresponds with psychological or mental states down on the earth, which in turn are mirrored by the geometry of the heavens. The scale of nobility is mirrored, too, by humans, who are part noble, part ignoble (most of them ignoble, it had to be said), as well as by the angels up in the heavens who move the stars and, if senior enough, can see the mind of God. They live in a world of light, where there is no darkness at all. God is, of course, outside the system – beyond space and time – in the very noblest part of the universe which the human soul longs to visit, the source of this intricate hall of mirrors. And that is where Dante is headed, away from gloom, ignobility and baseness towards bliss, light, Beatrice and God.

One of the first things he discovers is that he can now stare straight at the sun – 'no eagle could stare so fixed' – albeit for a short time. The experience is something like looking at 'molten iron as it pours from a fire'. He then travels, with Beatrice, beyond the earth's atmosphere into the sphere of fire above it ('ablaze with the sun's flames'), where he begins to hear the strains of harmony of the celestial spheres. She explains that the sensations of space travel are in some ways similar to moving about on the earth, but that 'lightning never sped downward from its home as quick as you are now ascending to your own'. They then start their ascent through all the spheres which carry the stars and planets around the earth – the spheres or heavens of the Moon, then Mercury, Venus, the Sun, Mars, Jupiter, Saturn, the Fixed Stars, the Primum Mobile, which are mirrored by the nine orders of Angels as they circle around God – Angels, Archangels, Principalities, Powers, Virtues, Dominions, Thrones, Cherubim and Seraphim. Above the Primum Mobile is the Empyrean, in which is the Rose of Paradise itself; above the Rose is the Supreme Being.

Did Dante really believe in space travel? After all, he had established credibility throughout the *Divine Comedy* not by asking for a leap of faith – the 'once upon a time' approach of most legends – but by piling on a mass of physical, verifiable details. One of the first questions he asks Beatrice on his travels through paradise is 'what the dark spots are' on the moon, to which she replies that it has very little to do with 'different densities' of matter – despite what human scientists think – and a lot to do with the fact that the angels who look after the moon are less senior than those in heaven, because the moon is so imperfect compared with the brightness of heaven. Well, says Dante, readers in little boats with little minds to match should 'go back now while you still can see your shores'. So the topography of paradise works, not because it always corresponds to things as understood on earth, but because it coheres as a system of perfect symmetry. Dante moves from sphere to sphere just by looking into the eyes of Beatrice, and her grace and radiance are enough to take him wherever he wants to travel. She must not smile too often, though. That experience would blast him right out of the solar system.

Dante sees his first souls in heaven and thinks they must be reflections:

> As faint an image as comes back to us
>   of our own face reflected in a smooth
>   transparent pane of glass or in a clear
>
> and tranquil pool whose shallow still remains
>   in sight – so pale, our pupils could as soon
>   make out a pearl upon a milk-white brow –
>
> such faces I saw there, eager to speak.

He asks the souls whether they are happy, or whether they yearn for a higher position in heaven. To which they reply that the virtue of their heavenly love tempers their will and makes them want no more than what they have: in short, 'in His will is our peace'. Dante can only wonder at this, and at the complexity of the whole system through which he is passing.

> Look up now, Reader, with me to the spheres;
>   look straight to that point of the lofty wheels
>   where the one motion and the other cross,
>
> and there begin to revel in the work
>   of the great Artist who so loves His art,
>   His gaze is fixed on it perpetually.

Beatrice will later encourage him to 'lower your sight, look down to see how far you have revolved' for the sake of comparison:

My vision travelled back through all the spheres,
    through seven heavens, and then I saw our globe;
    it made me smile, it looked so paltry there . . .

. . . the puny threshing-ground that drives
    us mad – I . . . saw all of it, from hilltops to its shores.

Then, to the eyes of beauty my eyes turned.

Compared with that 'puny threshing-ground', the inhabited sectors of the earth, it seems to Dante as if 'the whole of the universe turns to a smile: thus through my eyes and ears I drank into divine inebriation'. He flies, with Beatrice, into the higher reaches of the heavens, where the souls of the wise and learned live, and where 'even if I called on genius, art and skill, I could not make this live before your eyes – a man must long to see it there'. The souls, in the form of flashes of living light, or burning suns, form a circle around the two travellers, singing and dancing all the while:

When singing, circling, all those blazing suns
    had wheeled around the two of us three times
    like stars that circle close to the fixed poles,

they stopped like ladies still in dancing mood,
    who pause in silence listening to catch
    the rhythm of the new notes of the dance.

The soul of Thomas Aquinas steps out of the circle, to introduce his colleagues; he has read Dante's mind and recognizes 'it is your wish to know what kinds of flowers make up this crown which lovingly surrounds the lovely lady'. So the dance commences. There is Albertus Magnus, the teacher of Aquinas, who commented on all the known works of Aristotle (Dante's universe was to a considerable extent based on Aristotle, whom he had read in Latin translation); Dionysius the Areopagite, widely believed to have written *The Celestial Hierarchy*, on which the orders of angels in the *Paradise* were based and who is referred to as 'a burning candle' on account of his philosophy of light (later, Beatrice will conclude that Dionysius was quite right in all that he wrote); Isidore of Seville, encyclopedist of science and theology; the Venerable Bede, historian – the only Englishman Dante finds in heaven; and Siger of Brabant, who sailed close to the wind of heresy by doubting the immortality of the soul, but who is spectacularly proved wrong in heaven.

Thomas then pauses to tell the uplifting story of St Francis and his lover, Poverty, and the more depressing story of how the Dominican Order has strayed 'into alien pastures carelessly' since the death of its founder. Then another circle of wise and learned souls appears, and they move in harmony with the first as an 'echo'. This time Bonaventure – the third head of the Franciscan Order, and Francis's biographer – does the honours. While the first circle had an intellectual theme, this one is more inspirational. Bonaventure begins by celebrating Dominic of Guzman, founder of the Order of Friars Preachers who was given 'the right to fight . . . the barren thickets of heresy', in other words the Cathars or Albigensians, a right of which Dante evidently approved; and Francis of Assisi, whose Order, too, 'walks along by putting toe to heel' these days, unlike in the days of its founder.

Then, the dance begins again: Hugh of St Victor, the German theologian who coined the oft-quoted phrase 'Learn everything – later you will see that nothing is superfluous'; Nathan the Hebrew prophet; Joachim of Fiore, who, like Siger, had sailed close to the wind down on earth, but whose prophecies and visions of the end of the world had proved very influential; and seven others. Abbot Suger, Heloïse and Abelard are not among those mentioned in heaven, but Anselm of Bec *is*, and he was the man who taught the theologian Anselm of Laon – Abelard's much-abused teacher – which may give a clue as to where Dante's own sympathies lay in the debate between the saint and the scholar. Augustine of Hippo, Francis of Assisi and Bernard of Clairvaux (by now a venerable old man 'in the robes of Heaven's saints') will all be named, later, among the elect in the higher echelons of paradise itself.

In the two dances of the souls, which take place in the sphere of the Sun, the distinguished – and surprisingly light-hearted – masters of ceremonies mirror each other's behaviour, as in a square dance: a Dominican introduces St Francis while a Franciscan introduces Dominic; both of them introduce the greatest hits of medieval thought, from their own points of view; and the two circles mirror each other, too. They encourage Dante to reflect:

> Insensate strivings of mortality –
> how useless are those reasonings of yours
> that make you beat your wings in downward flight!

> Men bent on law, some on the *Aphorisms*,
> some on the priesthood, often in pursuit
> of governing by means of force or fraud . . .

> and I, relieved of all such vanities,
> was there with Beatrice in high Heaven,
> magnificently, gloriously welcomed.

In the sphere of the Fixed Stars, Dante sees the souls of the blessed rising to the Empyrean. This time he does not think of them as reflections but as 'frozen vapours':

> so I saw all of Heaven's ether glow
> with rising snowflakes of triumphant souls
> of all those who had sojourned with us there.

> My eyes followed their shapes up into space
> and I kept watching them until the height
> was too much for my eyes to penetrate.

Dante and Beatrice now fly even closer to the Rose of Paradise, to the ninth sphere, the Primum Mobile, which drives the whole universe. Beyond this, they have only one stage to go before actually seeing the mind of God. For, as Beatrice explains, it is the mind of God which 'contains this heaven, because in that Mind burns the love that turns it and the power it rains'. And it is symbolized by nine glowing circles of light, all circling around one another, and all travelling in a circle; on these, says Beatrice, nature and the heavens.

> By circling light and love it is contained
>   as it contains the rest; and only He
>   who bound them comprehends how they were bound.

For Dante, this is an image of all creation: small, simple, portable and circular. These circles of light are an image of the planets, their influences, the orders of angels who drive them, and the consciousness of God which is the motive force and rationale for the system itself. The primal light which somehow shines down through paradise.

But the circles of light must have seemed a very long way away from the real Dante who had, down on earth, lost his Beatrice and been permanently exiled from the city he loved. He worked as a kind of freelance diplomat and teacher, moving from city to city; as he travelled, he conscientiously broadened his knowledge of philosophy, cosmology and theology. His exile was made even more unbearable when he became alienated from his own allies, the 'Whites', back in Florence. His refusal to associate himself with a revolt and attempted takeover of the city led to him becoming, in effect, 'a party of one'. Eventually, he settled in the town of Ravenna at the mouth of the Po – reading, as he put it, the book of memory of his experiences and his love.

But as Dante was putting the finishing touches to his greatest work, the world into which he had been born, the world of the Middle Ages, was beginning to fall apart. The popes moved their headquarters to new premises at Avignon, to be closer to their French sponsors; the fortified walls of their new palace showed how far they were involved in the affairs of *this* world. Dante's dream of a 'just balance' was already so out of date as to be laughable. The French royal family perpetrated one of the great atrocities of the age, when they ordered the Templars, an Order of Holy Knights set up during the crusades to defend the Latin kingdom of Jerusalem and blessed by Bernard of Clairvaux, to be hunted down and

accumulated an enviable
for this, Dante called King
who drove his greedy sails
. One or two of the visionary
re Islamic in origin, and they
Dante by members of the Order
rusalem. There are even some sup-
plars in the *Comedy*, buried under
syn. ences; he had to be careful, especially as
he was a

Even the w against the Middle Ages. In 1315 it rained
for the entire summ. The crops rotted in the fields and livestock
starved to death. This started a series of famines which weakened
the population and made it easy prey to the Black Death when it
arrived. The political manoeuvrings that were to lead to the bloody
and relentless Hundred Years War also began at this time. The first
use of firearms as weapons of war was recorded in Europe while
Dante was writing.

Five years before he died, in 1316, there was an offer of pardon
from the city of Florence – in return for public humiliation and
payment of a fine. The humiliation involved wearing a mitre with
his crimes written all over it and walking through the streets to the
Baptistery, to be jeered at by all and sundry. Dante replied in a fury:

This is not the path by which I shall return to my native city . . . If some
other can be found . . . which does not detract from the fame and honour of
Dante, I will accept it eagerly. But if Florence may not be entered in such a
way, then I will never enter Florence again. Can I not gaze upon the face of
the sun and the stars anywhere? . . . Rest assured, I will not want for bread!

Although he never did see Florence again, it did not take long
after his death in September 1321 for the city to begin to honour
him as its great teacher and corporate symbol. To this day, the
people of Florence still send a flask of oil on the anniversary of his
death to the town of Ravenna where he died. He had lived some of
his exile in Verona, but spent his final years as a guest of Count

Guido Novella da Polenta, in Ravenna. (Guido was a nephew of that same Francesca da Rimini whom Dante had consigned to the whirling darkness of the second circle of hell, the circle of Lust. Perhaps *that* was why he was so sympathetic when she argued that it was all the fault of a soap opera.) Dante died on the way back from a political mission to Venice on behalf of the Count, most likely of malaria.

The story goes that when he died, the last part of his epic (it was only called the *Divine Comedy* later) was missing. Dante's ghost appeared to one of his sons in a dream and told him that the finale was so very special that it had been plastered into the wall of his study for safe-keeping. He had begun the *Comedy* around 1307, completed the *Inferno* by 1314 and was working on *Paradise* to the very end. Whatever the rationale of the story, when they found the last few cantos, they found some of the richest images in the whole work, images which were intended to re-enchant and re-harmonize a world which Dante knew from his everyday experiences was pretty thin on enchantment and harmony. To show how, despite all appearances to the contrary, things do cohere, and the centre *can* hold.

Dante's paradise – like his hell and his purgatory – was at the same time a work of art, with its creator playing the main part in the story, and about *God*'s work of art as well. That, in the end, was the message – the message he gleaned from all the sources in philosophy, theology, science, science fiction, cosmology and poetry which he had read since the death of Beatrice. The universe is a harmonious system, where people, angels and God have their rightful place: a quintessentially medieval message.

It is particularly ironic that Dante should be celebrating this huge idea at precisely the time when Christian Europe was falling apart. Ironic, too, that the *Comedy* has a happy ending – happy in the medieval sense of understanding the ultimate harmony and *rightness* of the universe, a harmony which is carried by one single principle, the key to the whole story. For, as Dante had promised faithfully at the end of *New Life*, 'if it be the wish of Him in whom all things flourish that my life continue for a few years, I hope to write of *her* that which has never been written of any lady'.

The *Divine Comedy* has been called 'a single crystal with 13,000 facets' and 'the work of the last man in history who was able to comprehend all the knowledge of his age'. But the point of the exercise was not just to amass details, or reduce the universe to bite-sized portions – which it would have been a hundred years later – or even to be progressive. Dante was on the whole happier looking backwards and was temperamentally committed to things as they used to be – just over the last hill; he was radical in the sense of exploring roots. The point of the exercise was re-enchantment. And the result of his personal tour of the cosmos was so strong and so influential that it even managed to do battle, for a time, with Renaissance forms of science – that other great vision of the universe. Dante's vision – and his map – can still, in the post-modern – or should I say post-Renaissance? – world, be a guide through the dark forest.

'If it ever happens,' wrote Dante at the end of the *Paradise*, 'that this sacred poem . . . wins over those cruel hearts that exile me from my sweet fold where I grew up a lamb . . . I shall return, a poet, and at my own baptismal font assume the laurel wreath, for it was there I entered in the faith.' So he finishes where most probably he began: with the Baptistery in Florence, whose mosaic ceiling he first saw and wondered at when he was eleven years old. As he says, on his first glimpse of paradise:

> No baby, having slept too long, and now
> awakened late, could rush to turn his face
> more eagerly to seek his mother's milk
>
> than I bent down my face to make my eyes
> more lucid mirrors . . .

Dante and Beatrice have watched the nine glowing circles fade away, and travelled to the Empyrean. Up to now it has been Beatrice who has seen the light of heaven and passed the experience on to her companion. Now Dante must be dazzled, so that *he* can see the light:

> Just as a sudden flash of lightning strikes
> the visual spirits and so stuns the eyes,
> that even the clearest object fades from sight,
>
> so glorious living light encompassed me,
> enfolding me so tightly in its veil
> of luminence that I saw only light.

With his power of new sight, he sees a flaming stream of pure light which 'turns its straight course to a circumference' and becomes a lake. Beside the lake are flowers painted by spring in miracles of colour, but on closer inspection ('as people at a masquerade take off the masks') the flowers turn out to be the souls of the Elect sitting in tiers of petals which have opened like a gigantic pure white rose. Not a rose of romantic love, or of chivalry, as in courtly literature, but a rose of divine love. Dante, like a child, cannot find the right words, and he sees as a child as well: all the petals of the rose seem to be equally in focus. It has taken him all his life to see as a child.

> And yet, by such enormous breadth and height
> my eyes were not confused; they took in all
> in number and in quality of bliss.
>
> There, near and far nor adds nor takes away,
> for where God rules directly without agents,
> the laws of Nature in no way apply.

So he has travelled beyond space and time. Distance and perspective have become useless visual guides. The goals towards which Dante's friend, the painter Giotto, was stumbling, rejecting Realism for Naturalism, were mere attempts to find a poor equivalent of 'the law of Nature' and reduce the experience to human-sized dimensions. Single-point perspective is no help at all in the Rose of

Paradise. Nor is physics: the thousands of angels who fly, like swarming bees, between the souls of the Elect and God never once 'impede the vision of glorious light'. And there is no noise: just one equal silence. Dante and Beatrice move to the centre of the Rose, and as the poet turns to ask her a question he discovers that he has a new and final guide – none other than Bernard of Clairvaux. Beatrice has moved to her proper place in one of the highest tiers of the Elect.

> . . . And she, so far away,
> or so it seemed, looked down at me and smiled;
> then to Eternal Light she turned once more.

Bernard asks Dante to look up even further, into the circles, until he can see the Queen of Heaven herself. He is the ideal guide at this moment, because he 'constantly burns with love's fire' for her, and because 'I am her faithful one, Bernard'. As Dante looks up, he can see that the petals of the celestial rose – moving outwards from the centre – consist of children, the blessed of the Old Testament and the saints of the New Testament, especially saintly men such as Francis of Assisi and Augustine of Hippo, with the Virgin Mary at the head of a row of Old Testament women which includes Eve. Mary is flanked on the AD side by St Peter and St John the Evangelist ('he who prophesied before he died') and on the BC side by Adam and Moses.

The effect is like a medieval court in the sky, with its kings, princes and princesses, barons, counts, ladies and commoners: hierarchical, ordered, segregated and preordained. Dante calls it 'an amphitheatre of the Elect'. And one of the miraculous aspects of his visit is that he feels for once on level terms with everyone. The Angel Gabriel salutes the Queen of Heaven 'with wings spread wide', and Bernard then asks Dante to look up to God. The word 'Christ' never once appears in the *Inferno*; now, amid a cluster of references, the poet must be made ready to see his face, as Bernard begs the Queen of Heaven to 'dispel the mist of his mortality'. Dante turns his eyes towards 'the sharp brilliance of the living ray' and sees three circles in three translucent colours bound together into one space. Each reflects the other, 'like rainbow on rainbow', and the poet tries to work out exactly how the three circles and colours of the Trinity can possibly relate to one another. Again, science – even the science of proportions – is of no use:

> As the geometer who tries so hard
>   to square the circle, but cannot discover,
>   think as he may, the principle involved,
>
> so did I strive with this new mystery . . .

Confronted by such perfection, where he sees 'the universal form, the vision of all things', Dante becomes a child once more:

> Now, even in the things I do recall
>   my words have no more strength than does a babe
>   wetting its tongue, still at its mother's breast.

And then arrives the moment of insight and illumination, which ends the poet's journey through the strange landscape of the Middle Ages:

> a great flash of understanding struck
>   my mind, and suddenly its wish was granted.
>
> At this point power failed high fantasy
>   but, like a wheel in perfect balance turning,
>   I felt my will and my desire impelled
>
> by the Love that moves the sun and the other stars.

THE WANING OF THE MIDDLE AGES
A note on the cover illustration.

Hieronymus Bosch's *The Garden of Earthly Delights*, painted halfway through the second millennium at a time when memories of the Black Death and the Hundred Years War were still fresh, is about the waning of the Middle Ages. A God-centred universe is giving way to a human-centred one; coherence is becoming fragmentation. In Bosch's triptych, an idyllic spring in the Garden of Eden – where Christ blesses Adam and Eve in their nakedness – turns into a ripe summer of forbidden knowledge and frantic sensual pleasure (the central panel – illustrated), which turns into the perpetual winter of a frozen hell where giant-sized musical instruments blast the atmosphere and puny human achievements go up in smoke. Maybe this cycle of history is supposed to be happening in the same place, where the Fountain of Life in the left panel becomes the tower-like architectural construction in the centre and the self-destroying treeman and burning city in the right. If so, by the end of the cycle hell is happening as much in this world as the next. Historian Johan Huizinga justly concluded of the era when Bosch was painting *The Garden of Earthly Delights*:

So violent and noisy was life, that it bore the mixed smell of blood and of roses. The people of that time always oscillate between the fear of hell and most naïve joy . . . between harsh asceticism and insane attachment to the delights of this world, between hatred and goodness, always running to extremes.

APPENDIX 1

UMBERTO ECO'S MIDDLE AGES

The following are Eco's ten loose classifications of the various re-inventions of the Middle Ages which have been happening ever since the Renaissance, mainly with my examples:

1. The Middle Ages as *pretext* – a mythological stage on which to place contemporary characters with little attempt at authenticity; operas, swashbuckling stories and television advertising are perhaps the best examples.

2. The Middle Ages as *ironic revisitation* – a way of commenting on today's less colourful mores, from Cervantes and Rabelais to Monty Python.

3. The Middle Ages as *barbaric* – a shaggy, dark era of brute force, Viking helmets and heavy metal, from Brunhild to Hell's Angels (the sort of Middle Ages Alain Minc has in mind in his *Le Nouveau Moyen Âge* (1994)).

4. The Middle Ages as *romantic* – an era of wind-swept castles, clank-ing ghosts in suits of armour, chivalry, ever-so-happy artisans and in general a golden age, from Horace Walpole via John Ruskin to *Star Wars*.

5. The Middle Ages as *perennial philosophy* – exemplified by pro-nouncements from the Vatican and secular system-builders of theory.

6. The Middle Ages as *national identity* – where a past model of cultural grandeur and independence is seen as a political possibility

(as in some of the republics of eastern Europe or in Ireland), when in fact it never happened that way.

7. The Middle Ages of *decadence* – from the Symbolists of the late nineteenth century (with their wallowing in the sadism of someone like Gilles de Rais) to millenarians and some gallery artists of today (who associate things medieval with what they call 'the abject').

8. The Middle Ages of *philological reconstruction* – the attitude of mind of the medieval scholar today, as he or she works through the vast collections of information which have become available in the twentieth century, perhaps in order to understand 'great events' but more likely in order to get inside 'the forms of everyday life', the *mentalities* of the period. (It has been estimated that between ten and twenty times more written texts have survived from the medieval than from the Greco-Roman world, mainly dating from 1000 onwards, partly because the texts were made of lambskin or calfskin parchment – a very durable material; for the post-1250 period, a lot of this material is still unpublished.)

9. The Middle Ages of so-called *tradition* – a ramshackle assemblage of loosely translated texts and over-hasty conclusions, which brings into its ragbag everything from the Druids, force-fields and earth-power to Solomon's Temple, Knights Templars, Rosicrucians, Hermetic philosophy, the Holy Blood and the Holy Grail, runic stones, buried treasure, numerology, self-actualization and, too often, a distinctly Old (as opposed to New) Age will to power.

10. The Middle Ages of the *Millennium and the Apocalypse* – which has been around since the waning of the original one, with its quickening tempo of change, and will be around until midnight of the Day After, when someone, presumably, will say 'I told you so . . .'

APPENDIX 2

MEDIEVAL STUDIES TODAY

Among the major scholarly works published in the last few years is Professor Norman Cantor's 450-page study of the lives, works and long-term contributions of the major medievalists of the twentieth century, which he calls *Inventing the Middle Ages*. In it he tells a fascinating story, which begins with the English legal historian Frederic William Maitland and continues by looking at the German cultural and intellectual historians whose careers were touched by Nazism, the French social historians of the interwar period who first studied economic conditions, then *mentalities*, and exiles such as Erwin Panofsky who redefined medieval art history. He has much to say about the 'Oxford fantasists', C. S. Lewis and J. R. R. Tolkien, and the American historians who studied the 'medieval origins of the modern state' in a hot and cold war climate; and he concludes with the Roman Catholic British historian David Knowles who devoted his adult life to the study of monastic and other religious orders in England, the French philosopher Étienne Gilson who interpreted Thomas Aquinas as 'a model for the progressive road that Catholic culture should take in the twentieth century', the Oxford-based Richard Southern, whose *The Making of the Middle Ages* (1953) remains *the* study of spiritual and secular sensibility in the twelfth century, and, as a postscript, the Dutch cultural historian Johan Huizinga who wrote the still influential *Autumn of the Middle Ages* (otherwise known as *The Waning of the Middle Ages*) over a single summer in 1919 – a book which speculated about the transition in fifteenth-century Holland and Burgundy from the coherence, 'idealism' and symbolic power of medieval art and culture to 'realism', the particular and the detailed, and used the evidence of popular culture to help support his case.

These historians have all, according to Cantor, *invented* the Middle Ages. He starts from the assumption that nineteenth-century historians of the period, however distinguished or talented as writers, tended to be 'sure of the relative simplicity of the medieval world and confident in making opinionated assessments of it'; in addition, they 'wrote about human relationships before the revolutionary cultural consequences of the emergence of social, behavioural, and psychoanalytic sciences in the modernist culture of the early twentieth century'. As a result, they regarded the behaviour of human beings in ways which twentieth-century readers find obsolete, or sometimes even offensive. So it was, to all intents and purposes, the historians of his story, the historians of the twentieth century, who invented the Middle Ages and, in doing so, they had a definite – if usually one-way – relationship with the perception of things medieval in the wider culture. As Cantor notes:

The medievalists' work is obviously divisible into distinct groups or schools of interpretation, and they differ among themselves, sometimes vehemently, on the essential character and the precise development of medieval civilization. To outsiders, such academic debate can seem to be the hair-splitting chatter of cloistered professors. But a closer look reveals much that is at stake in these debates, because during their course hypotheses are tested, ideas refined, and ultimately a consensus is reached. Academic medievalists contribute the interpretive community to which the popular writers about the Middle Ages, like Tuchman and Eco . . . defer in their highly imaginative writings.

One of the most important contributions of Cantor's book (which sometimes reads like a colourful tournament, the prize for which is the possession of the Middle Ages) is to locate the major developments in historical scholarship – which have been too often treated in isolation – within their proper social and political contexts. Thus, 'the medieval origins of the modern state' became important during the Cold War. Aquinas was and is important during debates about the Catholic Church's attitude towards contemporary culture. And so on. Cantor's 'great medievalists' (and Eco's 'philological tradition') can tell us as much about their own times as about the times they were studying.

A key example occurred in late 1920s Germany, when historian Ernst Hartwig Kantorowicz published his monumental, best-selling biography of Frederick II of the Hohenstaufen dynasty (1194–1250), who derived the German Imperial crown from his father Henry VI and grandfather Frederick Barbarossa, and the kingdom of Sicily from his mother Constance. At the height of his powers, and following wars on several fronts at once, Frederick's empire stretched from the borders of Denmark in the north, to Sicily in the south, to the Holy Land in the east. He was a figure of legend even in his own lifetime, partly because he himself was a gifted self-publicist, partly because successive popes countered his propaganda with their own (they were understandably apprehensive about being encircled), and partly because he was fascinated by the new knowledge from the east which entered Europe via Sicily and which looked to the uninitiated like the work of the devil. One enemy even claimed that he had dared to refer to Moses, Christ and Mohammed as 'the three great imposters'. Known in the mid thirteenth century as '*splendor mundi*' (the wonder of the world), '*mutator mirabilis*' (the amazing bringer of changes) and '*malleus orbis*' (the hammer of the world), Frederick also wrote the definitive book on hawking, his chancellor in Sicily invented the sonnet, he corresponded about the meaning of life with the wise men of Judaism and Islam, and he provided a safe haven for the Provençal love poets who had been driven south during the Albigensian Crusade. An extraordinary, larger-than-life subject for a biography. Kantorowicz was a member of the circle of intellectuals and romantic young men which surrounded the right-wing lyric poet and mystic Stefan George in Germany, and his book *Kaiser Friedrich der Zweite*, published in Berlin in 1927, was a brilliantly written hymn of praise to the concepts of charismatic leadership and national renewal. It began with the words 'enthusiasm is astir for the great German rulers of the past, in a day when Kaisers are no more' and ended, in high rhetorical mode, with an apocalyptic retelling of the medieval legend that this once and future king would return from his temporary resting-place within Mount Etna, flanked by five thousand flaming horsemen, to reunite his peoples: 'the greatest Frederick is not yet redeemed, him his people knew not and sufficed not'. According to Kantorowicz, Frederick had a master-plan which involved bringing together the effete southerners and the virile northerners in an empire which would challenge the power of the Papacy and eventually lead towards the modern, secular nation-state: no wonder Nietzsche referred to the Emperor as 'one of my nearest kin' and counted him a member of the select legion of super-heroes.

Whatever Kantorowicz's political intentions in writing the book (he was Jewish and, in common with several other members of the George circle, would have considered Hitler a vulgar upstart and/or a temporary annoyance), *Kaiser Friedrich der Zweite* was – in the context of the rise of Nazism – taken up as a sacred text in the new cult of medievalism. There had, of course, been such cults before in modern German history – most notably during the Napoleonic invasion and in the era of Bismarck and unification; but the mass media, and the Nazis' aestheticization of politics, ensured that the twentieth-century version would pack a nastier punch than ever before. Kantorowicz's biography was one of Hermann Göring's favourite books. In the last twenty-five years, various debunking biographies and studies have been published – the most effective of which is David Abulafia's *Frederick II, a Medieval Emperor* (1988) – which have sensibly and rationally questioned Frederick's uncanny ability to think the thoughts of future generations and stressed that, far from having a master-plan, the Emperor's main purpose in life was to cling on to his dynastic lands and titles as best and as brutally as he could. Plus the fact that he left the divided German principalities much as he had found them. But Kantorowicz's work still remains, as Norman Cantor concludes, 'the most exciting biography of a medieval monarch produced in this century'. The point is that Kantorowicz, great scholar though he was, inevitably viewed the Middle Ages through the spectacles of his own time – the disintegrating Weimar Republic and the then-fashionable reaction of neo-romanticism.

Another key feature of medieval scholarship which has been particularly significant this century has been the number of important scholars working from 'within' Roman Catholicism and thus approaching their task as one of tracing roots or nourishing a living as well as received tradition. Take, for example, this quotation from David Knowles's *The End of the Middle Ages*, volume II of *The Religious Orders in England*, first published in 1955:

In truth, intimate or detailed records of the nunneries are almost entirely wanting over the whole period between *c.* 1200 and the Dissolution [of the monasteries] . . . The religious historian of medieval England cannot help remarking, in every century after the eleventh, upon the absence from the scene of any saintly or commanding figure of a woman.

As a result, added Knowles, his study of English monasticism would not concern itself with nuns. Indeed, the most substantial work on the subject, Eileen Power's *Medieval English Nunneries, c. 1275–1535* (1922), was not even mentioned in Knowles's extensive bibliography.

Power's book *is* examined in Cantor's *Inventing the Middle Ages* – in a chapter headed 'outsiders . . . the dissenters, the eccentrics, the nonconformists' – but it is the only book by a female medievalist to make the grade (although Cantor does refer to four disciples, in a single line of text). Cantor adds:

Power's account of nuns in late medieval England, the distress and social marginality of their lives, and the lack of care and consideration they received even within the church hierarchy bears testimony to a downturn in the status of women in landed society in northern Europe in the later Middle Ages. It is not surprising that an enthusiast for the Middle Ages like

David Knowles passes over the history of women religious very quickly in his monumental four-volume work and had very little to add to Power's definitive account. It is not surprising that Dick Southern never addressed the issue of how modestly women actually benefited in the long run from the Virgin cult and the more humanistic theology of the twelfth century.

The work of Eileen Power – based at Girton College, Cambridge, in the pioneering 1920s – not only criticized patriarchal structures in the late Middle Ages, it provided a role model for women's history of half a century later. For, as Cantor concludes:

Eileen Power is the only woman medievalist who belongs in the array of the founders and shapers of our vision of the Middle Ages during the first seventy years of this century. As we look ahead into the twenty-first century, the story will be very different. Indeed, by 2020 medieval studies will be mainly in the hands of women scholars if current trends are sustained.

As researches over the last decade have revealed, there *is* information to be found on spiritual and personal life in the nunneries – and on the changing status of women between the early and later Middle Ages. David Knowles and others must surely have known of this information; it was a question of whether or not they were interested in it. Since the mid 1980s there have been surveys of women's work in the Middle Ages, the religious significance of food – involving fasting and what we would now call 'anorexia' – the meanings for women of self-mortification and, outside the convent walls, the feminine voice in medieval courtly romances and the place of sexual violence in aristocratic literature. There have been studies of such 'commanding figures' as Abbess Hildegard of Bingen (1098–1179) – visionary, dramatist, herbalist, the first woman composer of music in western history (her hymnal chants even made their way into the top ten classical records of 1993–5) and, we are now told, creator of 'theology of the feminine'; and Christine de Pisan (*c*. 1364–*c*. 1433) and her *Book of the City for Ladies*; together with studies of the changing image and meaning of the Virgin Mary at this time, with implications for the role and status of upper-class women. Nearly all of Abbess Hildegard's works had been in print for three hundred years; it was just that very few historians had picked up on them.

Perhaps the most radical contribution to this debate has been from the great French historian Georges Duby, who has argued that the code of courtly love in the twelfth and thirteenth centuries, the stylized submission of the unmarried knight to the married lady, was in fact a clever way of keeping the younger sons of aristocratic households busy (they had to remain unmarried to keep the inheritance intact and they had to learn about deferred gratification to keep out of trouble). Rather than giving the lady a special status, Duby concludes, the code of courtly love was really an affair between the young knight and the lord whose wife he was courting and whom he sought to impress with his loyalty – 'an affair between men', rather than an opportunity for the feminine voice to be heard. 'It is debatable,' says Duby, 'whether the sentiment of courtly love ever existed outside literary texts.' But once you do step beyond literary texts, it is extraordinarily difficult to establish how people actually behaved (as opposed to how they were *supposed* to behave or how people reacted to their supposed behaviour).

There have, of course, been countless other contributions to medieval scholarship which have reflected today's concerns every bit as much as yesterday's evidence. Among them is R. I. Moore's controversial study, *The Formation of a Persecuting Society* (1987), which argues that in the eleventh and especially twelfth centuries, in parallel with the attempt to make 'Christendom' cohere, came deliberate and socially sanctioned violence against groups of people defined by race, religion or sexual preference. This was a new feature of European history, coming from institutions 'above' and not necessarily from society at large, and it was the origin of countless atrocities which followed. Norman Cohn's work, too, on *Europe's Inner Demons* (1975) and the millenarians draws parallels with the mental sets which lead to ethnic cleansing today – a medieval nightmare coming true.

Cantor's overall point – that medieval studies, which seem on the surface to be thoroughly insulated from the concerns of the twentieth century, are in fact as deeply imbued with them as any other form of historical scholarship – would appear to be more and more explicitly acknowledged in recent contributions, which post-date the work of the philosopher Michel Foucault and others on the ways in which 'historical archives' are constructed and ordered. Whether or not such self-consciousness will mean that future medieval studies will do more than reproduce the assumptions of the present day, only time will tell.

SELECT BIBLIOGRAPHY

Titles marked with an asterisk were especially useful.

General

Barber, Richard, *The Penguin Guide to Medieval Europe* (Penguin, 1984)

Bishop, Morris, *The Pelican Book of the Middle Ages* (Penguin, 1971)

Brown, Peter, *The Cult of the Saints: Its Rise and Function in Latin Christianity* (University of Chicago Press, 1981)

Calkins, R. G., *Monuments of Medieval Art* (Phaidon, 1979)

Davis, R. H. C., *A History of Medieval Europe, from Constantine to St Louis* (Longman, 1988)

Geary, Patrick J. (ed.), *Readings in Medieval History* (Broadview Press, 1993)

*Gurevich, Aron, *Medieval Popular Culture: Problems of Belief and Perception* (Cambridge University Press, 1988)

Haren, Michael, *Medieval Thought: Western Intellectual Tradition from Antiquity to the 13th Century* (Macmillan, 1992)

Holmes, George (ed.), *The Oxford Illustrated History of Medieval Europe* (Oxford University Press, 1988)

*Le Goff, Jacques, *Medieval Civilization, 400–1500* (Blackwell, 1988)

*Loyn, H. R. (ed.), *The Middle Ages – A Concise Encyclopedia* (Thames & Hudson, 1991)

McEvedy, Colin, *The New Penguin Atlas of Medieval History* (Penguin, 1992)

Martindale, Andrew, *Gothic Art* (Thames & Hudson, 1988)

*Moore, R. I., *The Formation of a Persecuting Society: Power and Deviance in Western Europe, 950–1250* (Blackwell, 1990)

*Murray, Alexander, *Reason and Society in the Middle Ages* (Oxford University Press, 1985)

Southern, Richard, *Western Views of Islam in the Middle Ages* (Harvard University Press, 1962)

*Southern, Richard, *The Making of the Middle Ages* (Pimlico, 1993)

Storey, R. L., *Chronology of the Medieval World, 800–1491* (Helicon, 1993)

The Middle Ages Today

Abulafia, David, *Frederick II, a Medieval Emperor* (Pimlico, 1992)

Bennett, Judith M., 'Medievalism and Feminism' (*Speculum*, April 1993)

Bretèque, François de la, *Le Moyen Âge au cinéma* (Perpignan, 1985)

Brynum, Caroline W., *Holy Feast and Holy Fast: The Religious Significance of Food to Medieval Women* (University of California Press, 1987)

Campbell, Joseph, *The Hero with a Thousand Faces* (Paladin, 1988)

*Cantor, Norman F., *Inventing the Middle Ages: Lives, Works and Ideas of the Great Medievalists of the 20th Century* (Lutterworth Press, 1992)

Ciment, Michel, *John Boorman* (Faber, 1986)

Cohn, Norman, *Europe's Inner Demons* (Pimlico, 1993)

Day, David, *The Tolkien Companion* (Mandarin, 1993)

Duby, Georges, *Love and Marriage in the Middle Ages* (Polity Press, 1994)

Eco, Umberto, *Art and Beauty in the Middle Ages* (Yale University Press, 1986)

*Eco, Umberto, *Faith in Fakes: Essays* (Secker & Warburg, 1986)

Eco, Umberto, *The Aesthetics of Chaosmos: The Middle Ages of James Joyce* (Hutchinson Radius, 1989)

*Eco, Umberto, *The Name of the Rose* (Secker & Warburg, 1983; Mandarin, 1992)

Eco, Umberto, *Reflections on The Name of the Rose* (Minerva, 1994)

*Frayling, Christopher, 'Conversation with Umberto Eco' (full transcript, May 1984)

Frayling, Christopher, 'In Search of a Logic of Culture' (*The Listener*, 11 October 1984)

Frayling, Christopher, 'Conversation with Terry Gilliam' (BBC World Service, 12 November 1991)

Gablik, Suzi, *The Re-enchantment of Art* (Thames & Hudson, 1994)

*Girouard, Mark, *The Return to Camelot: Chivalry and the English Gentleman* (Yale University Press, 1985)

Griffin, David Ray, *The Re-enchantment of Science: Postmodern Proposals* (State University of New York Press, 1988)

Hobsbawm, E., and Ranger, T., *The Invention of Tradition* (Cambridge University Press, 1992)

Jencks, Charles, *The Post-Modern Reader* (Academy Editions, 1993)

Kantorowicz, Ernst H., *Frederick the Second, 1194–1250* (Constable, 1958)

Knowles, David, *The Religious Orders in England*, 3 vols. (Cambridge University Press, 1948–59)

*Ladurie, Emmanuel Le Roy, *Montaillou: Cathars and Catholics in a French Village* (Penguin, 1990)

Macdonald Fraser, George, *The Hollywood History of the World* (Michael Joseph, 1988)

McLuhan, Marshall, *The Gutenberg Galaxy* (Ark Publications, 1988)

Marcus, Greil, *Lipstick Traces – A Secret History of the Twentieth Century* (Penguin, 1993)

Minc, Alain, *Le Nouveau Moyen Âge* (Gallimard, 1993)

Mottram, Eric, *Blood on the Nash Ambassador: Investigations in American Culture* (Radius, 1991)

Power, Eileen, *Medieval English Nunneries, c.1275–1535* (Cambridge University Press, 1922)

Rose, Mary Beth, *Women in the Middle Ages and Renaissance* (Syracuse University Press, 1986)

Sheldrake, Rupert, *The Greening of Science and God* (New York, 1991)

Stone, Norman, 'The Return of the Dark Ages' (*Sunday Times*, London, 17 April 1994)

Strong, Roy, *And When Did You Last See Your Father?: The Victorian Painter and British History* (Thames & Hudson, 1978)

Tuchman, Barbara, *A Distant Mirror: The Calamitous Fourteenth Century* (Macmillan, 1978)

Twain, Mark, *A Connecticut Yankee at King Arthur's Court* (Penguin, 1987)

★White, Lynn, Jr, *Medieval Religion and Technology: Collected Essays* (University of California Press, 1978)

The Jewelled City

Bony, Jean, *French Gothic Architecture of the 12th and 13th Centuries* (University of California Press, 1985)

★Brooke, Christopher, 'The Cathedral in Medieval Society', in Wim Swaan, *The Gothic Cathedral* (Elek, 1969)

Coulton, G. J. G., *Life in the Middle Ages*, 4 vols. (Cambridge University Press, 1928–30)

Friedman, John, *The Monstrous Races in Medieval Art and Thought* (Harvard University Press, 1981)

Frisch, Teresa G., *Gothic Art 1140–1450: Sources and Documents* (University of Toronto Press, 1987)

★Geary, Patrick, *Furta Sacra: Thefts of Relics in the Central Middle Ages* (Princeton University Press, 1990)

★Gimpel, Jean, *The Cathedral Builders* (Pimlico, 1993)

Harvey, John, *The Gothic World 1100–1600: A Survey of Architecture and Art* (Batsford, 1950)

★Hogarth, James (trans.), *The Pilgrim's Guide: 12th Century Guide for the Pilgrim to St James of Compostela* (Confraternity of St James, 1992)

★James, John, *Chartres – The Masons who Built a Legend* (Routledge & Kegan Paul, 1982)

Katzenellenbogen, Adolf, *The Sculpture Programs of Chartres Cathedral* (The Johns Hopkins Press, 1959)

Lasko, Peter, *Ars Sacra 800–1200* (Penguin History of Art, 1978)

Macaulay, David, *Cathedral – The Story of its Construction* (Collins, 1974)

★Miller, Malcolm, *Chartres Cathedral* (Pitkin, 1992)

Oursel, Raymond, *Lumières de Vézelay* (Zodiaque, Yonne, 1993)

★Panofsky, Erwin (ed.), *Abbot Suger on the Abbey Church of St Denis and its Art Treasures* (Princeton University Press, 1946)

Panofsky, Erwin, *Gothic Architecture and Scholasticism* (Thames & Hudson, 1957)

★Simson, Otto von, *The Gothic Cathedral: Origins of Gothic Architecture and the Medieval Concept of Order* (Princeton University Press, 1988)

Sox, David, *Relics and Shrines* (Allen & Unwin, 1985)

★Turnbull, David, 'Inside the Gothic Laboratory' (unpublished conference paper, Bath, 1991)

Ward, Benedicta, *Miracles and the Medieval Mind: Theory, Record and Event 1000–1215* (Wildwood House, 1987)

Wilson, Christopher, *The Gothic Cathedral* (Thames & Hudson, 1990)

Zarnecki, George, *Romanesque Art* (Weidenfeld & Nicolson, 1972)

Fires of Faith

Barber, Malcolm, *The Two Cities: Medieval Europe, 1050–1320* (Routledge, 1993)

Cohn, Norman, *Europe's Inner Demons* (Pimlico, 1993)

Cook, William, and Herzman, Ronald, *The Medieval World View* (Oxford University Press, 1983)

Gumley, Frances, and Redhead, Brian, *The Christian Centuries* (BBC Books, 1989)

★Habig, Marion A. (ed.), *St Francis of Assisi – Writings and Early Biographies* (SPCK, 1973)

★Hamilton, Bernard, *The Medieval Inquisition* (Edward Arnold, 1981)

★Johnson, Paul, *A History of Christianity* (Penguin, 1990)

Lambert, Malcolm, *Medieval Heresy: Popular Movements from the Gregorian Reform to the Reformation* (Blackwell, 1992)

Leclercq, Jean *(et al.), The Spirituality of the Middle Ages* (Burns & Oates, 1968)

★Leff, Gordon, *Heresy in the Later Middle Ages: The Relation of Heterodoxy to Dissent, 1250–1450*, 2 vols. (Manchester University Press, 1967)

★Little, Lester K., *Religious Poverty and the Profit Economy in Medieval Europe* (Elek, 1978)

Oldenbourg, Zoë, *Massacre at Montségur: History of the Albigensian Crusade* (Dorset Press, 1991)

Rouquette, Yves, *Cathares* (Portet-sur-Garonne: Loubatières, 1991)

Sorrell, Roger D., *St Francis of Assisi and Nature: Tradition and Innovation in Western Christian Attitudes toward the Environment* (Oxford University Press, 1988)

Thomas, Keith, *Man and the Natural World* (Penguin, 1984)

★Wakefield, Walter, *Heresy, Crusade and Inquisition in Southern France, 1100–1250* (Allen & Unwin, 1974)

Wakefield, Walter (ed.), *Heresies of the High Middle Ages (Selected Sources)* (Columbia University Press, 1969.)

The Saint and the Scholar

Barber, Richard (ed.), *The Arthurian Legends* (Boydell Press, 1987)

Brooke, Christopher (ed.), *The Medieval Idea of Marriage* (Oxford University Press, 1994)

Chibnal, M. (trans.), *John of Salisbury's Memoirs of the Papal Court* (Nelson, 1956)

Cobban, Alan B., *Universities in the Middle Ages* (Liverpool University Press, 1991)

Gilson, Étienne, *Héloïse and Abélard* (University of Michigan Press, 1960)

Grane, Leif, *Peter Abelard: Philosophy and Christianity in the Middle Ages* (Allen & Unwin, 1970)

Haskins, C. H., *The Renaissance of the Twelfth Century* (Harvard University Press, 1990)

Kenny, Anthony, *Aquinas* (Oxford University Press, 1980)

Knowles, David, *The Historian and Character and Other Essays* (Cambridge University Press, 1964)

Le Goff, Jacques, and Fagan, Teresa, *Intellectuals in the Middle Ages* (Blackwell, 1993)

*Matarasso, Pauline (ed.), *The Cistercian World: Monastic Writings of the 12th Century* (Penguin, 1993)

*Murray, A. Victor, *Abelard and St Bernard: A Study in Twelfth Century 'Modernism'* (Manchester University Press, 1967)

Pennington, Basil (ed.), 'St Bernard of Clairvaux' (Cistercian Studies, no. 28, Cistercian Publications, 1977)

Pullan, Brian, *Sources for the History of Medieval Europe* (Blackwell, 1966)

*Radice, Betty (trans.), *The Letters of Abelard and Heloise* (Penguin, 1974)

*Scott James, Bruno (trans.), *The Letters of St Bernard of Clairvaux* (Burns, Oates & Washbourne, 1953)

Warner, Marina, *Alone of All Her Sex: The Myth and the Cult of the Virgin Mary* (Pan, 1985)

Circles of Light

*Anderson, William, *Dante the Maker* (Hutchinson Educational, 1983)

Auerbach, Eric, *Dante – Poet of the Secular World* (University of Chicago Press, 1961)

Baxendall, Michael, *Giotto and the Orators* (Oxford University Press, 1988)

Gilson, Étienne, *Dante the Philosopher* (Sheed & Ward, 1948)

Heer, Friedrich, *The Medieval World: Europe 1100–1350* (Weidenfeld & Nicolson, 1962)

Hollander, Robert, *Allegory in Dante's 'Commedia'* (Princeton University Press, 1969)

*Huizinga, J., *The Waning of the Middle Ages* (Penguin, 1990)

Hyde, K., *Society and Politics in Medieval Italy: The Evolution of Civil Life 1000–1350* (Macmillan, 1973)

Jerman, James, and Weir, Anthony, *Images of Lust: Sexual Carvings on Medieval Churches* (Batsford, 1993)

Le Goff, Jacques, *The Birth of Purgatory* (Scolar Press, 1991)

*Musa, Mark (trans.), *Dante: The Divine Comedy – Inferno* (Penguin, 1984), *Purgatory* (Penguin, 1985), and *Paradise* (Penguin, 1986)

*Pope Hennessy, J. (ed.), *Paradiso* (Thames & Hudson, 1993)

Reynolds, Barbara (trans.), *Dante – La Vita Nuova (Poems of Youth)* (Penguin, 1969)

Sayers, Dorothy, and Reynolds, Barbara (trans.), *The Comedy of Dante Alighieri*, vol. 3, *Paradise* (Penguin, 1974)

NOTES ON SOURCES

Displayed extracts on the pages listed below come from the following sources:

Page 43: *The Chronicle of Jocelin of Brakeland*, trans. L. C. Jane (Chatto & Windus, 1925)

Page 46: Panofsky, *Abbot Suger*

Page 54: Abbé Bulteau, *Monographie de la Cathédrale de Chartres*, I, 1887. Translation by Christopher Frayling

Page 58: Robert Willis, *The Architectural History of Canterbury Cathedral* (London, 1845). Quoted in Frisch

Page 68: J. M. Neale and B. Webb, *The Symbolism of Churches and Church Ornaments* (Leeds, 1843). Quoted in Frisch

Page 74: Quoted in Wakefield, *Heresies of the High Middle Ages*

Page 81: Quoted in Wakefield, *Heresy, Crusade and Inquisition*

Page 83: From *La Chanson de la Croisade Albigeoise*. Translation by Christopher Frayling

Pages 86, 91, 93, 94: Quoted in Habig

Page 108: Matarasso

Page 114: Radice

Page 115: Gottfried von Strassburg, *Tristan and Isolde*, trans. by A. T. Hatto (Penguin, 1960). Quoted in Barber, *Arthurian Legends*

Page 116: 'Cistercian Fathers Series', No. 18, Cistercian Publications (Kalamazoo, Michigan)

Page 127: Pullan

Full details of books and authors mentioned above (if not given here) and of books and authors referred to in the text are given in the Select Bibliography.

The quotations from the writings of and about St Francis in Chapter 2 are taken from *St Francis of Assisi – Writings and Early Biographies*, edited by Marion A. Habig (SPCK, 1973). The quotations from the writings of Heloise and Abelard in Chapter 3 are taken from *The Letters of Abelard and Heloise*, translated by Betty Radice (Penguin Classics, 1974), © Betty Radice, 1974. The quotations from Dante's *Divine Comedy* in Chapter 4 are taken from Mark Musa's translation, first published by Indiana University Press, and subsequently published in the Penguin Classics series. (Vol. I, *The Inferno*, © Indiana University Press, 1971; Vol. 2, *Purgatory*, © Mark Musa 1981, 1985; Vol. 3, *Paradise*, © Mark Musa 1984, 1986).

INDEX

A SELECTION OF BOOKS FROM BBC/PENGUIN

Great Railway Journeys
Photographs by Tom Owen Edmunds

Against all the odds – despite the aeroplane and the motor car – trains are still the best way to travel to discover a country. In *Great Railway Journeys* six travellers write about their railway journeys through terrain for which they have a particular attachment, curiosity and affection.

Mark Tully takes the Khyber Mail from Karachi to the breathtaking Khyber Pass; Clive Anderson explores the route from Hong Kong to Mongolia; Natalia Makarova journeys through her Russian past, from St Petersburg to Tashkent.

Whether by steam or diesel, on cattle trucks, double-decker coaches or the luxury City Gold service, each of these journeys – as well as those undertaken by Lisa St Aubin de Terán, Rian Malan and Michael Palin – turns into an adventure.

Crusades Terry Jones and Alan Ereira

In 1095 Pope Urban II made an announcement that would change the world. He called upon Christians to march under the banner of the Cross and save their brothers in the East from the advance of Islam. This vision of crusading Christianity dominated the events of the next two centuries. With wit and humour, making the history of the Crusades accessible to all readers, Terry Jones and Alan Ereira bring vividly to life the compelling, often horrific, story of the fanatics and fantasists, knights and peasants, corrupt clergy and duplicitous leaders who were caught up in these fervent times.

A SELECTION OF BOOKS
FROM BBC/PENGUIN

The Watchdog Guide to Getting a Better Deal
David Berry

Watchdog is probably the most famous and effective consumer-protection programme on television. Although it has inevitably focused on the most dramatic cases and worst abuses, the research team has developed the tools to help ordinary citizens see through the scams and fight back against the sharks. In this invaluable guide to getting a better deal, David Berry gives clear and concise advice on topics such as shopping and what to do about faulty goods, getting good services from public utilities, dealing with hospitals, the police and local authorities, borrowing and investing, holidays and pensions.

Crimewatch UK   Liz Mills

Six true crime stories are recorded in this compelling volume, including the infamous Michael Sams case, which the police have been able to solve thanks to *Crimewatch UK*, now celebrating its tenth successful year. The result is a fascinating behind-the-scenes glimpse into *Crimewatch* and the world of modern detective methods.

The Underworld   Duncan Campbell

From the racetrack gangs and safe-crackers of the 1930s to the hitmen and drug smugglers of today, *The Underworld* is the remarkable story of modern British crime. *Guardian* crime correspondent Duncan Campbell tells of infamous and feared gangsters, unarmed 'gentleman' criminals, the growth in the use of firearms and the role of prisons and borstals in providing the underworld with heroes, and gives accounts of the major players in gun fights, drug rings and clubland carve-ups. Gangland empires, police corruption, shocking headlines and legendary ringleaders all play their part in this gripping and revealing chronicle of crime.

A SELECTION OF BOOKS FROM BBC/PENGUIN

Who Learns Wins Phil Race
Positive Steps to the Enjoyment and Re-discovery of Learning

It's never too late to learn. School may have been dreary and left us with a low opinion of our abilities, but with *Who Learns Wins* it's never been easier to make a fresh start. In this stimulating book Phil Race demonstrates with humour and understanding that we are capable of far more than we ever thought possible. Whether we want to speak a new language, understand mathematics, assemble a piece of furniture or grow chrysanthemums, this invaluable book helps us to rediscover the thrill and excitement of learning.

In Search of the Dead Jeffrey Iverson
A Scientific Investigation of Evidence for Life after Death

What lies beyond death? For over a century scientists have searched for proof that we survive death. In this book, based on a BBC television documentary series, Jeffrey Iverson examines the evidence for this and other aspects of the paranormal through a fascinating variety of case studies.

In Search of the Dead calls for a greater understanding of the scientific framework for the paranormal, and convincingly argues that the future could see a new science of Mind. And though the ultimate reality of the universe remains a mystery at present, transcending death may be the next stage in the evolution of human consciousness.

A Guide to Parliament David Davis MP

Have you ever wondered why the Speaker has to be dragged to the Chair? Who is Black Rod? And what is a three-line whip? Combining amusing anecdotes with invaluable information, David Davis chronicles the history of Parliament, and illustrates how committees function and the roles of the Prime Minister, Cabinet and Departments of State, giving a fascinating insight into Britain's greatest institution.

A SELECTION OF BOOKS FROM BBC/PENGUIN

Plato to NATO
Studies in Political Thought

The question 'Why should I obey the state?' forms the basis of all political philosophy from the time of the earliest civilizations to the present day. It has provoked much debate over the centuries on topics including the definition of liberty, the laws of nature and the intervention of divine power. *Plato to NATO* contains fourteen essays on prominent political thinkers that provide a tantalizing introduction to the works of figures as diverse as St Thomas Aquinas, Hobbes, Machiavelli, Rousseau and Russell. *Plato to NATO* contains an introduction by Brian Redhead, and is ideal reading for students of political history.

Against the State Janet Coleman
Studies in Sedition and Rebellion

In 399 BC the philosopher Socrates was charged and condemned to death by fellow citizens who believed he had acted against the Athenian democracy. In the seventeenth century Cromwell and the regicides chose the same punishment for Charles I. In *Against the State* Professor Janet Coleman looks at the enduring tradition of rebellion against official authority, studying the violent activities of religious martyrs and terrorists, oppositional movements like feminism, and the radical social analyses of Thomas More, Karl Marx and Sigmund Freud. With an incisive introduction by Brian Redhead, *Against the State* is an excellent companion volume to *Plato to NATO*.

A SELECTION OF BOOKS FROM BBC/PENGUIN

Greek as a Treat Peter France
An Introduction to the Classics

We can get through life nowadays without Greek. Yet, as Peter France argues, we are missing out on the best of it. Shakespeare, Byron, Shelley, Dr Johnson and Winston Churchill are unlikely all to have been wrong. In this exhilarating book Peter France opens our eyes to classical Greece and to the 'greats' – Homer, Pythagoras, Aeschylus, Socrates and Plato – ready and waiting to enrich our twentieth-century lives.

John Dunn's Answers Please

Amazing answers, fascinating facts, tantalizing trivia: *John Dunn's Answers Please*, from John Dunn's popular BBC Radio 2 programme, is a wonderfully entertaining compendium of general knowledge questions and answers. What is Amaretto made from? How much water is there in the world? Why do geese fly in a V-formation? Who was Big Bertha?

Arranged in A–Z order, *John Dunn's Answers Please* is a treasure trove of fact, information, detail and knowledge that will keep the whole family amused and entertained for hours.

A SELECTION OF BOOKS FROM BBC/PENGUIN

Great Journeys
Photographs by Tom Owen Edmunds

Here seven great travellers of our time rediscover some of the world's most spectacular and inhospitable terrain, tracing these remarkable journeys with idiosyncratic style and humour. Colin Thubron returns to the Silk Road; Naomi James sails amongst the Polynesian islands; Hugo Williams travels the Pan American Highway; Miles Kington uncovers the old Burma Road used by Chaing Kai-shek; Norman Stone follows the Viking route from the Baltic to the Black Sea; William Shawcross traces the Salt Road in the Sahara and Philip Jones Griffiths revisits the Ho Chi Minh Trail twenty-one years after photographing the Vietnam War.

Living Islam   Akbar S. Ahmed

Although there are around a billion Muslims in the world, most discussion of Islam is based on clichés or outright prejudice. This lively and compelling book sets out to bridge gulfs of misunderstanding. Going back to the sources of Islam, to the Prophet Muhammad and the Quran's 'five pillars', looking at Muslim communities from Samarkand to the Outer Hebrides, Akbar S. Ahmed explores the issues with insight and sympathy, penetrating beyond the stereotypes to the realities of Islamic life.

A SELECTION OF BOOKS FROM BBC/PENGUIN

The Death of Yugoslavia   Laura Silber and Allan Little

While the western world stood by, seemingly paralysed, and international peace efforts broke down, the former Yugoslavia was witnessing Europe's bloodiest conflict for half a century. *The Death of Yugoslavia* is the first account to go behind the public face of battle and into the closed worlds of the key players in the war. Laura Silber, Balkans correspondent for the *Financial Times*, and Allan Little, award-winning BBC journalist, plot the road to war and the war itself.

Drawing on eye-witness testimony, scrupulous research and hundreds of interviews, they give unprecedented access to the facts behind the media stories. Could anything have been done to prevent this terrible tragedy? What will be its lasting effects? The authors consider these questions and assess the present situation and its implications for future international relations.

States of Terror   Peter Taylor
Democracy and Political Violence

Terrorism is the scourge of most modern democracies, but how can governments fight back without adopting the same terrorist tactics and trampling on those human rights they claim to uphold? In this vivid and disturbing book, based on an acclaimed documentary series, Peter Taylor takes readers inside Irish Cabinet meetings and IRA courts martial. He examines the aims and methods of Palestinian radicals and their Mossad pursuers, and talks to the sons of assassinated enemies who may provide a glimmer of hope. His findings bring fresh insight into one of today's key moral and political issues.

A SELECTION OF BOOKS FROM BBC/PENGUIN

Storm from the East   Robert Marshall

Genghis Khan left an empire more than twice the size of Alexander's; his successors went on to conquer and govern an empire stretching all the way from Korea to the River Danube. Robert Marshall examines the Mongols' breathtaking rise from nomadic herdsmen to world conquerors in just two generations. He describes their devastating invasion of feudal Europe, and Christendom's clumsy attempts to understand these alien invaders, and ends with the empire's decline and fall, after Khubilai Khan's triumphant unification of China.

In Search of the Dark Ages   Michael Wood

One thousand years of invasion by Romans, Anglo-Saxons, Vikings and Normans have helped to define the myths, culture and spirit that shape Britain today. Here Michael Wood gives us a vivid portrait of the early kings and conquerors of Europe's oldest kingdom. He charts the facts and legends surrounding the Celtic Queen Boadicea and King Arthur, and the three great Anglo-Saxon kings, Offa, Alfred and Athelstan, and explores the failure of Ethelred the Unready to defend England against renewed Viking invasions, paving the way for the Norman Conquest of 1066.

In Search of the Trojan War   Michael Wood

Did Troy actually exist, and did the Trojan War really take place? In this incisive study Michael Wood takes us back to the Greek Age of Heroes. In the Aegean, Turkey and ancient Egypt he follows in the footsteps of the travellers and adventurers who tried to locate the lost cities of legend. He takes a fresh look at some of the most famous and exciting discoveries in archaeology, and chronicles dramatic new developments in the search for Troy, including the rediscovery in Moscow of the so-called Jewels of Helen and the re-excavation of the site of Troy which began in 1988.

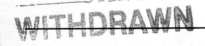